Thirty Paths to Stillness

An Introduction

Thirty Paths To Stillness was originally intended for local Yoga Tutors, Teachers and anyone working in the field promoting relaxation. I have taught Yoga for over 10 years and I found it difficult to source a little handbook which I could use in class, so I decided to write my own.

This is the result, Thirty basic simple visualisations, which have been tried and tested on my own students, therefore Thirty Paths is dedicated to all those who are continually seeking that still small voice within, that which is.

OM SHANTI.

Susan Johnson

June 2002

Thirty Paths to Stillness

Written and devised by Susan Johnson

Designed by The Art Room
Some Photography by David Johnson
and Lucy Reynolds

Printed in England by CP Offset Limited, Darlington.
Telephone 01325 462315
First printed and published August 2002
Published by Susan Johnson

Published by Susan Johnson
© Susan Johnson 2002
E-mail: susan@thirtypaths.com
website: www.thirtypaths.com

Contents

Yoga Nidra

Yoga Nidra precedes visualisation. Before we start to imagine, the body must be totally relaxed. Begin the relaxation technique by allowing the body to totally let go.

Feel the body sinking into the mat, allow the shoulders to spread across the floor, move the head from side to side to release the neck, allow the head to let go. Imagine a cool blue light surrounding your body from the crown of the head to the tips of the toes, feel this light widening outwards, creating an aura of light around you. Feel it pulsating with life and energy, allow this light to be a healing light, if you feel in need of healing either mentally, emotionally, or physically allow this healing to take place whilst you relax.

Take the attention to the breath and allow the belly to slowly rise and fall with each breath, do not try and alter the breath in any way just witness the in and out, the flow, the slow coming and going, the evenness, the quiet rhythm. Allow the body to just be.

Now you are aware of melting down onto the floor, and you feel quite safe and secure,feel the colour blue soaking into the body, drenching all your cells with fresh life force, with energy, with balance, allow yourself to surrender to the healing.

Now take the attention to the feet, and allow the toes to spread and separate. Turn the toes inwards, flex and release, allow the instep to let go, the sole of the foot, the ankle, and feel the feet as solid and heavy, feel as though the feet are moving away from you, dense and heavy so heavy that you feel as though you are unable to move them. Allow the feet to relax and let go, feel them flopping out to the side. Allow the legs to release, the shins, the calfs, the knee and the kneecap, the thigh and the back of the thigh, allow the legs to release and let go, feel as though the legs are moving away from you solid, heavy and dense. Take the attention to the hands, to the back of the hand touching the floor, to the fingertips, the fingers and the palm of the hand, feel the softness in the palm of the hand, allow the lower arm to let go, the elbow, the upper arm, the whole of the arm releasing down, moving away.

Take the attention to the back and feel the vertebrae release from the base of the spine to the crown of the head visualise each vertebrae letting go and release onto the floor. Feel the whole of the back spread outwards, feel the back widen,at the same time feel the length, the stretch, the whole of the back spreading across the floor, and be aware of the amount of space the body takes up, the small amount of space.

4

ake the visualisation to the belly and be
ware of the softness in the belly, the
low steady breath, the calm quiet
oming and going of the breath, witness
he rhythmn,
he separation
f the breath,
he pause, and
he still point,
eel as if the
whole body is
breathing, that
he breath is
breathing the
ody.

llow the
bdomen to let
go and feel the
oftness in the
belly, allow the
hest centre to
open out and
on each
nhalation feel the division of the breath,
llow this openness to create a space
within the chest centre allowing you the
reedom to breathe mentally and
physically, allow this freedom to open out
he heart centre creating a releasement, a
eeling you may not have felt for a long
ime, allow this centre to be filled with
peace.

Feel this openness now spreading to the
throat to release the voice, to move
around the neck, the back of the head,
the crown of the head, the scalp, the
space between
the scalp and
the skull, and
even the hair
on the head, as
you allow the
face to let go
and soften, the
lower jaw
slightly drops,
feel the entire
face release,
the forehead,
the eyes, the
eyebrows, the
eyelids relaxing
in pools of
darkness, the
temples, the
nose, the tip of
the nose, the
cheeks, the cheekbones, the upper lip
and the lower lip, the jaw and the hinges
of the jaw, the chin and even the ears
and earlobes, feel the whole body release
and sink down onto the floor all you are
aware of is the steady breath, the rise
and fall of the belly as the breath moves
in and out, the stillness, the journey to
visualisation.

Creating your own haven of peace

One of the first things to do when you are serious about visualisation is to create your own special place. You can then go to this sanctuary any time you feel like it, you may go in times of stress or times of peace, the results should be the same. First of all your place needs to be peaceful, quiet and still, it needs to feel safe and secure, so you need to choose a place to meditate where you are not going to be disturbed, to allow you to create.

Close your eyes and settle down into a slow rhythmic breathing pattern, try and visualise a place that makes you feel happy and peaceful, it could be a holiday moment, a chapel, a perfect beach, a mountain, a large crystal, wherever or whatever. Now be aware of the sounds, the scents, the colours, the emotions, anything that comes into your mind allow it to happen. Be patient, be a witness to your own

thoughts, try not to intellectualise them, just allow them to be there and to flow, be aware of your own impressions, your own instincts, your own intuition, stay and just allow the mind to just be.

If you feel happy with this visualisation keep it for a while, and then maybe change it after a few weeks.
From now on this is your own personal creation, it is a place of peace and quiet, it is your secret haven from the outside world, it is your own meditation.

OM SHANTI.

Rotation of consciousness

Following relaxation the student follows the voice, and visualises the object or scene.

VISUALISE.

Sunshine and warmth.

Summer rain.

A rainbow of colour.

The blue sky.

The blue sky meeting the ocean.

The horizon.

Dolphins playing

A lonely yacht drifting along on the breeze.

Seagulls gliding.

Feel the cool ocean breeze

The salt in the air.

Waves lapping on the seashore.

The soft golden sand supporting the body.

The warmth and stillness.

The breath flowing.

The in and out of the breath, the still point and the pause between the inhalation and exhalation.

The sound of the breath creating a mantra.

The deep quiet rhythm, the evenness of the breath.

Allow the body to become suspended by the breath.

I AM BREATHING THE BODY.

Autogenic Training

When using this technique, the person lies down or sits in a comfortable position with the eyes closed and progressively concentrates on six fundamental stages.

Heaviness
The right arm is heavy.
The left arm is heavy.
Both arms are heavy.

The right leg is heavy.
The left leg is heavy.
Both legs are heavy.

Warmth
The right arm is warm.
The left arm is warm.
Both arms are warm.
My right leg is warm.
My left leg is warm.
My legs and arms are warm.

Heart
My heartbeat is calm and regular.
(repeat five times)

Breathing
My body breathes itself.
(repeat five times)

Abdomen
My abdomen is warm.
(repeat five times)

Forehead
My forehead is cool.
(repeat five times)

This is a hard relaxation technique to master but once learned it can be done anywhere.

Affirmations

An affirmation is a positive thought repeated as many times a day as you like, in relaxation we repeat this positive thought three times. The idea is to allow one's mind to be influenced by a command.

A selection of affirmations

I am strong.
I am healthy.
I know no fear.
I am in charge.
I am peaceful.
I am brave.
I have courage.
I am better today.

ALWAYS USE A POSITIVE STATEMENT.

CREATING ENERGY

Invocation is a technique to summon any type of energy or quality to come to you.

When you feel relaxed say silently and firmly, I will now summon the quality of strength, allow yourself to feel strong, powerful, full of courage, try and experience this feeling.

To enhance the quality of strength, think of an old oak tree.

To enhance the quality of compassion think of a Mother Superior and serenity.

To enhance the quality of softness, imagine lying on a bed of soft sand.

To enhance the quality of clarity, think of clear running water.

To enhance the quality of intelligence, think of the Universe.

To enhance the quality of healing, think of a higher source, a universal power.

Simply make a strong clear statement to encourage this strength to surround you. Always ask for empowerment of the highest.

A Relaxation Technique

A RELAXATION TECHNIQUE TO USE PRIOR TO VISUALISATION

Be aware of the breath, allow it to slow down, feel yourself sinking into the floor, feel the body spreading across the mat the shoulders widen, the buttocks spreading, the whole back widening at the same time the body lengthening . Allow the earth to support the body. Be aware of a rainbow of light, an arc of colour, a spectrum of colour, across the centre of your body, see the colours clear and bright, and walk into one of those colours that most appeal to you at this moment in time, be aware that you are responding to this colour, this colour has a vibration of healing energy, allow this healing to take place whilst you relax.

Imagine:
breathing into the soles of the feet
I relax my feet
Breathe into the calves
I relax my calves
Breathe into the thighs
I relax my thighs
Breathe into the hip joints
I relax my hip joints
Breathe into the belly
I relax my belly
Breathe into the abdomen
I relax my abdomen
Breathe into the chest and open it out, feel the expansion in the chest, the release, feel the freedom in the chest centre.

Allow the body to breathe.
Breathe into the throat.
(Continue to relax each part of the body)
Breathe into the crown of the head.
Breathe into the base of the spine.
Breathe into the shoulders
Breathe into the arms.
Breathe into the hands.

Relax and let go of the face, the forehead, the temples, the cheeks, the chin, the jaw, the ears, the mouth. Relax the eyes in pools of darkness, the eyelids become heavy with relaxation, and now the entire body is relaxed.

REPEAT YOUR AFFIRMATION

And now you are ready for visualisation.

10

Meditation on strength

The affirmation is I am strong. Close the eyes softly and visualise yourself sitting against a large old oak tree, feel strength in your back, from the base of your spine to the crown of the head. Allow that strength to enter your mind and repeat the affirmation, I am strong.

Think how this tree grew from a small acorn, sprouting forth a shoot, visualise this shoot coming up through the earth developing into a small tree, growing strong through the seasons, feel your body widening out at the shoulders and lengthening upwards, feel the body growing, be aware of a strong tree trunk moving upwards towards the light always looking and searching towards the light.

Feel the warmth around the back, and now visualise this tree deep down to the roots, how they spread out hard and gnarled, how the roots taper and soften as they sink deeper into the earth, and how they finally end up as threads searching out for food and moisture, feel how strongly they bond the tree to the earth, how the roots become the firm foundation for growth. Now be aware of the name of this tree, the colour of the leaves, the deep shades of brown the crust of the bark, the texture, and even the smell of the earth. How old is this tree, and how many people have sat here against the trunk, feel the strength again, feel the steady support, and repeat again the affirmation, I am strong.

Now be aware of the steady beating of the heart, the in and out breath, the length of the exhalation the slow evenness, the complete integration of the breath with the heartbeat. Feel the link between the breath, the life force and strength.

Repeat the affirmation, I am strong, three times.

OM SHANTI

The Breath

For all Pranayama techniques the back is held straight this allows the free flow of prana, or energy to flow unimpeded up the spine. You can sit in the Adept position, or any position which will hold the back comfortable. Feel well grounded by taking the concentration to the sits bones, these are at the very bottom of the spine, feel at ease and rooted to the spot, as in all meditative work the body must feel comfortable. Hands can rest in the lap or in The Mudra of Knowledge, finger and thumb connected, this creates the circuit of energy and keeps it well into the body instead of allowing it to become dissipated.

Sit for a few moments and allow the body to just be, feel as though the breath is breathing the body and you are just witnessing the breath, the breath is just coming and going, breathe in, and think of a golden dot on the left shoulder and as you breathe

out take a golden thread across to the right shoulder, from a golden dot on the right shoulder breathe in and on an exhalation take a golden thread down to the base of the spine. Take another in breath thinking of a golden dot at the base of the spine then as you breathe out take a golden thread up to the left shoulder, so completing a golden triangle.

The next in breath is directed to a golden dot on the right knee. Breathe in, and on an out breath take a golden thread to your left knee and visualise a golden dot there. Breathe in, and on your next out breath take a golden thread up to the point between your eyebrows, visualise this point, breathe, then as you breathe out take the golden thread to your right knee, so forming a second triangle.

Feel the interconnection of the two golden triangles, the points of the triangles and what they represent, the two interlocking triangles are visualised, one having the apex in the Muladhara centre and the other in the Ajna centre. Allow the body to remain in the stillness of the image, as the breathing is slow and even this position can be held as a long meditation as long as there are no contraindications related to the lower limbs.

OM SHANTI

The Mantra is the Breath

Follow the relaxation and allow the body to just be. Feel the entire body spread out across the floor, the body is sinking into a deep state of relaxation. feel as though the body is drifting away and all you are aware of is the breath coming and going. Visualise the colour Indigo Blue surrounding the body imagine this colour as a healing light , feel the coolness, the stillness, the peace that surrounds and enfolds you. You feel as if you are in a blue cocoon, a cape of blue velvet holding you, supporting you, allowing you to feel safe and secure, this healing light surrounds your aura whilst you relax. It is safe to allow the earth to support you, release and dissolve, surrender to the moment.

Now just let the breath come and go, feel the rise and fall of the belly, do not interfere with the sensation of the breathing just witness the coming and going, the in and the out flow, the coming and going. Now take the attention to the nostrils and allow the breath to come into the nose, hear and feel the sensation in the back of the throat, this is the Ujjayi Pranayama the sound is deep, still, steady, and relaxed, like a baby snoring. Drift into the rhythm of the sound. You are beginning to feel the sound resonate deep within, allow the sound to become a vibration, allow the sound to become your Mantra. The Mantra is the sound of your breath, let the breath sigh, feel it spreading throughout the chest centre, into the abdomen, down into the arms and into the legs. Allow the body to feel open to the sound, to the vibration as the breath breathes the body.

Now as the breath deepens feel the body go deeper into the sound, so that all you are aware of is the sound and the vibration, allow the sound to be your Mantra. The breath is harmonising the body, the breath is calming, the breath is balancing, the breath is healing, the breath is life.

Feel now the pause between the inhalation and the exhalation. Be aware of the still point, allow the whole body to breathe in harmony with the sound, link into your Mantra your own vibration.

Visualisation with a Partner

This visualisation is done with a partner.

Begin the visualisation by sitting upright, allowing the shoulders to touch and if possible the base of the spine. Close the eyes and consider this as a giving experience. Feel comfortable allowing the back to remain straight throughout to encourage the free flow of prana.

Begin to be aware of the breath coming and going, take the attention to the sits bones, to the base of the spine and feel well settled, grounded and rooted in this centre, feel strong. Visualise the colour red spreading around your lower back, feel the heat, the warmth ,feel as though you are generating a glow of energy, and be aware of this energy being transferred to your partner. Take time to allow this to start happening.

Now take the attention back to the breathing and you will observe that the breath is almost synchronised, feel as though you are breathing together in harmony. The breath is slow, relaxed, and even. Take time to allow the body to tune in.

Now take the attention back to the lower back and imagine the spine as a thermometer, and the mercury is a silver light, as you breathe in and out the silver light moves up the spine, be mindful of any blockages, observe these areas and create a fine silver mist to move through these blocked areas. Observe what areas you are having difficulty with, and gently encourage the fine mist to move along.

As you continue to merge with your partner's energy, feel now the energy moving all the way up the back, creating warmth, creating heat, creating healing, this energy can now be directed to any part of your body that may be in need at this moment in time.

You may be in need mentally, emotionally or physically, you have generated by thought enough healing energy to move between you.

Sit still and allow the healing to happen.

When you feel ready to bring yourself out of the visualisation imagine this silver light returning to the base of the spine, still and quiet back to the source.

Sit still and allow this to happen

OM SHANTI.

Absent Healing

Go to your own chosen place, your own haven of peace, and begin to meditate on the breath, allow the sound of the breath to be heard in the back of the throat, the ujjayi breath, deepen the breath and allow the breath to become the mantra. For the next 10 minutes allow the breath to breathe the body, to still the mind, just observe the coming and going of the breath, feel the sound resonate throughout the body creating a vibration.

Now bring the focus into the heart centre, and visualise if you can, the person you wish to send healing to. If you are working together with this, you can even set a time when you link in together, in thought.

Imagine this person sitting in front of you, you know them well, so they are able to trust you, they feel secure. Visualise placing your hands on this persons hands, feel them relax into your firm hold, completely steady, allow your hands to be relaxed, to feel confident, enabling your partner to feel reassured, to trust.

Ask your higher energy source to allow you to be used as an instrument of healing.

Now visualise both of you being surrounded in a orb of blue light, and allow this light to surround and protect you. Ask for protection, that you may receive healing from the highest, be conscious that you are coming from the heart centre. Allow the feeling of compassion, of empathy, of a stillness, of peace to come into your aura. Feel the energy as heat, coming into your hands, allowing this person to receive, visualise a two way blending of positive energy, allow yourself to transmit this energy by thinking of it being drawn away from you, visualise the negative energy being drawn out and away back into the earth. Allow the healing to take place, just be still and breathe, sit like this for another 10 minutes.

When you are ready to come out of the healing meditation, visualise this same person lying on a soft bed covered by a blue velvet cloth, resting, and recovering. Thank your healing helpers for visiting.

You also have received, as the healing energy was transmitted, you were left with the residue, so feel as though you have been blessed by that higher source, by that universal power, that which we are all part of.

Remembering that you should not feel in any way drained of energy, you are simply being the messenger, the go-between, the instrument, so your own energy is not at all in jeopardy.

OM SHANTI.

The Colour Red

Red is the colour which dominates the base chakra. Red represents life, strength, vitality, fire and energy. It rises from this centre through all the chakras, spinning the wheels of energy. When working with the energy centres we have to be aware of our intent as red can also represent danger, anger, fury and fear, it can be a powerful stimulant therefore red can keep the mind buzzing. The base chakra is connection, we are connected to the earth with roots and it is from being earthed in this centre we can begin to work on ourselves with energy. Red is connected to the life force and therefore it is not surprising we think of blood red, this is the circulation, the circling around the spine, the connection with oxygen, the movement of prana. Therefore this is a good colour to work with if we are feeling depleted, anaemic or iron deficient. Through the effect on the blood corpuscles we become more energised. Red is also warm it makes us feel warm and cosy and yet empowered.

Allow the body to feel as though it is sinking into the mat, feel the peace and stillness and allow the breath to just flow. Allow the body to just Be. Take the attention to the base of the spine and feel in this area a warmth, a heat starting to move around the lower back, feel the heat and the slow pulsing of energy as the colour red begins to take form allow the colour to deepen, and change into a brilliant red the colour of poppies, visualise this crimson flower, the delicate petals, the shimmer, the red glow, feel the energy generating, feel the vibration of the prana, be aware of any sensations, or any shifting in energy, and now imagine a field of crimson poppies, and you are walking through this field, feel the vitality, the energy the upliftment, the joy. Stay for a while in this field of crimson poppies and enjoy.

You are now beginning to feel this warmth spreading around the whole of the body, moving and filling the entire body, take the attention back to the base of the spine and be aware of a slowing down, think of the spinning wheels losing speed, slowing down, coming back into its centre, settling down to a slow pulsating a gradual letting go and consciously allow this chakra to return to the natural state of stillness and well being.

Be aware of the belly and allow the breath to normalise the body back to here and now. Take time to readjust and take notice of how the body feels.

In a class, if you are back to back with a partner this breathing technique can generate a lot of energy and healing.

OM SHANTI

The Colour Orange

Orange is the colour connected to the Sacral chakra. It is related to the Adrenals. This energy centre helps to create balance and harmony within the central nervous system, because of the near proximity of the base chakra it also has to do with feelings and the release of thought, however it can also harbour unwanted thoughts and feelings, therefore keeping blockages well hidden, these unwanted areas of our life can manifest as anxiety or depression, the opposite of joy and dance, because orange is such a vibrant colour bursting with energy it is a good colour for people who have deep seated emotional problems, anxieties or depression or just in need of upliftment.

Allow the body to let go and imagine a beam of orange light going straight and deep into the lower abdomen. Think of the common African Marigold the huge round orange ball of light, see how all the petals are formed exactly in proportion, the layers, the shape of the flower, how perfect the flower has been formed, how did this colour take form, see how the flower is joined at the stem, the centre of the flower, note the stamens laden with pollen, remember how this is collected and used by bees in the long lazy days of summer. Be aware of the heady scent of these flowers, feel yourself become drowsy with the perfume. See how this flower attracts many insects, butterflies, bees, ladybirds.

Now breathe in the colour orange, take in the life force, the strong vibrant colour, the joy, you have no need to be unhappy or sad, think of this flower, the brilliance, so full of sunshine, so full of upliftment, allow this healing light and energy to sweep through your body, filling you with positive thought, with clarity of thought, with a willingness to let go and move forward. When you feel ready, release the colour orange, allow the light to return to the second energy centre, back to the normal state, slow down, release and allow the breath to breathe the body.

OM SHANTI.

The Colour Yellow

Yellow relates to the solar plexus centre, the belly. Related to the mind and intellect it represents the power of thought. The belly is a storehouse of energy, and a lot of feelings are felt in this area. This colour stimulates mental activity it is therefore a good colour to use in a study or any workplace or station. When we centre on the solar plexus as in abdominal breathing we are also slowing down the body. We are trying to still the mind, increase equilibrium, therefore as in all energy centres they have a two fold effect, creating energy and creating relaxation. In visualisation the colour yellow always reminds us of the sun, solar, solar plexus. The yellow rays bring energy, vitamins upliftment, and a general feeling of well being, the yellow rays carry positive ions, and magnetic currents which stimulate the nerves and strengthen us mentally. Yellow is a good visualisation colour because it holds so much upbeat energy.

Begin the visualisation by taking the concentration to the belly, be conscious of the breath, the slowing down of the breath, think of the breath in four parts, the inhalation, the exhalation, the pause and the still point, feel the gentle rise and fall of the belly and know that you are receiving.

Now visualise a beam of yellow light like a laser coming directly into your solar plexus, imagine this beam as a search light or a shaft of pure energy, feel as though the warmth of the sun is penetrating your belly, filling you with new and vibrant energy, allow this warmth to now spread around your body going deep within, until you feel as though you are melting into the sunlight, dissolving onto a bed of golden yellow sand, feel as though you are just suspended in light ,allow this warm sand to support you, to mould into the body to hold you safe, warm and at ease.
Feel as though the colour yellow is now around you, all over the body, you are bathed in a golden yellow light, and you feel completely relaxed and at peace.

When you feel ready begin to bring the body back to the space you are occupying on the floor.

The Colour Green

Green is the colour midway in the spectrum. It is neither hot or cold, we could call it the centring colour the harmonising colour, the balance. As the chakras move up from solid colours, they become more pastel, less gross, more lighter and spiritual. Green is the colour connected with the heart centre it has the power to unite the positive and negative energy and transform into harmony. When we think of the colour green we are reminded of fresh green fields, a lawn after summer rain, Prana, life force, and the fresh intake of energy. The colour green also reminds us to try and stay in the heart centre , when our feelings and intuition come from the heart centre we are generally in the right place.

Allow the body to just Be. Feel the breath breathing the body, be aware of the four part breath, the intake, the pause, the out breath, and the still point. Feel as though you are just witnessing the breath, be an observer. Now take the attention to the heart centre, and feel as though the breath is parting the chest, like waves on a seashore, coming and going, in and out, feel the chest expand, widen, open out, and in this opening is space, a space that allows you to breathe more easily both mentally and physically, deep down within this space is a tiny

seed of emerald green light, as you breathe in and out allow this seed to grow into a ball of emerald green energy, allow it to soak into the chest centre, to bathe the lungs in green light, to bring energy, harmony and balance, allow the whole body to be healed by this green light, allow the whole body to breathe in this emerald light.

Now feel as though you are sinking into a lush green carpet of springy grass, allow the earth to support you as the whole body is bathed in a green luminous light.

OM SHANTI

The Colour Blue

Blue is the colour associated with the throat centre, it governs communication. Space is represented here in the form of sound, allowing the voice to be heard, walking your talk, expression, confidence, allowing the voice freedom. All sound is vibration and vibration resonates, sound moves through the vibration and energy of the body and helps to lift the spirit and mood, that is why singing and chanting, all voice work ,is such a liberating force, it is such a tonic to the whole energy system.

As we focus on the colour blue, feel it as a strong vibrant glow, allow this colour to go around your body like a aura of light, feel it expanding outwards on each in breath, feel the colour radiate healing, allow this colour to surround the body and as it grows around you it forms a cloak of protection. Be aware of the breath just coming and going with quiet ease, the body is feeling comfortable, rested, warm, and you are beginning to feel completely relaxed.

You find yourself waiting beside a lakeside, it is a warm day, the lake is still and placid, and a small boat is coming towards you, you recognise the boatman as your friend, he is slowly drawing the oars together as he comes to the lakeshore, he invites you inside the boat and you sit down and admire the view, the fine day, the crystal clear water not a ripple in sight only the movement the oars make, gently moving in and out of the water. The boat is steady and drifts along. All you are aware of is the blue sky, the blue lake, and the sound of the oars skimming the water.

Eventually you come to a small island, and on this island is a small castle, someone is waiting to greet you at the door, you are being made very welcome, do you know this person, you are directed into a large room, blue light fills the room, it seems to filter down from the ceiling, cascading onto a deep blue velvet chair, you are now guided to sit down, this guide seems to know you, and yet, you are not quite sure, as you sink down into the deep velvet chair, you feel a cloak being draped across your shoulders, how soft this deep blue velvet cloak feels, it completely covers your body, how warm, how safe, how secure it feels, how comforting, you feel as though the guide is saying allow this cloak to be your protection and put it on any time you feel as if you are in need of help or healing. Feel now as though the entire body is being bathed in light, in healing, energised and protected, allow the warmth of the cloak to help you relax deeper and deeper into the velvet chair.

All too soon you find yourself back in the rowing boat, drifting along, back to the lakeside, you know you have healed, you know you have been comforted, and you know that anytime, anytime at all, you can ask to wear that deep blue velvet cloak.

The Colour Indigo

The colour Indigo is associated with the third eye. This centre is the Intuitive, the seat of guidance, the meditative state, concentration, contemplation, and Prana merges at this point both negative and positive.

When we try to meditate or engage in Pranayama, we try and take the attention to the eye brow centre. By increasing the awareness in this centre we can get a clearer insight and focus.

Imagine that you are lying down looking up into a deep dark velvet indigo sky . The stars are bright and shining and you can make out shapes and constellations, some stars are very bright, and some are just twinkling, some are close together, they seem to hang in clusters and some are very far apart they go on, endless, forever, in fact we do not have a concept of them ending.

See the brightest star ,how are you able to see it, and yet how many light years away it is, how large is this star, and how fast is it travelling, be aware of the mass of energy it contains, all the different types of energies, if you were near it, how would it sound, how would it feel, visualise the power, the force, how it converts and transforms, how transformation is change, change to another energy or force. How long will this energy form last, how many more millions of years, how will it then look.

Look and compare yourself, the amount of space your body is taking up on the floor, how small you are, and yet you yourself are continually changing, your energy is constantly moving, you are continually growing, progressing, as a whole we are all a mass of vibrant energy, a huge life force. on our own we feel insignificant. Contemplate once again the grandness of the Universe, the movement of the planets, without any interference from man.

Feel the colour Indigo merge around your body, creating a aura of light, protection, and healing, as You travel to the nearest star. The brilliant white light forms a tunnel for you to move through and as you go along this tunnel of light, you become infused with healing, with positive thought, with a lightness, a deep understanding and recognition that you feel completely safe, secure, peaceful and content, you come through the tunnel of light, and you find yourself floating back through the indigo sky, back onto your own mat. You are peaceful, relaxed, at ease, the body is still ,the breath is slow. I Am.

OM SHANTI.

The Shining Lotus

The crown chakra is the highest centre in the body. It is situated at the crown of the head. It is not a chakra as such but the seat of higher consciousness. We are looking for pure light, energy, spirituality, union with self, thought, the still small voice, and that which we are, I am.

Energy is a powerful source, to raise energy through the chakras to the crown centre is maybe too much for westerners, after all, we have in many ways adapted yoga to meet our western needs, we cannot all be into meditation every day, we are on this earth and of this earth, therefore our physical body has to be lived in a material sense, we still have to be well grounded and earthed, we can strive for aspects of complete peace, we can visualise this happening to us, we may never attain it, but our goal is to try and experience it.

Begin the visualisation by allowing the body to completely let go, feel the body releasing, follow the yoga nidra technique. Feel the body sinking into the floor, allow the earth to support you. You are free, safe and secure, the body is comfortable and warm, feel the back spread out across the mat, to widen, at the same time elongate, feel a loosening up, flexibility, a freedom that surrounds you, protects you, as you surrender onto the floor.

Be aware of the amount of space you are taking up on the floor, the amount of space you take up on this planet, surround yourself now with a pure blue healing light, allow this aura of light to pulsate with energy and light, as you breathe in and out, allow the aura of light to grow, to widen, to touch the person next to you and merge your energies. Think of the room being filled with a circle of blue light, a healing energy, a vibrant upliftment, comfort and solace for anyone who may be in need at this moment in time either physically or mentally.

Visualise the crown of the head, and place in the centre of the head a shining lotus with a thousand petals, this pure white flower is shining with luminous light, it is spiritual energy, it is peace, it is contentment and comfort, feel the compassion, the softness.

The opening out of the petals now creates within you an opening which allows a stream of pure white crystal mist to flow through the crown of the head into the body, feel as though the crown of the head is allowing a stream of pure white light to enter your body, and with this light comes complete surrender, you are now able to let go, let any restrictions or blockages be released, recognise that part of you that has been lost or fragmented, feel the crystal mist now flooding into the whole of your body, as it goes into the arms and legs feel the lightness, feel the whole of the body being released of weight, release any heaviness, any density, feel the body sinking deeper and deeper into the relaxation, all you are aware of now, is the stillness, the peace, the warmth and the contentment.

As you bring the body back from the visualisation, imagine the lotus flower on the crown of the head, closing into itself. Be aware of the petals folding back into a bud, feel the light shimmer until the stillness returns, and allow the body to slowly return.

OM SHANTI.

Balancing the Energy

When you are feeling completely relaxed, take your attention to the base chakra, the lower spine. Into this centre create the colour red, think of a field of crimson poppies, be aware of the vibrant colour, the deepness of the red, how it makes you feel, the upliftment, the boldness, the courage, and the strength. Be aware of these positive feelings emanating from the base chakra, feel as though you are drawing these feelings upwards, you now feel strong, fearless, and full of courage, still visualise the colour red.

Hold it for, a few moments.

Move your attention to the sacral area a few inches above the base of the spine and be aware of the colour orange. Visualise this colour flooding into the whole of the lower pelvis area. The vibrant colour orange represents expression, joy, releasing of unwanted thoughts and feelings, feel alive, imagine a cottage garden full of marigolds, see the brightness of the colour, the different shades of orange, feel the upliftment, the joy, and allow this colour to be drawn upwards, feel as though the colour orange is pulsating with life, spreading across the entire lower body.

Hold it for a few moments.

Now be conscious of the belly, the solar plexus. In the whole of this area think of the colour yellow flooding into the belly, imagine a beam of light like a huge search beam going directly into the abdomen feel it flooding across the centre allowing the belly to soften, to feel relaxed, to feel as though a golden light is healing you.

Hold it for a few moments.

Next bring your visualisation into the heart centre, and be aware of the breath, feel as though the chest centre separates each time you breathe in and out. With this separation comes space.

Deep down in the chest centre, in this space, create a seed of emerald green light, each time you breathe in and out feel this emerald green light growing, expanding, until it becomes a ball of emerald green energy, allow this green energy to soak into the heart centre and create peace, harmony, and balance.

Feel an openness in the chest centre that you haven't felt for a long time, feel free, and allow this freedom to breathe you both mentally and physically.

Open out the heart centre and allow

he chest to breathe.

Hold it for a few moments.

Now be mindful of the throat centre, the colour blue, the freshness and openness of blue, allow the voice to be heard, release the tightness with song, with chant, with mantra, be mindful of always walking your talk, have and enjoy the freedom of speech, allow the colour blue to go into the throat centre, to massage the thyroid, to heal, to create a balance in this centre.

Hold it for a few moments.

The brow centre is our direct link to intuition, and our ability to become more in touch with our self development, usually known as the psychic centre, we come into this centre with the colour indigo, be aware of a deep blue, and as you try to imagine this colour think of space, the endless night sky, the awesome power of the universe, direct this light into the third eye, the brow centre, think of a slender beam of pure blue light going directly into the forehead, imagine piercing into the brow centre, bringing intuition, concentration, contemplation, allow this centre to cease the chattering monkey, focus the mind and allow this colour to create stillness.

Hold it for a few moments.

Finally bring your imagination to the crown of the head and visualise pure crystal light, imagine a stream of pure crystal light filtering into the crown of the head, this beam of light is directly above you, this laser of light is pure energy, allow it now to return to the source.

Be still and know that I am.

OM SHANTI.

Fire

Sitting in your chosen place, visualise yourself walking to a small cottage on a cold winters evening. The snow lies thick on the ground, you can hear the crunch of your feet as you walk along the hard ground. The trees are covered in a blanket of snow, the boughs hang laden with ice, silence fills the air, the wind blows cold penetrating the clothes that serve to protect you.

In the distance is your cottage, you approach the gate, lift the old latch and walk up the snow covered path to the front door, open the cottage door with the key provided, and you find yourself in a dimly lit hallway, feel the warmth as you entered the cottage, feel a sense of relief at being away from the cold night air, feel safe, feel secure.

Walking from the hall into the sitting room, you find a blazing log fire, feel the warmth as you walk into the room. The only light is from the log fire. Take a seat beside the fire, allow the body to sink down into the comfortable arm chair, position the cushions to allow the head to relax, the shoulders to widen, the back to release, sink deeper into the cushions feel as if the body has moulded itself into the chair. Relax and let go.

As you sit gazing into the fire you are aware of the flickering flames dancing around the walls, the light, the darkness, be aware of the sounds from the open fire, the crackling of the logs, the sparks, the kindling burning, smell the scent of pine, of fresh burning wood, of forest and earth, see how the flames change shape, how the colours dance and dart around, feel the warmth from the fire now spreading around your body, feel the eyelids heavy, feel as though you are sinking deeper and deeper into a state of relaxation, it feels safe, you are safe, relax and let go.

Now gradually come back to this room away from the visualisation, be aware of how you feel, where you have been and if you followed the visualisation, continue to feel the peace and the stillness of the moment.

OM SHANTI.

A walk in the country

Be aware of the blue sky, the shades of blue, the healing colour of blue,the blue sky.

Be aware of the sun shining down on your body, the golden yellow sun, the energy, the vitality.

Be aware of gentle moving clouds, fluffy clouds hanging like cotton wool, clouds drifting.

Be aware of passing green fields, the freshness, feel the colour green drenching the body, breathe green.

Approach a kissing gate and gently lift the latch, walk through the gate and find yourself in a field of bright crimson poppies, be aware of the tall green stems, the central black eye, the delicate petals, a field of crimson, feel the bright red lift the spirits, feel a surge of joy.

You hear the sound of running water.

Approach a gentle stream, feel the coolness in the air, the clarity, the energy, be aware of the gentle sound of om.

Cross the stream by way of stepping stones and arrive in a field, two horses are watching your approach, you pass slowly by.

In the distance you hear the sound of church bells chiming, stop for a moment and listen to the slow clear chime, a small church appears, very pretty, very old.

Enter the church, it is empty and quiet, take a seat and breathe in the peace and tranquillity, feel the presence of all those souls who have gone before you, walked the same walk, the same walk as all of us, seeking peace and stillness.

Rest for a while and enjoy the stillness.

When you are ready open the eyes and slowly bring the body back here and now.

Bluebell Wood

It is a clear warm spring day and you are walking through the woods, see the shafts of sunlight dapple through the branches of the trees, showing up all the new buds, tiny leaves are forming, the woods are alive with energy and life force. Feel the earth under your feet, the damp mossy leaves, the newness of the grass, the fresh green shoots. Here and there ferns are unfurling opening gently, the smell of wild garlic is in the air, a musty damp smell. Be aware of the birds busy nest building, the snowdrops beginning to lose their purity for they are snow lovers, the feeling of expectation and renewal has began.

As you walk on you come to a clearing and it is as if a paintbrush has been swept across the ground covering it in all shades of blue, from the palest shade, to deep indigo, you find yourself surrounded by bluebells, you are in a bluebell wood.

Finding a fallen tree trunk, you sit down and look at the spectacle, the shades of blue, how all the flowers differ in stages of development, some are tight buds and some are fully open. How intricate they are, how each tiny bell possesses its own shape and colour. Close you eyes, feel the warmth of the sun on your face, visualise one of these bluebells, be aware of the deep heady scent, as you look closely, you discover the bell expanding, until it completely surrounds and enfolds you and you find yourself lying inside the huge bell.

How comfortable it feels, lie back allow the head to rest on the pale blue petals, feel the petals surround you like a soft mantle. The blue rays emanating from the petals play upon your body, releasing, dissolving, melting, allowing you to let go and surrender. Feel safe and secure, you are safe and secure you are completely at peace, allow the blue light to circle you with a healing light, for any part of the body or mind that may be in need of healing at this moment in time.

Take your time bringing the body back to lying in your own space.

OM SHANTI.

Changing Seasons

Allow the body to completely let go, and feel the earth supporting you. Be aware of your body and the amount of space it is taking up on the floor. Try and visualise this planet earth and draw a cord from the base chakra into the earth, imagine going deep down through various layers to the very core and centre, feel the cord being earthed, anchored, imagine how this earth has evolved over billions of years, and yet the seasons still seem to come and go, the sea and oceans remain tidal and nature has her way, we are all dependant on change.

Imagine the season of winter, the air blows cold, frost skims the ponds, the trees are white and frosted, the air is crisp and the earth is cold and hard. All is quiet and still, the days are long and dark, animals hibernate, the earth seems to sleep, and yet below the ground bulbs are growing, roots are searching, and the first green shoot of a snowdrop pushes itself forward and upwards towards the light.

The pure white snowdrops are the welcome sign that growth and renewal are both part of the natural cycle of life. As the ground warms up the snowdrops lose their purity and the daffodils herald the spring, the days lighten up, the earth starts to rapidly prepare for growth, and all around, all of a sudden we seem to see new life forming, all the spring flowers bring with them the message of renewal, of hope, of life force and in this burst of growth we understand the cycle of nature.

This is the time when nature is busy, the birds are nest building, frogs are mating, the blossom is forming, and we feel a sense of expectation, we long to be released from the long dark days of winter, our bodies are needy of sunshine. Suddenly we find ourselves looking at a wonderful summer cottage garden, the pond is full of water lilies, the borders are full of lupins, lilies, foxgloves, the smell of wallflowers fill the air, lavender bushes create a safe haven for bees and butterflies, the cottage wall is full of honeysuckle and the branches flow down to the open doorway allowing the heady scent to flow through the cottage.

Imagine yourself in this cottage garden swinging slowly on a garden hammock, the warmth of the sun creates total relaxation, all you are aware of is the steady humming of the bees, the singing of the birds. The rocking movement of the hammock is like the in going and outgoing tide, back and forth in and out, the slow steady beating of the heart, the slow steady breath, feel yourself drifting, melting into the hammock, feel as though you are suspended in relaxation, allow the body to become very heavy, slowly sinking into the hammock.

Soon you are aware of the rustle of leaves, of the breeze catching the trees, of fallen leaves, of flowers that have lost their vigour, of a slowing down, and you find yourself looking at a broody Autumn sky, the trees have changed, the leaves are crisp and dry, they are now the colour of burnished copper and there seems to be a chill in the air, the nights are closing in, the time has come for hibernation, for storing energy, for slowing down, and in this slowing down the body changes, there is a need to nurture, to look after, to pamper through the dark November days, this is the time of suspension, for sleep, for we need our body reserves of energy to help us through the dark, long days of winter, once again the season has changed.

Every season has wonder, and as nature begins her cycle once again, we know that transformation is change, and in that change is balance.

OM SHANTI

The Rose

Complete the yoga nidra and feel yourself drifting into deep relaxation. The body is warm and comfortable and you feel safe and secure. Take the attention to the breath and be aware of the slowing down of the breathing. Relax like this for a few minutes before beginning the visualisation.

Now take the attention to the chest centre and be aware of your open chest, as you breathe in and out feel the expansion, the wideness of the chest centre, feel it opening out, in that opening you have created space, room to breathe, to visualise, to release and let go. Remember an open chest allows you to breathe.

Visualise in front of you three long stemmed red roses, the stem is long and graceful, the leaves are bright green, the thorns are sharp, and the rose is tightly closed. As you look at this rose, you are aware of the tightness of the bud, how all the petals tightly fold around each other perfectly, no creases or folds, just perfectly folded around each other. Be aware of tiny droplets of dew clinging to the petals, the colour, the softness of the bud, and now imagine those buds slowly opening, how the petals unfold, be aware of the deep colour red, of the slight perfume, the delicacy.

As the rose fully opens you marvel at the changing colour, the different hues of red, the perfect shape, the strong heady perfume. Look deep into the centre of this rose, look at the size, how the petals have spread, how the flower has widened be aware of the perfection in each of the three roses.

Now visualise these roses folding back into themselves becoming once again the perfect bud, see these three long stemmed roses clearly, and if you feel you would like to give someone one of these roses, consciously bring into your mind that person, and visualise them holding the rose.

When you feel ready to leave this visualisation, slowly bring the body back to where you were, take a few deep breaths and relax.

OM SHANTI.

Dolphins

Find yourself on a balmy tropical beach at sunset, the coconut palms swaying gently in the warm breeze, the sand warm , soft and golden under your feet, the sea is calm and so blue, all you can hear is the quiet lapping of the waves as they break on the sea shore, see clearly the blue of the sea, the light sparkling through the waves, the shafts of sunlight, the silvery light reflected on the sandy bottom. See clearly the horizon.

You are aware of movement, you hear sounds, and as you look out into the distance, you see shapes moving, dolphins, dancing amongst the waves, twisting and turning, diving under and over the waves playing with each other, chasing and twirling up into the air, see how nimble they are, how full of life, how playful, how they invite you to come and join them, hear their call, the high whine, the low humming sound, they are calling you to come and join them, and suddenly you are in the warm blue ocean, and you feel the dolphins gliding around you, you can actually feel them welcoming you, inviting you to be childlike again. You feel as if you are dissolving in the blueness, that you are surrounded by love and light, suddenly you feel playful again, lighter, you feel as though a weight has been lifted, and you can be free again, in and out of the waves you frolic, turning and twisting, look how

these dolphins smile at you, how they laugh, hear them speaking to you , they are calling out your name. Stay for a while and play, be childlike again.

Now they are reminding you that you have to be on your way. Suddenly it is time to go, and you feel sad to be leaving, but they tell you that you can come and swim with them any time, they will be waiting.

When you feel ready bring the body back from the visualisation, lie still for a while and be aware of where you have been and how you feel.

OM SHANTI.

Flight of a Seagull

Allow the body to let go and feel completely relaxed. Imagine you are lying on a bed of warm, soft sand. The body is moulded into the sand, every part of your body is completely relaxed. You feel warm, comfortable and free, feel as though you are just sinking deep down into the sand, the whole of the body is releasing and relaxing, feel the sand beneath your hands, the softness, the warmth, the ease.

You are able to open the eyes and look up into a deep blue cloudless sky, the sky goes on forever, and the blue of the sky meets the blue on the horizon, joining the sky and the ocean together.

All around you, surrounding you, is the blue of the sky and the blue of the sea. The sea is endless, a vast amount of water, the sea is calm, peaceful, still and silent, all you are aware of is an odd seagull diving into the clear blue sea. Feel the warmth of the sun on your face, the warmth of the sand supporting your body, be aware of feeling completely relaxed and at ease. You feel as though you are floating, suspended, lifting and moving upwards towards the sky, towards the seagull, imagine you are this seagull , gently floating along over the tops of the foam, tasting the sea salt, feeling the air under your arms, flying high, allowing the arms to become your wings, giving you the freedom in the chest centre, the freedom to fly, the freedom to soar, higher and higher, now you are free.

You fly near to land keeping close to the cliff edge, and dart back out to sea, you can soar up into the sky and dart down with ease, the warm thermal breeze helps you to drift along, helps you to drift and rest. Drifting and resting. Just be aware of drifting, of drifting.

Soon you find yourself slowing down, and you stop for a while near the rocks on the shoreline, you observe the rock pools, the sea life that the incoming tide will revive, the limpets clinging tightly to the rocks waiting for the fresh salt water to wash over them, the seaweed beginning to dry out, waiting, everything waiting, for the turn of the tide.

Slowly now the tide begins to turn, bringing back fresh supplies of food, life force, and energy, the slow in and out of the waves trickling into the rock pools, moving over the dried out seaweed, moving up to the shoreline, bringing flotsam, different types of seaweed, shells, pebbles, and bits of driftwood, completing the whole cycle once again.

lying backwards and forwards has red you out, and now you need to est for a while, drift down once again , nd feel your wings lose the power, feel our arms back down by your side lying omfortable on the warm sand. Stay for while and then gently bring the body ack from the visualisation. Be aware of where you have been on this visualisation, did you fly upwards, see how you feel mentally and physically, and lie still enjoying the peace and the tranquillity.

OM SHANTI.

Seaside Meditation

Lie still and feel completely relaxed, completely at ease. Feel the warmth of the sun penetrating your entire body, feel the colour yellow, the energy, soak up this sunshine, allow the colour yellow to drench into your body, releasing, relaxing, feel your body melting into the floor, dissolving into relaxation, feel your entire body, mould into the mat, feel as though you are being supported, cushioned by sand, feel the warmth of the golden sand, feel the grains of sand slipping through your fingers.

Visualise yourself walking along a sandy beach on a warm summer day, feel the firmness of the sand, the coolness, the damp sand, be aware of the tide receding, you are aware of the footprints you have left, slowly now being erased by the water.

Listen to the sound of the waves as they gently lap on the seashore, in and out, in and out, feel as though you are breathing in unison with the tide, be aware of the in and the out of the breath. Feel the freshness of the ocean, the energy, the life force, the clarity of the air, allow yourself to breathe, how good it feels to be free, well, and healthy, to be able to do exactly as you wish at this moment in time, on this warm summers day.

The beach is quiet, you are alone, and all you can hear are the seagulls, as they swoop and dive see how the water shimmers, sparkles, how the sun settles on the water creating rainbows of light. Stop for a moment, look and listen, all you can hear is the gentle rush of the wave as it moves across the shingle, and recedes back, in and out, in and out, without any interference by man, look now at the tiny pebbles, the tiny beautiful shells, that are lying by the waters edge, how they are anchored by tiny bits of seaweed, where did they come from, what animals lived in their shells, they are all different, some may have travelled for many miles, perhaps from a foreign shore, think of the journey, maybe they came in a storm, how they were washed into different countries until they came to rest right here on this beach, look at the different shapes and colours, every tiny shell had a life journey.

Feel the water now swirl gently around your feet, the tide is slowly turning, feel the coolness over your feet, the movement, the salt on the breeze, the coolness in the air, lift up your arms to the sky and stretch be aware of the stretch, feel the opening out of the heart centre, feel the freedom, feel as though you have been released, how light you feel, how content. Be aware now of the seagulls swooping down for food on the incoming tide, see them weaving in and out of the water, some are bobbing up and down on the waves, how good it feels just to observe, to have the time to wander, to be able to watch.

Now you approach some sand dunes, from this point you are able to watch the tide as it slowly comes in, lie still and allow the eyes to look out to the blue horizon, see an endless ocean of blue sea, feel at peace, feel at ease, relax and let go, feel the healing as the energy is released from the incoming tide and breathe in that energy.

OM SHANTI.

Space

Lie still and imagine you are looking up into a dark blue sky, the night is cool and still. Be conscious of the mat you are lying on, the amount of space you are taking up on this planet. Focus your attention on the universe, the vastness of space, the universal energy, the movement of the earth and all the planets without any interference from man, how the universe just is.

Be aware of this huge energy and imagine it as a vortex of light, this light you can draw down as lifeforce and energy to heal yourself.

Look up into this dark blue sky and draw down towards you showers of silver stars, feel that sparkling energy rush through your body creating a tingling sensation, a lightness.

Visualise shooting stars racing across the sky, and draw down a shaft of energy.

Visualise a full moon, feel the magnetic energy, the strength and draw it down towards you.

Visualise a bright golden sun, see the bright yellow, and feel a warmth of energy beaming down towards your solar plexus, be aware of receiving vital prana.

Visualise a rainbow, see all the colours of the rainbow, and see yourself walking through one of those colours that most appeals to you at this moment in time.

See now a double rainbow, a most magical experience, and feel uplifted.

See an orange disk forming on the horizon, a ball of colour, see this large disk increasing in size until it becomes the most glorious sunset

See the same orange disk on the horizon as it heralds a new dawn, a new start, a new beginning, a new day.

Feel the glow of the colour orange spreading into your body filling you with a lightness, a freedom, the strength to start a new day.

Allow this healing visualisation to wash away any worries, any blockages, anything that you no longer need to hold onto. To clear and cleanse the mind, to allow us to be clear about our intentions, to allow us to go forward without fear, feel now the heart centre opening out, allowing you to receive healing, hope, courage, and strength.

A Christmas Visualisation

Begin with Yoga Nidra completely relaxing the body and feeling the body sinking into the mat. Allow the body to completely surrender.

Imagine that you are lying on a thick Arabian rug. This rug has a deep soft pile and is navy blue, painted with silver stars, moons and golden suns, you can feel the tassels on the edges of the rug they hang like thick golden threads. Now sink into the rug and let it hold you safely and securely, allow it to take your weight, surrender and trust. This is a magic carpet and you are going on a journey, so relax and let go.

Feel the rug now rising up into the clear night sky. There is a full moon and the stars are out, the night is crisp and still. You feel yourself rising upwards , and it feels safe. You are moving along steady, and secure. Begin to feel the warm air on your face as you travel over foreign lands. On and on you travel, the warm breeze moving you gently along. Far away in the distance you begin to sight land, this is the land of the Arabian Nights.

As you peep over the side of the rug you begin to see lights in the desert, Bedouins in their tents, camel trails and the sound of Eastern music fills the air,

as you float along, you are able to see women in eastern dress dancing around camp fires, further on you trave over homesteads, colourful bazaars, stalls, and villages, you can smell the aroma of the orient as exotic oils waft up on the breeze, musk, amber, frankincense, and the deep heady smell of incense burning, cedarwood and sandalwood, breathe in the orient, breathe and relax. Allow these sensuous oils to deepen your visualisation, to heighten your awareness, to work on your higher energy ,To give you deeper insight, a clarity of thought, and intuition.

PAUSE FOR A WHILE AND JUST FEEL SUSPENDED.

Now feel yourself slowly turning back towards your homeland, the night is still dark, and you feel a sense of knowing as you travel back the way you came. The moon is behind the cloud now, but some bright star is guiding the way, look deep into the night sky, and allow that star to guide you home.

You are now back on your own space on the mat, take a few deep breaths to centre and feel grounded.
You are safe, secure and at peace.

OM SHANTI.

Printed in Great Britain
by Amazon

NICKEL

Elise Noble

Edited by Nikki Mentges

Cover by Abigail Sins

www.undercover-publishing.com

www.elise-noble.com

If I had a nickel for every time you got on my nerves...
I'd have a sock full of nickels to beat the shit out of you
with.
- *Emmy Black*

CHAPTER 1 - SLOANE

"STOP CALLING ME at the office," I hissed.

"You leave me with little choice, Sloane. You won't answer your cell phone."

And there was a darn good reason for that. I didn't want to talk to Kenneth. I didn't even want to think about him. What I did want to do was run his testicles through a wood chipper right before I removed his vocal cords with the dental pick he insisted on using in front of the mirror every morning.

"Because I'm busy. Just give me back my stuff."

"I will, when you come over and get it. We need to talk, pumpkin."

I'd once thought it cute that he gave me a nickname, but a rotund orange Halloween decoration? Really?

"I've got nothing to say to you."

"Look, I made a mistake. I realise that, and I'm prepared to apologise if you'll only sit down and discuss this like an adult."

"A mistake? *A mistake?*" Heads turned to stare at me, and I lowered my voice to a harsh whisper. "Forgetting to buy milk is a mistake. Burning dinner is a mistake. Sticking your cock into your secretary is not a freaking mistake!"

"I've explained that." His reasonable tone made me

want to throw the phone across the room, but I prided myself on remaining professional at all times. "We won a big advertising contract, and I had a little too much to drink with lunch. Sherilyn drove me home, and we got carried away. I told you I've fired her."

And I felt weirdly guilty about that. Sherilyn couldn't have been more than twenty—wrinkle-and-love-handle-free—and it wasn't her fault that her boss had been a complete jerk. Still, she was probably better off without him. We both were. I just wanted my freaking belongings back.

"Yes, I understand you left the girl unable to pay her rent this month, but that doesn't change how I feel. It's over."

"Why don't we take a vacation? Hawaii? You always wanted to go to Hawaii."

Which part of "it's over" did he not get? Was this how he'd made it to assistant vice president at the big advertising firm he worked for? Did he simply wear down any potential clients until they signed the contract to make him go away?

"I don't want to go to Hawaii."

"How about the Bahamas?"

"Or the Bahamas or anywhere else with you. I just want you to pack up the things I left in your apartment so I can get out of your life. I'll send a courier at a time that's convenient."

"As Benjamin Franklin once said, 'Take time for all things: great haste makes great waste.' This is a big decision, and you've barely thought it through."

Give me strength.

"Kenneth, I can't talk about this right now. I'm at work."

"Tonight, seven o'clock, my place. I'll buy one of those French apple tarts from Claude's that you're so fond of."

"Fine. Seven o'clock. But we're not talking. I want to get my stuff and leave."

"I'll open a bottle of rosé."

I slammed the phone down so hard it fell onto the floor. Leah, the friend and colleague who sat next to me, picked it up and set it back on my desk.

"You okay?" she asked.

"Kenneth's totally delusional. He still thinks that if he buys me enough gifts and ignores everything I say, I'll conveniently forget I walked in on him cheating."

"I don't know why you haven't asked Emmy to get your stuff back. You know she would."

Emmy and her husband, Black, were my two bosses at Blackwood Security. I'd started working there at the age of twenty-two, seven-and-a-bit years ago, following a brief spell at an accounting firm in Richmond. Brief because one of the partners had followed me into the stationery cupboard and tried to put his hand up my skirt, and I'd walked out the door without stopping to pick up my final pay cheque. Luckily, Emmy had taken a chance on me, and I'd been at Blackwood ever since. I never wanted to leave.

And as the female version of Superman, she'd help me to collect my things if I asked her—of that I was certain—but I was equally sure that Kenneth would end up with a few dents along the way.

"I don't want to get Emmy involved. Kenneth's best friend is a personal injury lawyer and his uncle's a cop."

"So? Emmy won't care about that."

"But my mom will when she hears about it, and she

will hear about it. If Kenneth gets so much as a bruise, he'll make sure the entire neighbourhood knows, and Mom hates any sort of violence."

Go figure. I'd been brought up on a diet of rainbows and pacifism, and my bosses were both highly paid assassins. Mom thought I worked for a company that installed burglar alarms. I loved her dearly, but sometimes she could be really, really hard work.

"Do you have much to pick up from Kenneth?"

"Enough that I can't let it go. Clothes, shoes, books, half of my bakeware including the pans Grandma gave me before she died two years ago, and I can't ever replace those."

"Tell me again, why did you date Kenneth?"

"You have no idea how many times I've asked myself that same question over the past month."

I just didn't want to admit to the answer. My next birthday—in only four short months—would be the big three-O, and between Mom's comments about grandchildren, internet ads for dating sites, memes about crazy cat ladies, and my own biological clock ticking away in the background, I may have ended up a teeny bit unhinged. That and I was sick of spending all my spare time alone. So when Kenneth asked me out at one of the church fundraisers both of our moms had a hand in organising, I'd said yes even though he didn't exactly make my heart skip. Mom once said she hadn't much liked my dad when they first met in high school, but thirty-five years later, they were still together, for better, for worse. Mostly worse, if I was truthful. When I was younger, he'd hurt her badly, and even now they bickered a lot and he acted like a scumbag most of the time. But perhaps that was an extreme example? Even

regular relationships were supposed to take effort, right? And men needed a translation manual.

"So, are you gonna go over there tonight?" Leah asked. "I'd come with you, but it's my sister-in-law's baby shower."

Tick, tick, tick.

"Honestly, it's fine. No, I'm not going, not tonight. Maybe another day when I'm less likely to throw things at Kenneth."

If only I hadn't thrown back the key to his damn apartment, then we wouldn't be having this conversation. It didn't even hit him, just bounced off the sheet his secretary was clutching around herself.

"You *should* throw things. Like a grenade."

"I—"

A shadow fell across my desk, a big shadow, and I knew who it was before I turned my head. The light aroma of Hugo Boss aftershave that barely masked the woodsy musk of *man* made my heart race. How did I know it was Hugo Boss? Because I'd spent hours picking it out when I drew the wearer in the office Secret Santa the year before last. *Hours.* I'd tested so many fragrances that I lost my sense of smell for three whole days. The original bottle must surely have run out by now, which meant he'd liked it enough to *buy more.* Therefore the effort had been worth it.

"Everything okay?" Logan Barnes asked.

As well as having great bosses, did I mention the other perk of working at Blackwood? *The men.* We didn't just have eye candy, we had the visual equivalent of ice cream sundaes, glazed donuts, and chocolate caramels walking through our office every single day, dressed in everything from custom-made suits to

combats.

And Logan? Logan was a banana split with chocolate sauce, whipped cream, and sprinkles. Emphasis on the banana part.

Not that I'd ever admit he made my mouth water. Men like Logan—sculpted visions of tanned skin and smooth muscles topped by tousled dark-brown hair— didn't go for girls like me. Sure, he could be a bit of a dick on occasion, like the time he bought me diet chocolates for Christmas, but he still made my insides do somersaults whenever he came near. And men like Logan dated heiresses and CEOs and the lingerie model he'd brought to last year's Independence Day celebration.

Girls like me, well, we got Kenneth. A thirty-three-year-old advertising executive who answered every question with a question and freaked if he ran out of clean socks.

And guess who was supposed to wash the socks? That's right: me.

But right now, I had a hot man leaning over my desk and a pulse that thought it was sprinting for gold, so I shoved Kenneth to the back of my dirty mind and tried to smile.

"Everything's fine. Totally fine. Couldn't be better."

"You sure? You were looking kinda pissed."

"Honestly, there's no problem. Uh, my cat scratched my leg this morning, and it stings a bit."

Nickel had done nothing of the sort, and I felt slightly guilty for blaming him, but I didn't want Logan to know just how bad I was at making decisions.

"Have you had a tetanus shot?"

"All up to date." I forced a smile. "Can I help with

anything?"

"I was hoping for a favour, but if you're not feeling good..."

"Sure, I'll do it," I said a little too quickly. "I mean, things aren't busy this afternoon, so I've got time."

Let's be truthful—if Logan wanted me to fetch him coffee or type up a report or tidy his desk or run an errand, I'd do it in a heartbeat.

"You're a lifesaver. It's my niece's birthday tomorrow..." He looked uncertain for a moment and checked his phone. "Yeah, fifth of June. I need to FedEx her a gift."

"What sort of gift?"

"I have absolutely no idea."

"How old is she?"

Panic flashed across Logan's face, which made me smile inside because normally he was super tough.

"Six? Seven?" He tapped at his phone screen again. "Eight. She's eight."

"Okay, eight years old. What kind of stuff does she like?"

Logan just shrugged.

"I need a tiny clue."

"I think she takes ice-skating lessons. And she keeps asking for a pony."

"FedExing a pony isn't really practical."

"Plus my sister would probably kill me if I bought her one."

"So, ice skating. Anything else? Do you know her favourite colour?"

If only Logan's sister had owned a cat instead. Buying kitty treats was one of my fortes, and I knew every pet store from Richmond to Norfolk.

"When Fantasia used to draw on the walls, she mostly picked blue."

"Wait a second... Your niece is called Fantasia?"

Logan groaned as he perched one taut ass cheek on the edge of my desk. "Don't go there."

"Can't she shorten it?"

"To what? Fanny? Fanta?" Logan shook his head. "My sister was married to some weird hippie for six months in her twenties. The smartest thing she ever did was divorce him."

"Does he still help with Fantasia?"

"He's serving ten years for fraud."

"I'm sorry to hear that."

"I'm not. He was a devious son of a bitch. Took me three months to find enough evidence to get him put away."

Oh. "Uh, congratulations?"

"Thanks, but that's all in the past." He glanced at his watch. "Sorry, I've got a meeting. About this gift..."

"Yes, the gift. If she was decorating the walls, maybe Fantasia likes art as well?"

"I guess."

"Leave it with me, and I'll find something, I promise. Can you email me the address?"

A few more taps on his phone. "Done." Then he leaned down to kiss me on the cheek, catching me by surprise. "I owe you one, kitten."

I felt my blush spread up my cheeks, possibly over my head and down my neck too. Had my ears gone red?

"Kitten? Is that appropriate?"

He smirked as he pointed at my T-shirt, which may have had a sparkly cat on it. Emmy's other assistant,

Bradley, had gifted it to me for my last birthday and while I'd loved it at the time, now I felt like a gawky teenager in front of her high-school crush.

"I didn't buy this. I mean, I've had it for ages, and..." Really, I had no more words.

"Cute."

One word, and Logan strolled off. I leaned my head on the desk and wrapped my arms around it, although I couldn't help peeking at Logan's butt as it headed for the conference room.

Perhaps I'd borrow a desk on a different floor tomorrow.

CHAPTER 2 - LOGAN

"WHAT'S UP WITH Sloane?" Logan asked Leah as he waited for the machine to make his coffee.

"What makes you think anything's up? She said everything was fine."

Which was bullshit. Normally, Sloane's smile brightened the entire office, but today, she looked as if she'd swallowed a hornet's nest.

"Yeah, she did say that, but she was also lying."

"She'll kill me if I say anything."

"How about I kill you if you don't?"

"Now *you're* lying."

Leah laughed and leaned past him to take a donut, but Logan grabbed the box and held them out of her reach. Since he stood six feet one compared to Leah's five feet nothing, that wasn't a difficult task.

"Oh, no you don't." He stood on tiptoes as she jumped to grab them. "I'll eat every single one of these if you don't tell me why Sloane's upset."

"You wouldn't dare."

"Try me. Mmm, I'm so hungry."

Leah narrowed her eyes, and for such a tiny lady, she looked disproportionately scary.

"Why do you even care about Sloane?"

"Because we had a management meeting the other day, and Black asked me to head up the new employee-

welfare program."

Black, of course, had done no such thing. No wonder Leah looked sceptical. The big man's idea of monitoring staff well-being was to check they were all still breathing from time to time. Why didn't Logan think before he opened his mouth?

"Well, it was Nick's idea, but Black signed off on it," Logan clarified. Nick was another of the directors—the only one out of the four rumoured to have a soul. There, that sounded more plausible.

"Sloane's issues outside work aren't any of your business."

Ah, so there *was* a problem. Logan reached into the box blind and pulled out a donut. Boston Creme. He bit into it, never taking his eyes off Leah.

"This is delicious. Are you sure you don't want one?"

"You're such an asshole, Logan."

"Tell me something I don't know, like why Sloane looked as though she wanted to put her pen through someone's throat earlier."

The prospect of refined sugar won out, and Leah sighed. "Man trouble."

"Man trouble? Sloane?"

"Don't sound so surprised. She gets plenty of interest. It just so happened that the last guy was a prick. Still is a prick."

Didn't Logan know it? A prick with gelled hair, a fancy condo, an electric BMW, and—most likely—a limp dick. The mystery wasn't why he was interested in Sloane, but why she'd been interested in him.

"What did he do?"

"Cheated on her. But you didn't hear it from me,

okay?"

That little cocksucker. Logan dropped the box of donuts on the counter and cracked his knuckles.

"I'll have a word. Nobody does that to Sloane."

"No! Why do you think she kept it quiet? She doesn't want anyone here taking things into their own hands."

"I promise I'll be nice."

"Seriously?"

"Sure."

"Just don't do it. *Please?* He'll probably take all her stuff to Goodwill if you antagonise him."

"What stuff?"

Leah dropped into one of the weird plastic chairs that had appeared in the kitchen the previous week. Lime green, kind of triangular, but at least the wheels on the bottom made it easier to tug her towards him.

"Tell me everything, or I'll have to ask Kenneth."

"You know his name?"

Shit. "I may have heard Sloane mention it a time or two."

And he may also have got Kenneth's number from Sloane's cell phone when she wasn't paying attention, then persuaded Mouse, one of Blackwood's data geeks and a man of questionable morals, to dig up everything he could find on the sleaze. Kenneth spent a hundred dollars on a hairstylist every fourth Saturday, regular as clockwork. What sort of man did that? In fact, Logan couldn't even remember the last time he got his hair cut. He stroked his chin absent-mindedly—yeah, he might have trimmed his beard a couple of weeks ago. Maybe a month.

Leah ate two donuts while she spilled everything,

but Logan had lost his appetite. That arrogant little troll was trying to bully Sloane into continuing their relationship after what he did? The guy was deluded. He'd had everything and lost it through his own stupidity. Sloane was sweet as cotton candy, loyal, hard-working, not to mention pretty. No, Kenneth wouldn't be getting her back.

"So he's expecting her at seven?"

"Yes, but she's not going."

"Make sure she doesn't. I'll go instead."

"Logan..."

"I won't leave any marks. Cross my heart."

Logan left Sloane in the office hunting for Fantasia's birthday present, and at five minutes to seven, he pulled up outside Kenneth's apartment building with Slater in the passenger seat of his truck.

"We're just picking up Sloane's stuff?" Slater asked. "That's it?"

"That's it."

Before they'd left, Leah had fetched them a bunch of those big cardboard boxes with lids from the archive room, and they were sitting in the back seat.

"Sounds straightforward," Slater said.

"Yeah, it should be. In and out. Half an hour at most."

"Beers afterwards?"

"Sure thing."

Logan grabbed the stack of boxes, and they headed for the communal entrance. A leggy blonde was on her way out, and when Slater flashed her a shit-eating grin,

she tripped over her own feet to hold the door open for them.

"Thanks, babe," he said as they strolled past, and the girl turned scarlet.

On the fourth floor, Logan stopped outside apartment 406, where Kenneth actually had his name outside on a tiny gold plaque. Talk about pretentious. Logan rapped on the door with his knuckles.

A minute passed.

Two.

Eventually, the door opened and the greasy little shit peered out through the crack.

First, Logan went for nice. He may have spent seven years in the military—three in the regular army, one as a Ranger, and three attached to a CIA unit so elite he wasn't allowed to mention its name—but his momma had brought him up well.

"Kenneth Perkins?"

From the sportswear and the towel around his neck, it seemed as though they'd interrupted his workout, if you could call it that. He wasn't sweating much.

"Who are you?"

"Friends of Sloane's. She asked us to pick up her stuff." Okay, so that was a tiny white lie. "Hope we're not late."

"How did you even get into the building? Did you buzz the intercom? I didn't hear you buzz the intercom. And I'm not speaking to you. I've already told Sloane I'll return the items she left with me for safekeeping, but she's got to come over herself. What, you think I'll simply hand her things over to a pair of thugs like you? Get lost. Just get lost! Crawl back under your rock and

stop disturbing people while they're in the middle of important things, you condescending pair of slimeballs. Don't you have anything better to do with your time? Because I do."

Kenneth ended on a yell and slammed the door in their faces. Slater looked at Logan.

"I thought you said this would be easy?"

Logan unclenched his jaw for long enough to speak. "Obviously, I was mistaken."

"So, what now? We go for beers?"

"Give up? Never." Logan chewed on his bottom lip as he mulled the problem over. "You know what it is? We're not scary enough."

"Dude, you look like you just escaped from the zoo."

Was that supposed to be a compliment? Logan wasn't sure. "Well, you look like you just escaped from the Tommy Hilfiger catalogue."

Slater may have had over one hundred confirmed kills, but most of them had been with a high-powered sniper rifle rather than hand to hand, and he'd been scouted by modelling agencies at least four times that Logan knew of.

"Ralph Lauren, actually. You have a plan?"

"Yup. Gonna call for reinforcements."

They sat in the hallway, legs crossed at the ankles with the stack of boxes beside them as they waited. What had Sloane ever seen in Kenneth? Logan struggled to find a single redeeming feature. Why did chicks dig guys like that? Boring apartment, boring job, boring to talk to, boring in bed... Yet Kenneth had hooked two girls, according to Leah, while Logan had been single since the lingerie model he'd been dating ditched him in a snit for prioritising work over a visit to

Pottery Barn. Not that he'd been devastated. Yeah, she was pretty to look at, but it'd been like fucking one of those porcelain dolls. Cold, soulless, and a tiny bit creepy. At least his hand didn't insist on calling him Logie.

Half an hour passed before Jax and Evan trooped up the stairs. Evidently, they'd used the same trick as Slater.

"Okay, we're here," Evan said. "Now what?"

"Just stand behind us and act intimidating. I'll do the talking."

"I think we can manage that."

"And don't touch the guy. The deal is no violence, no marks."

"Are you kidding? Where's the fun in that?"

"I promised Sloane." Well, Logan had promised Leah, which was practically the same thing.

"We're doing this for Sloane? Why?"

"Because her ex is being a douche."

"Half the women in the office date douches, but we don't visit all of them to rescue their stuff."

Oh, no way was Logan about to admit his true feelings. That he'd liked Sloane for years but always from afar. Sure, he'd been tempted to make a move, usually after copious quantities of alcohol, but each time, he'd come to his senses before he did something irreversibly stupid. Like kissing her, for example. Because girls like Sloane didn't go for assholes like him. They picked the regular guys, preppy men who worked nine-to-five jobs and held family cook-outs on the weekend. Country music, Bud Light, five kinds of salad... Last time Logan and his buddies had decided to grill, half of them had chopped a tree down for the

firepit while the others went to hunt dinner.

"Uh, Sloane was crying earlier, and I hate it when women cry." Logan was gonna pay for this later. "I promised I'd help her out. Believe me, I'd rather be in the bar."

"In that case, shall we get it over with?"

Logan knocked on the door again, and a whole five minutes later, Kenneth yanked it open.

"Now what do you want?" He peered past Logan and saw Evan and Jax standing behind Slater. Evan was a former Army Ranger too, while Jax fought MMA in his spare time. Kenneth's tone softened a tad. "Look, I already told you, I'll give Sloane her stuff back personally. No offence, but I'm just not going to hand it over to strangers."

"We're not strangers to her."

"Well, bring her with you. Sorry, but I'm not wasting any more time on this. I'll have to ask you to leave."

The door clicked shut, leaving the four Blackwood men on the wrong side of it.

"Slightly better," Slater said. "At least he didn't tell us to crawl under a rock this time."

"I don't get it," Jax said. "I've had street thugs throw down their knives when I've asked them nicely."

"Are you sure we can't maim him?" Evan asked. "Just a little?"

Nothing would have given Logan more pleasure than twisting the shitbag's arm off and inserting the soggy end up his rectum, but he had to respect Sloane's wishes. Plus Leah was the chihuahua of executive assistants—tiny but vicious.

"No maiming. Who else was left in the office? A

couple more people should do it."

Jax and Evan looked at each other.

"Nate," Jax said.

"Anyone else?"

"Ana," Evan blurted, and Jax tried to cover it up with a cough.

"No no no no no no no." Slater shook his head. "Not Ana. Don't call Ana."

Logan considered the options for a few seconds. Ana was new to Blackwood, a Russian assassin who legend said could stop a man's heart with a well-timed glare.

"It might solve our problem. I'd hand Ana my firstborn child if she asked, wouldn't you?"

"Probably your balls too," Jax muttered.

"Ana's not that bad," Logan said. "I mean, I even saw her smile a month or two ago."

Yes, she had just broken a man's arm, but it still counted, right?

"If you think it's a good idea, then *you* call and ask her to come."

What, just phone her up? Was Jax crazy?

"Okay, what I'm gonna do is call Nate and ask him to bring her along when he comes."

Yes, that would work. And in the meantime, they could all run down to their cars and put on their body armour, just in case.

CHAPTER 3 - LOGAN

HALF AN HOUR later, footsteps sounded on the stairs. Only one set—Nate's—because Ana wasn't even human. Nate strolled around the corner with the bitch herself stalking behind him. She didn't look happy. Nothing new there.

"So, we're here," Nate said. "But you were light on the details. We need to persuade a creep to return items belonging to Sloane?"

"That's right."

"You didn't elaborate on why?"

"Because it's the right thing to do."

"Because Logan likes Sloane," Slater piped up from behind him.

"Shut up. I'll buy everyone beers when we're done, okay?"

"Wait, you like Sloane?"

"She helped me buy a birthday gift for my niece. Figured I owed her a favour."

"That's all?"

No. "Absolutely."

Nate stared at Logan for one long beat, then nodded.

"Okay, let's do this."

Logan took a deep breath and knocked on the door for the third time, Nate alongside him. A minute passed

before Kenneth opened it, this time wearing a pair of chinos and a polo shirt.

"You can bring as many people as you want, idiot, but I'm not letting you in. If you'll excuse me, I'm in the middle of watching a movie."

Kenneth tried to shut the door, but Nate blocked it with his foot.

"We're reasonable men. Just give us Sloane's belongings, and we'll leave you alone."

"You can't make me."

"Wanna bet?"

"Lay one finger on me and I'll call the cops. And my lawyer."

Nate took one pace to his left, and Ana stepped forward. Her freaky violet eyes locked onto Kenneth's, and she stared at him for a full minute in total silence. You could have heard a cockroach fart. Although the only cockroach in the building was Kenneth, and from the way Ana was looking at him, he was more likely to shit himself.

A bead of sweat ran down his forehead as Ana uttered a single word.

"Move."

Kenneth moved, opening the door wide as he did so.

"Fine, take whatever you want. Just hurry up."

Logan owed Ana a whole case of beer. Did she even drink the stuff? Or did she merely feast on the blood of her helpless victims?

She followed Kenneth through the apartment, close, too close, invading his personal space. "Unsettling" didn't even begin to cover it. From the way Kenneth kept glancing over his shoulder, he was one

step away from leaping off the balcony.

In the living room, she tapped him on the shoulder, and he jumped a clear foot in the air. Logan resisted the urge to laugh as Ana waved at the couch.

"We sit, *da*?" Today, she didn't bother to hide her Russian accent, or the large knife she wore clipped to her belt. "We watch movie together."

Fuck. How did her boyfriend manage it? Living with Ana must be like sharing a very small tank with a great white shark.

Slater interrupted Logan's musings. "Right, what are we picking up?"

Logan now realised the fatal flaw in his non-plan. "Uh, girl stuff."

"She didn't give you a list?"

"It was a spur-of-the-moment thing."

Slater blew out a long breath. "Then can you call her?"

No chance. "Sure. I'll get right on it." He stepped a few feet away and pretended to dial. Listened. Let out a hopefully realistic sigh. "Straight to voicemail."

"How did you ever survive forty-seven trips to the Middle East?"

Simple. Logan kept any photos of Sloane securely hidden away on his phone and only looked at them when he was off duty.

"Pure dumb luck, buddy. Okay, just pick up anything that looks like it might belong to her. If it doesn't, she can send it back later."

Or set fire to it. Logan would gladly lend her a lighter and a gallon of gas.

The men assembled their boxes and traipsed around the apartment. Under the bed, Logan found a

bra that was far too small to be Sloane's and a pair of panties that possibly might have been hers. Black lace. Did Sloane wear black lace? He got a half-chub just thinking about it.

Still, he didn't want to take a chance they might belong to another girl and risk upsetting the delectable Miss Mullins, so he stuffed them into Kenneth's closet instead. Now, what else could he take with him?

In the kitchen, he found Evan stacking cupcake trays into a box and Nate making a sandwich.

"What the hell are you doing?"

"I didn't think Kenneth looked like much of a baker," Evan said.

"I was asking Nate, not you."

Nate sliced his chicken-on-rye down the middle. "What? I got hungry, and you guys seemed to have everything under control."

Well, Ana did, at least. When Logan walked through to the living room, Kenneth was squashed up against the arm of the sofa, fists clenched. Every few seconds, he cut his eyes in Ana's direction. What were they watching?

"...Luminol revealed a large pool of dried blood under the bedroom carpet. The Redwood Ripper had attempted to scrub it away, but it had seeped through..."

True crime? They were watching a true-crime documentary?

Ana pointed at the screen. "Stupid man. He should have stabbed her through eyeball. Much cleaner."

Kenneth's eyes rolled back in his head as he passed out. Ana merely shrugged.

"He's not very good company."

"Just don't give him a heart attack, okay?"

"Then hurry up."

"Almost done."

Logan finished in the bathroom, then went to round up the others. Except when he got into the bedroom, something looked different. Hmm... Yes, what once had been a king-size wood-framed bed with flashy carving on the headboard was now just a mattress.

"Evan, where's the rest of the bed?"

Please, say they hadn't tried to fit it into Logan's pickup.

Evan pointed to the balcony. "These Leatherman multitools are surprisingly versatile."

He'd reassembled the bed outside, and better still, it was starting to rain.

"Nice work. You ready to go? Ana's getting restless."

"Jax and Slater just took the last boxes down to your truck."

Half an hour later, the back of Logan's Ram was stuffed full and he was sitting in the Brotherhood of Thieves, the Richmond bar he co-owned with two of his old high-school buddies. They'd both gone straight, they always kidded—Christian managed the place day-to-day and covered the occasional evening shift, while Trey did the marketing when he wasn't busy being married with two kids and a Pomsky called Graham. Yeah, a Pomeranian crossed with a Husky. Graham shed hair everywhere and escaped at least once a week.

Tonight, Trey was at a parent-teacher conference, but Christian was on duty while the Blackwood guys propped up the bar beside Logan. Ana excepted—she'd borrowed Nate's car and driven back to her crypt.

"What are you drinking?" Christian asked Logan.

"Coke."

"Coke?"

Usually, Logan had a beer, ate dinner, and then drove home. More than one alcoholic beverage, and he caught a ride. Never did he drink Coca-Cola.

"Yeah, Coke."

"Are you sick?"

Lovesick, possibly. Fuck. Logan quickly shook his head. Was Ana's insanity contagious?

"I need to go somewhere else afterwards."

"Still working?"

"Not exactly."

But keeping a clear head was more important than ever tonight. He never knew what to say around Sloane. More often than not, he vomited out the wrong words and ended up insulting her by accident, like the time he'd said she looked as if she enjoyed eating candy. He'd meant because she smiled, but...yeah, he wouldn't forget her hurt expression in a hurry. Now he tried to limit himself to business-related stuff and small talk, but sometimes, like tonight, he couldn't resist becoming more involved.

Still no wiser over how to explain his actions, he drained his glass, left the guys to their drinking, and headed for his truck.

Chapter 4 - Sloane

DON'T CRY, SLOANE.

I slammed the front door and shoved my gym bag into the hall closet. If I never saw it again, it would be too soon. A low groan escaped my lips as I crumpled to the floor, still clutching the bag of salad I'd bought on my way home.

What had I been thinking? Had Kenneth destroyed every last one of my brain cells?

The courier had picked up Fantasia's gift at six thirty, and as the clock ticked closer and closer to seven o'clock, I'd berated myself for being such a coward. The part of me that wanted to be more like Emmy told me to woman up and face him, but Sloane the scaredy-cat refused to move from her desk. To appease my conscience, I'd come up with the fabulous idea of doing something even worse than facing my cheating ex so I wouldn't feel guilty.

Which was how I'd ended up at a yoga class.

Yes, all of those subtle jibes from Kenneth had finally got to me. The way he always requested low-fat salad dressing for me in restaurants. The exercise infomercials he left playing in the background while we ate dinner at his apartment. That little black dress he'd given me for my last birthday—the one that was two sizes too small so I'd "have something to aim for."

I might have owned twenty pairs of yoga pants, but I rarely wore them out of the house, and until this evening, I'd never heard of downward-facing dog. Leah always talked about the benefits of yoga, but she'd never mentioned the drawbacks. Such as the complete and utter embarrassment.

While I prided myself on my flexibility at work, that skill didn't extend to the physical, and I'd been the only girl in the class who shopped in the plus-size section. Probably even the entire building. But that wasn't the worst of it. I'd huffed and puffed my way through several warrior poses and a dozen sun salutations when it happened. The teacher told us to bend forward, my sweaty hands slipped, and one boob popped out.

And *everyone* saw.

Probably because I shrieked.

Emmy always told me I should stay positive, and I tried. I really did try. On the plus side, I suppose, I'd never known I could run so fast until I sprinted out of Wanda's Workout World this evening.

The salad was my punishment.

The salad was also disgusting. Even Nickel's cat food looked more appetising, and probably tasted better than the limp lettuce, tomato, and carrot too. There wasn't even any dressing. Ugh. I'd forked half of it down when somebody knocked on my door, and I didn't know whether to cheer at the interruption or grab my pepper spray. Apart from Edna who lived next door and Kenneth, I never got visitors. He'd shown up sixteen times since we split, and I always hid behind the couch.

Tonight, I shuffled over to the window on my hands and knees and moved one corner of the drapes aside,

only for my eyes to bug out all of their own accord. Logan? What the hell was Logan doing at my house? He'd only been there once before, when he dropped me off after a staff get-together, and he'd never been inside.

Should I pretend I was out?

That would be kind of rude, but I was still wearing yoga pants and the stretchy top of doom. Perhaps if I crawled, I could make it upstairs and leap into the shower? I wouldn't feel so bad about fibbing then. Yes, that was an excellent plan.

An excellent plan with one tiny glitch. I forgot I was dealing with Logan.

Thirty seconds later, the front door opened, and he got a perfect view of my oversized ass, barely constrained by pale-pink Lycra as it headed for the stairs.

"What are you doing down there?"

Oh, heckety heck.

"Uh... I lost something."

"What did you lose?"

Quick, Sloane. Think!

"My...my cat."

"You mean this cat?"

Too late, I realised Nickel was looking at me from the living room doorway.

"Yes! That's him." I scrambled to my feet, heat spreading up my cheeks. "What are you doing here?" Hold on, Logan had *broken into my freaking house.* Anger would be appropriate. "And how dare you just walk in? What did you do, pick the lock?"

Stupid question, of course he picked the lock. Logan worked in the Special Projects department at

Blackwood. He'd probably learned to pick locks in kindergarten, right after he got his first gun.

"I thought you were in the shower or something."

"How does that make it better?"

He pointed behind himself at a box on my front porch. "Well, I figured I'd just leave this stuff in the hallway."

"What stuff?"

"Your stuff. From Kenneth."

"Back up. *Back up.* Why did Kenneth give you my stuff?"

Did the two of them know each other? Oh, hell, did Logan know about Sherilyn?

"He didn't give it to me, exactly. We went over and collected it."

"What? Why? Who's 'we'?"

"Me, Slater, Evan, Jax, Nate, and Ana."

"Ana?" I sank to the floor, visions of Kenneth's bloody corpse floating before my eyes. "How bad is the damage?"

"Don't worry; we were nice."

Nice? *Nice?* Logan didn't know how to do nice. He knew how to do sexy and he knew how to do scary, but nice was far, far removed from his repertoire. What should I do? Did my mom know yet? I really didn't want another lecture on how violence was never the answer. Like the talk she gave when ten-year-old me got sent home from school in disgrace for pushing one of my bullies into a wall—Mom had made me take the little witch cream cakes the next day to apologise, and I'd ended up wearing them.

Logan dropped down beside me. "Don't worry, kitten. There's not a mark on him."

"How did you even know Kenneth had my stuff?"

"Heard a rumour." He draped an arm over my shoulders in a stiff hug. "Picking your shit up was the least I could do after you dug me out of a hole with Fantasia's gift."

"I got a jewellery-making kit and a doll on ice skates. And a card. I signed it from you."

"See? I owed you big."

Slowly, it started to sink in what he'd done. Logan had rescued my stuff, and if he really hadn't hurt Kenneth, that meant my nightmare was over. I didn't have to face my asshat of an ex again. A little of the tension that had been building up inside me for the past few weeks seeped away, but in hindsight, I should have held onto it because a tear escaped too.

"Hey, don't cry."

Logan wiped my cheek with his thumb, but I couldn't stop more from coming, a veritable waterfall of embarrassment. Humiliation: complete.

"Sloane? What did I say? Look, we left Kenneth on the sofa watching TV. Ana only glared at him."

"I'm f-f-fine."

"Oh, shit."

I sniffled loudly as Logan got to his feet in one graceful movement and backed towards the door, muttering into his phone. Who was he calling? The asylum?

"I'm s-s-sorry." I struggled to my knees. "Please don't go."

Great. Now I sounded desperate too, and the tears fell harder. Mom always said I got too emotional, and I tried to hold everything back, really I did. More than anything, I wished I could be like Emmy. People called

her the ice queen, and she'd mastered that perfectly blank mask so nobody knew what she was thinking. Me? I was an open book. Well, more of a magazine—easy to read and unmemorable.

"I'll be back, okay?"

Logan dragged the box in through the door, gave me an awkward pat on the head, and practically ran to his truck. Ten seconds later, I heard the engine growl into life, and he floored it down the street.

Congratulations, Sloane. First a conversation with Kenneth, then boobgate, and now I'd freaked out the guy I'd secretly crushed on for years so badly that he literally ran from my house. Today was officially the worst day of my life.

Nickel rubbed along my leg, purring, and I reached out to scritch his head. At least I still had my cat. He didn't care that I was socially awkward and twenty pounds overweight. Okay, thirty. As long as he got his dinner in the evenings and fresh litter in his tray, he liked me just fine.

CHAPTER 5 - LOGAN

LOGAN HAD THOUGHT that Sloane would be happy to have her belongings back, but then she'd started crying and he'd panicked. Terrorists, cold-blooded killers, and knife-wielding maniacs didn't faze him, but tears scared him stupid.

He'd called Trey in desperation. His wife had gone through a crying phase last time she was pregnant, and according to Trey, he'd cured the problem with cheesecake and pickles. Logan wasn't sure about the pickles, though, so he figured he'd try wine instead.

At the 7-Eleven, he leapt out of his pickup and ran inside. Desserts...where were the desserts?

"Cheesecake. I need cheesecake," he blurted at the cashier.

"Aisle three, sweetheart."

"And the wine?"

"Aisle five."

Lemon cheesecake, chocolate chip cookie dough cheesecake, strawberry cheesecake, peanut butter cup cheesecake. Logan grabbed one of each and speed-walked to the wine section. Did Sloane drink red or white? He had no idea, so he grabbed a Merlot and a Sauvignon Blanc plus a bottle of rosé for good measure.

At the checkout, the lady gave him a sympathetic look. "Celebration, apology, or the wrong time of the

month?"

"Honestly? I have no idea."

She gave him a look that said, *Really?*

"So I dropped some stuff off at her house, and she started crying. I'm just trying to make her stop."

"Four different kinds of cheesecake should work."

Logan handed over his credit card. "Should I get candy too? Or ice cream?"

"It wouldn't hurt."

Five minutes later, he was speeding back to Sloane's duplex with an overflowing grocery bag on the seat beside him. But where was she? Logan picked the lock in double-quick time, only to find an empty hallway. No Sloane, no cat, just the box he'd abandoned earlier. He paused, holding his breath, and in the silence, he heard a quiet sniffle from the back of the house.

"Sloane?"

Nothing.

Her house wasn't huge. No, it was cosy, stuffed with too much furniture for the small rooms. What Laverne, the last model he'd dated, had called shabby-chic, only Sloane's decor tended towards the shabby side. Not a lack of money, surely? Blackwood paid well. More likely a lack of time. Sloane worked all hours, and Logan bet Kenneth had never lifted a finger to help her at home.

Logan went past a tiny dining room and through the door at the far end of the hallway. The kitchen had seen better days too, but Logan only had eyes for the woman sitting at the counter, staring at a bowl of salad. Sloane had changed her V-neck top for a sweater that buttoned up to her chin, but she still looked utterly

miserable.

"Hey," he said.

She stared at him through red-rimmed eyes. "Why did you come back? Didn't I embarrass myself enough the first time?"

"Huh? I just hate seeing you upset." He slid the salad away and replaced it with a cheesecake. "You don't really want lettuce, do you?"

"Yes." She grabbed the bowl and pulled it back again. "It's h-h-healthy."

Oh, shit. That little stutter didn't sound good. Had Trey got things totally wrong and Sloane *didn't* like cheesecake? Women needed to come with an instruction manual, one written in really, really basic language rather than the riddles they tended to speak in.

"Hey, let's forget the food altogether. Where do you want all the boxes? I've got a truck full of your stuff."

"Boxes, plural? There's more than the one you brought in earlier?"

"Sure. We brought clothes and bathroom shit and those little tray things you make cakes in."

"My bakeware?"

"Yeah, that."

Oh, thank goodness: a smile. Sloane got off her stool with an ungainly hop and clutched at the counter to steady herself. Low blood sugar? She really needed to eat something, but Logan would broach that subject again later. If bakeware made her happy, he'd stick with that for now.

"You must think I'm such a mess," Sloane muttered as they walked through to the hallway.

Honestly? Yeah. Sloane was always so put-together

at work, the queen of executive assistants who somehow managed to juggle Black's and Emmy's schedules as well as training the newbies and ensuring the office never ran out of anything. When she'd taken a vacation the year before last—with her tree-hugging ex—they'd had to borrow three people from other Blackwood branches to cover for her.

But right now, Sloane was absolutely a mess. In a way, Logan liked that better because it made her more human, but he also wanted to know why. Had Kenneth done that bad of a number on her head?

"Forget about that. Let's get these boxes. I'll carry; you decide where you want me to put them."

Logan schlepped in the crap they'd liberated, and Sloane peered into the top of each carton like a kid on Christmas morning, which made Logan even more pissed at Kenneth. His ex-girl shouldn't have been so excited to get her own stuff back.

"Hey, it's my casserole dish! My grandma gave me this. Can you put it in the kitchen?"

Forget cheesecake—household goods were definitely the way to go. Logan learned something new every day. He thought he'd cracked the code, at least until they got to the last box.

"What's this?" She pulled out a laptop charger. "This isn't mine."

"No, it's Kenneth's."

Plus all of his dress socks, his razor blades, the lightbulb from his bathroom, the batteries from his remotes, the fuse from his toaster, his scissors, a single Salvatore Ferragamo shoe, and a dozen odd cufflinks. It had taken Logan ages to go through the boxes and pick out one from each pair.

"You stole Kenneth's stuff?"

"He said to take whatever we wanted."

Sloane's face crumpled, and Logan's heart seized for a moment, but then she burst out laughing.

"I can't believe you took his socks. He's gonna freak."

"Call it karma. Do you want any of this stuff, or should I throw it straight into the trash?"

"Better not. He'll want it back."

"And you'll give it to him?"

"Well... Uh... I guess."

This girl was far too soft. Had she learned nothing from working with Emmy for all those years?

"Burn it. Not the batteries because they'll explode, but the rest. Want me to help?"

"I'm not sure..."

"Have a glass of wine and think about it, okay?" Logan slung an arm over Sloane's shoulders and steered her back towards the kitchen. "Red, white, or pink?"

She gave that shy smile that always made Logan's cock harden. "Pink."

The same colour as her cheeks.

Sloane sat on a stool while Logan uncorked the bottle of rosé. Evan was right. The multitools Bradley had put in last year's Christmas crackers *were* surprisingly versatile.

"Where are your wine glasses?"

The tabby cat leapt onto the counter as Sloane pointed to the cupboard next to the stove.

"Top shelf."

Except Logan never even got the door open. Sloane shrieked, and he turned in time to see a mouse take a

running leap from the countertop into her lap.

"Get it off! Get it off! Get it off!"

Logan didn't know whether to laugh or dive for the rodent or get his gun out. The thing was fast, he'd give it that. It ran down Sloane's leg and dashed into an open cupboard while the asshole of a cat just stood there watching.

Sloane clambered on top of the stool. "Where did it go?"

"You don't like mice?"

"Last time Nickel caught one, the darn thing bit me and I had to get a tetanus shot, so no, I'm not very keen on mice. Or spiders. Or snakes. And now I'm babbling."

Yes, she was, and she'd gone all flushed and breathless and... *Stop it, Barnes. Now is not the time.*

"Hey, it's okay. Sit down here..." Logan helped Sloane to perch on the counter with her feet on the stool. "And I'll hunt for Mickey."

The mouse may have run into a cupboard, but when Logan emptied the dishes out and piled them next to the sink, all he found was a loose panel at the back and no mouse.

"Is it in there? Tell me it's in there."

"No, kitten, but I'll find it." Logan got to his feet and leaned against the counter, one hand each side of Sloane's knees. His thumbs itched to caress her thighs, but he gripped the Formica instead. "Just relax and have a glass of wine."

"I'm so, so sorry about this."

"What did you do last time the cat brought you a gift?"

"Uh, stayed at Kenneth's for five days while a pest-control guy pulled the house apart. Fifteen hundred

dollars, he charged, and he didn't even find the darn mouse. I had nightmares for weeks afterwards. Even now, I swear I can still hear tiny feet pitter-pattering when I'm lying awake in the dark."

"Well, Mickey can't have got far." Logan filled the wine glass to the brim and slid half a cheesecake onto a plate. "Relax."

He couldn't resist brushing one hand across her hip, and she jumped as though he'd electrocuted her.

"Sorry. Hand slipped."

Office Sloane and off-duty Sloane were two completely different people, weren't they? At Blackwood, Sloane was unflappable, always composed even in the worst crisis. This new Sloane was skittish, nervous, and cute as hell.

Logan gave his head a little shake to dislodge his dirty thoughts and dropped to his knees for all the wrong reasons. Time to find this tiny four-legged fiend.

An hour later, Sloane had eaten a whole cheesecake and the wine had done its job. She giggled as he removed another panel and stacked it with the others. Yes, it turned out one multitool could dismantle an entire kitchen.

"This looks worse than the office after Bradley decided to refit the break area last year," she said. "My landlady's gonna go crazy if she sees it like this."

So far, Sloane had stuck to safe topics, work mainly, but Logan wanted to change that.

"Does she share your fear of mice?"

"I doubt it. She used to be a bit fierce, but then her husband died three years ago and she lost her fire. Until then, I'd been planning to move out, but I realised Edna needed me around to help."

Sloane always had been a generous one. "Does she live far away?"

"Right next door." Another giggle followed by a groan. "I'll need to clear this mess away super quick because she'll probably have a heart attack if she looks through the window."

"Are you serious? She looks through your windows? That's kind of intrusive, kitten."

"I don't like it, but at least I don't need to worry about burglars, right?"

Logan hated nosy neighbours, which was why he'd bought a house in the middle of nowhere. A ranch-style home tucked away in the woods beyond Rybridge, surrounded by whispering trees and a high fence. Growing up in Anaheim squashed into a two-bedroom apartment with his parents and three sisters, he'd craved space, or at least somewhere to sleep that wasn't a fold-out bed in the living room. Now he had sixteen acres of land, but it got lonely there sometimes.

"I guess that's a positive. Edna aside, you like living here?"

"It doesn't cost too much, and Nickel likes the yard."

"That doesn't answer my question."

Oh, shit. Another tear. Cheesecake. More cheesecake. Logan grabbed another box from the counter and tipped the chocolate chip cookie dough version onto a plate, then poured Sloane another glass of wine just to be on the safe side.

"Hey, hey, it's okay." He slid a forkful of gooey goodness into her mouth. "Here, eat this."

"It's not okay. The bathroom faucet drips, the roof leaks, and the yard turns into a jungle every spring. I

only moved here because of the cats, but Dime got run over last year by the cable repair guy. And I got so upset that I shouted at him, so now I don't have cable either."

"Kenneth didn't help?"

Sloane choked on a mouthful of cheesecake, and Logan thumped her on the back.

"Oh, sure, he helped. By insisting we always stay at his place because the dripping noise annoyed him. He wanted me to move in with him, did you know that?" She knocked back the wine and held out the glass. "I need another drink."

Logan picked up the bottle. Was this a good idea? Probably not, but at least Sloane was opening up. Every time he talked to her in the office, she turned the conversation back to the job, and in seven years, he'd only become more intrigued by the quiet, pretty girl who hid away behind a curtain of light brown hair and an ultra-professional attitude.

"Well, at least you didn't move in with him. I'd have had to rent a bigger truck to get your stuff back."

"Right! And I'd have been homeless."

"Nah, that would never happen. I've got—" He'd been about to say "a spare room," but what if that freaked her out? "I've got an idea that Emmy would have come up with a solution."

"Asking my boss to rescue me? I'd never have lived that down."

"Come on, Emmy's more than just a boss. She's a friend too."

"I suppose." Sloane picked up the bottle and chugged back the last of the rosé.

"You want the white next?" Logan asked.

"I think so. Yes."

Definitely not a good idea. Logan reached for the corkscrew.

"So, why do you only 'suppose' Emmy's a friend?"

"Look at everyone in the office."

"I do, most days."

"Well, I don't exactly fit in, do I?"

"Why not?"

"Those women are all so...so...capable. So smart and elegant. And then there's me."

"I don't get it."

And Logan genuinely didn't. Never had he suspected that Sloane suffered from such a crippling lack of self-confidence, and one that was completely unwarranted. Sure, she may not know how to shoot a gun or jump out of an airplane, but few girls did. And Sloane had Emmy beat hands down in the sweetness stakes.

Sloane ate another mouthful of cheesecake and washed it down with Sauvignon Blanc. "My boob fell out at yoga tonight." She went to clap a hand over her mouth but poked herself in the eye instead. "Ouch. This whole day has been a disaster. Whole week. Year."

But Logan had already heard the first part, and he couldn't stop laughing. "What? How?"

"Forget I said that."

"Not happening." Despite Emmy's friend Fia extolling the benefits of yoga, he'd always written it off as a bit girly. But now he saw that attending a class could have benefits. "Where do you go to yoga?"

"Doesn't matter. I'm not going again."

He flicked the zipper on her sweater. "Is that why you changed into this?"

"Yup. I'm never— There's the mouse!"

Shit. The little bastard shot across the floor and dived under the refrigerator. Logan moved it an inch, and the mouse ran out into the corner and sat there, whiskers twitching.

"Don't kill him," Sloane squeaked.

Logan grabbed a plastic container and advanced, arms outstretched. The mouse was quick, but years of special forces training had made Logan's reflexes quicker. Two seconds later, he had Mickey trapped in the box.

"Got him. I'll put him out in the yard."

Or better still, the landlady's yard. She took Sloane's money and didn't bother to repair her roof, yet the woman managed to fill her yard with an expensive patio set and a bunch of ugly-ass statues.

"Welcome to your new home, Mickey," Logan muttered as he released the mouse over the fence. "I hear she's got cheese inside."

Back in the kitchen, Sloane had keeled over sideways onto the counter, narrowly missing the remains of the cheesecake. Seemed the alcohol had finally caught up with her.

"You're so damn beautiful, kitten," he whispered.

His only answer was a quiet snuffle.

"Let's get you to bed."

CHAPTER 6 - SLOANE

MY HEAD HURT, my stomach hurt, and I'd already puked twice this morning. With Nickel as my witness, I swore I'd never eat cheesecake again.

Pride wouldn't let me call in sick, so I stumbled into the office at nine a.m., just in time to rearrange Emmy's flight back from Barcelona. Apparently, she'd gotten delayed by an unplanned excursion and missed her departure. Then Black called from Washington to say his meeting at the White House was going to overrun and would I please rearrange his meetings for the rest of the day.

One of the people who got bumped was a CEO who needed me to grovel a bit and stroke his ego, and by the time I'd moved Black's dinner with him to next week, my headache had turned into a migraine.

But it wasn't all bad. With the scheduling issues, I'd barely thought about what happened last night. The mouse, the kitchen, the wine... How would I ever face Logan again? If my hazy memory served correctly, I'd told him my boob escaped from my yoga top. Death seemed like an attractive option.

Lunch didn't.

In fact, the mere thought of eating made me feel ill, which was probably a good thing since I'd consumed about six thousand calories yesterday. I fetched a glass

of iced water and a package of Tylenol from the kitchen and groaned as another email popped into my inbox.

"Logan was looking for you," Leah said.

Fantastic. My day was now complete.

What on earth should I say to him? An apology, obviously, but that was totally inadequate. He'd picked up my stuff from Kenneth, bought me comfort food, removed my unwanted visitor, and when I'd woken up in bed this morning—fully clothed, I hasten to add—my kitchen had been restored to its former rickety glory.

The only evidence Logan had been there at all were the cheesecake wrappers in the trash and the wine bottles in the recycling bin.

Oh, and the mortification permeating through my veins like a slow-acting poison.

Since Emmy and Black were away, I gathered up my laptop and phone and decamped to their private office. Yes, the walls were glass, but if I ducked down behind Black's giant computer screen, perhaps Logan wouldn't notice me? Only one more presentation to finalise before I could go home and crawl back under my duvet.

And I so nearly made it. My mouse was hovering over the "save" button when the door cracked open, and a groan escaped my lips when I realised who it was.

"Sorry! So sorry. I was groaning about work, not you."

Logan dropped into Emmy's chair and wheeled it closer.

"I wanted to check you were okay. You seemed a little, uh, unconscious last night. I stayed for a while to make sure you kept breathing, but..."

"Oh, I'm fine. Perfectly fine." My fingers nudged the

Tylenol package underneath Black's keyboard. "Thanks for catching the mouse and rebuilding my kitchen. And bringing food. And I guess you carried me to bed? You didn't hurt your back, did you?"

"Stop doing that."

"Doing what?"

"Putting yourself down."

"Huh?"

"My back's fine. There's no reason why it shouldn't be. Carrying you to bed was the decent thing to do, as was helping with your rodent problem. Want me to come over at the weekend to fix your leaky faucet?"

"No! I mean, no thank you. It's kind of you to offer, but you've got that trip to New York, and you're not scheduled to come back until six on Sunday evening."

"You've been checking my calendar?"

Perhaps just a tiny peek. "Leah mentioned it earlier."

Dammit, I needed a distraction. Something. *Anything.*

My phone rang.

Okay, anything except Kenneth. Technically, it was an unknown caller, but the last ten times that had happened, it had been my pig of an ex withholding his number. Because it was my work phone, I had to answer in case a client was calling, and the slimeball knew that.

"What's wrong?" Logan asked.

"Nothing."

"Then why are you glaring at the phone like it murdered a puppy."

"Because there's a ninety-eight percent chance that it's Kenneth."

Before I could stop him, Logan snatched it up.

"Blackwood Security."

A pause.

"Sorry, Sloane can't talk right now. Her mouth's otherwise engaged." Logan waggled his eyebrows and grinned. "That's it, kitten. All the way down."

His low, drawn-out moan sent heat rushing south before I realised what he was insinuating. How dare he?

"Stop it!" I hissed.

Logan merely tucked my phone into the crook of his shoulder, reached out, and put a hand over my mouth. One eyebrow quirked at whatever Kenneth had said.

"Really? You ever stop to think that maybe it was just *your* dick she didn't like sucking?"

Did he...? Tell me he didn't. Tell me Kenneth didn't just inform Logan that I hated giving blow jobs. Yes, it was true, but Kenneth always wanted me to go down on him late in the evening, and he insisted on wearing tight-fitting briefs that gave him sweaty balls. The smell made me gag. Yeuch.

In my dreams, on the other hand, Logan tasted of chocolate cake and red wine, a proverbial buffet of well-hung man.

But today, I had no time to dream, not when that same man was currently ruining my life. I wrenched his hand away and made a dive for the phone, but the asshole twisted sideways and I ended up plastered against him, my back to his front. That delicious bulge pressed against the top of my butt. Was it my imagination, or did it feel a tiny bit hard?

For a brief second, I relaxed against Logan's chest, but then I came to my senses, what little was left of

them.

"Logan!"

"That's it, lovely. Scream my name."

Before I could say another word, his hand clamped over my mouth again, and his other arm came around my chest like a steel band. I could barely move an inch, and now I was close enough to hear Kenneth spluttering through the phone.

"Sloane would never do anything so vulgar in her workplace."

"Beg to differ."

"What would your boss say if he heard you speaking like that in the office?" Had Kenneth always been so whiny? "In fact, I've got a good mind to call him."

"Sure, go right ahead. His—"

"No!" I tried, but it came out as a mumble.

Rather than tighten his grip, Logan perched on the edge of the desk so I had no choice but to tilt back against him. When I tried to protest again, he ran his thumb over my bottom lip, which theoretically shouldn't have stopped me from speaking, but it did because I couldn't think of anything other than sucking it.

Don't you dare, Sloane. Just don't.

"As I was saying, my boss's extension number is six-six-five—" I felt Logan shrug. "Kenny hung up. Score one to us."

Us? *Us?* Logan finally removed his arm and I scrambled away, panting worse than the pervert who'd started calling my home number six months ago. I didn't know his name, but he phoned every Wednesday, the only man in my life who demonstrated any kind of commitment.

Apart from Mr. Barnes, possibly. Right now, he seemed committed to being a jackass.

"Logan, what the heck are you playing at? Why did you say that to Kenneth?"

"To stop him from talking shit to you again. And don't tell me you haven't thought about it."

"No! You... You... You utter pig! Never once have I done that."

My mouth spouted denials, but my eyes weren't on the same page. Despite my attempts to focus on Logan's face, my gaze dropped all of its own accord. And Logan was wearing sweatpants.

Ohmigosh. Did he go commando?

By the time I realised what I'd done, it was too late. Logan had caught me looking, and he didn't bother to hide his smirk.

"Don't sweat it, kitten. It wasn't that bad. Just a little play-acting."

"Wasn't that bad? How could it possibly have been worse?"

Logan shrugged, totally unrepentant. "I could have mentioned anal."

I stormed out, slamming the door behind myself as I muttered nasty things about men in general and Logan in particular, then I realised I'd left my laptop on Black's desk. Logan held it out to me when I slunk back in to pick it up.

"Need this?"

"Why can't you just act like a normal guy?"

"Like Kenneth, you mean?"

"Well, no, but... Why did you do it? Say all that?"

"A man can dream, can't he?"

"Don't be ridiculous. Can't you at least stop messing

with me?"

"You want the truth? Truth is, I'm an asshole."

I couldn't argue with that, not today.

"Thank you, I guess."

I'd got halfway out the door for the second time when I heard Logan's final words.

"Fifty bucks says Kenny won't bother you in the office again."

CHAPTER 7 - SLOANE

"STILL FRETTING OVER Logan?" Leah asked.

Three days later? Yes. The man was born to wear sweatpants, but why, oh why, had I looked at the bulge?

"Of course not."

"It's just that you've put five sugars in your coffee."

"Huh? Oh, darn it."

When I kept getting distracted on Tuesday, I'd had to come up with an explanation for Leah, one that didn't involve mice or cheesecake or blow jobs in the office or getting horrendously drunk. So, I'd told her my jitters were Kenneth's fault. That he'd been rude to Logan, first in person and then on the phone. Seeing as it was Kenneth who'd caused this whole mess with his inability to keep his dick in his pants, I figured he should shoulder some of the blame.

"Honestly, Logan won't care that Kenneth told him to screw off. I don't suppose Logan was all that polite when he picked up your stuff on Monday."

If Mom caught me bending the truth, I'd be going straight to hell. The only saving grace was that Logan was already there. Well, Iraq. After some rearranging of schedules, Cade had taken the New York job while Logan flew to the Middle East on Tuesday night to oversee a hostage rescue, which meant I'd spent every

day since then alternately worrying and hoping he stayed there. At least it was Friday now. The office would be quieter at the weekend. Yes, I could have taken Saturday and Sunday off like a regular person, but I got lonely at home, okay?

"I still feel bad for dragging Logan into my problems in the first place," I said.

"Trust me, he's dealt with far worse. And Kenneth hasn't called you since, right?"

"No." Logan had been absolutely right about that.

"So, problem solved."

I disposed of my overly sweet coffee in the sink and poured myself a fresh cup from the filter jug. Normally, I could do my job in my sleep, but this week had been a challenge.

"I hope you're right," I told Leah. "I just want to forget I ever met Kenneth."

"And I've got the perfect thing for that."

Leah fished her phone out of her pocket and turned to face me. That gleam in her eye had me worried.

"What have you done?"

"I've got you a date."

"Like, with a man?"

If she'd rolled her eyes any harder, we'd have had to retrieve them from the shooting range out back.

"Of course with a man. I signed you up for online dating."

"You've done *what?*"

"I've signed you up for—"

"I heard the first time. Do the words 'invasion of privacy' mean nothing to you?"

"But you'd never have done it yourself."

"Exactly. Because I don't want to go on a date.

Kenneth put me off men for life."

Well, mostly. I may have spent a little too much time daydreaming about Logan's abs, but I didn't *actually* want to lick them. Not at all.

"Don't be too hasty. Just because you got mixed up with Kenneth-the-prick doesn't mean there aren't decent guys out there."

"I'm not sure I'll find one on the internet."

"Sure you will. My friend Lydia married a guy she met on Tinder. And if these men are hanging out online, then at least they're not technologically inept like...like... What was his name? The guy before Kenneth?"

"Lyndon."

"That's it. Tree guy. Is he still finding himself in Venezuela?"

"As far as I know. He sent a postcard a month ago."

Not an email like a normal person, because Lyndon didn't have a phone or a computer. But while he may have come across as slightly odd, like the time he'd gone through a phase of refusing to wear shoes, he'd always been kind to me. And faithful. We'd split up eighteen months ago when he got the urge to volunteer at an eco-project in the South American rainforest and I'd opted to stay in Virginia. I still kind of missed him, but at least I didn't have to pretend to be a vegan anymore.

"A postcard? Sheesh. Well, this guy's wearing a leather jacket in his profile picture, so he's not gonna freak out about your purses, and better yet, he wants to see you tomorrow night."

"Tell him no."

"Cancelling would be rude."

"You've already told him yes?"

"I couldn't leave the poor guy hanging." Leah scrolled through her phone. "Take a look—apart from the nose, he's quite handsome."

Curiosity got the better of me. According to his profile, Laurence was two years older than me, worked as an architect, and loved dogs, Italian food, and classical music. His blue eyes sparkled as he smiled, and I had to admit, a butterfly or two may have fluttered in my stomach.

"What's wrong with his nose?"

"It's crooked."

I peered closer at the screen. "Really?"

"To the right. See? And I'm not sure about the blond hair, but if he's got a good personality, you could overlook that, right? Does that sound shallow?"

Now, Leah was one of my best friends—okay, one of my only friends—but she wasn't just shallow, she was a puddle in the Mojave Desert. Luckily, she knew this.

"Yes, it sounds shallow."

Any man who wanted to date Leah had better have a seven-figure bank account, a modelling contract, and a whole closet full of designer suits. Currently, she was single, but with her determination, she'd find her perfect match someday. Of course, it didn't hurt that she still looked like the cheerleader she'd been in college.

"Okay, so let's think positive. It says here that he enjoys going out for dinner with friends. At least he's not some weirdo who lives in his basement."

"You're really selling this."

"Seven p.m. at Il Tramonto. I've booked you a table for two. And don't forget, Oliver lives on the top floor in

the same building, so if Laurence does turn out to be a mad axe murderer, you can call for help."

Oliver was Emmy's lawyer—sexy, way out of my league, and now engaged.

"I haven't even said I'll go."

"Wear something pretty. That navy-blue dress you had on at Bradley's Memorial Day party will be perfect, but not with the beige shoes. You need to go brighter."

Quite honestly, it was easier to meet Laurence than argue with Leah, and Il Tramonto did serve excellent pizza, so at least I wouldn't have to cook. What was the worst that could happen?

What was the worst that could happen?

Well, let's see... First, Laurence squinted a bit and said he almost hadn't recognised me because I looked thinner in my profile picture. Then he talked about the nitty-gritty of sustainable development for an hour and a half, and when I ordered a second glass of wine, he frowned and asked if I normally drank that much. I was still trying to think up a witty retort when he went outside to take a phone call, and after fifteen minutes, it slowly dawned on me that he wasn't coming back.

Gianni, the manager of the restaurant, always had a kind word and a friendly smile. I'd chatted with him lots of times in the past when I stopped to grab takeout on my way home from the office, and now he slid into the seat opposite and passed me a glass of...

"What's this?"

"Tuaca. You look as if you need it, *bella*."

Fire burned down my throat as I knocked it back,

and my eyes watered. "Thanks, I think."

"Your date left?"

"I'm not sure whether to be upset or relieved."

"None of the staff liked him. Angelo put extra chillis on his pizza."

I thought Laurence had gone rather red at one point. "He deserved it."

"First date?"

"Yes. My one and only attempt at online dating."

Gianni patted my hand. "*Mi dispiace* it didn't work out. But don't give up. My cousin met her husband in an online chatroom, and now they have two beautiful *bambini*."

Was I literally the only person in the world who couldn't meet a man that wasn't an eco-warrior, a cheater, or a weirdo? Because it sure seemed that way.

"I think I'll stick with cats."

"My sister and her husband have two beautiful kittens, almost three months old... What is it? Why are you so upset? Here, have another glass of Tuaca."

By the time Gianni heaved me into a cab, it was almost midnight and I could barely walk. So much for my hot date. This time, I didn't even have Logan to carry me up the stairs, so I had to crawl.

Maybe I just wasn't destined to be one half of a couple. Perhaps that was why I favoured blouses and pencil skirts and spent most of my waking hours in the office, because at least then I could claim to be a career girl. A career girl and a cat mom.

Oh, wait... What was that on my pillow? I clicked on the light and peered closer. Half a dead bird? Yeuch! I had just enough energy left to stagger to the bathroom and throw up before collapsing downstairs on the sofa.

At the moment, I didn't even want to be a cat mom anymore.

"So, how did it go?" Leah asked.

I held the phone away from my ear as I rolled over and nearly fell off the sofa, leaving a trail of drool behind on the cushion. "What time is it?"

"Almost nine."

"My head hurts."

"Good night, then? I half expected you to be doing dirty things with Laurence."

"Oh, yeah, it was a great night. Laurence did a runner and stiffed me with the bill."

"He what?"

I garbled through the details, and they sounded even worse the second time around. Luckily, as well as getting me drunk, Gianni had given me a fifty percent discount and called me a cab, otherwise I'd have woken up in a gutter somewhere. Such a shame he was gay.

"So you see," I told Leah, "this is why I'm better off staying single."

"Don't be silly. You just need to step it up. If you go on enough dates, they can't all be bad. Probability and the law of averages and that sort of thing."

"No way."

"I've got you a date with Desmond tonight. Seven thirty. He's going to get back to me with the place."

"Did you not hear a word I said?"

"Sure I did. I just chose not to listen. Desmond's thirty-three years old, five feet nine, and he works on a ranch out near Chesterfield. A cowboy! And he sure

looks good in jeans, even if he's a little on the short side."

"I'm not going."

"I get that last night could have turned out better, but that's no reason to write off all men."

"Says the woman who turned down a date with an investment banker because he drove a Toyota Prius."

"It wasn't only a Toyota Prius. It was a *brown* Toyota Prius."

"Forget it. I'm staying at home this evening. If you like Desmond so much, then you can go out for dinner with him."

Yes, I'd curl up on the sofa with a pint of ice cream and a romcom. No cheesecake. As long as Nickel didn't decide to bring me any more dead things, it would be bliss.

"I'll give you a couple of hours to change your mind. Nobody should make important decisions when they're half-asleep."

For goodness' sake—didn't Leah ever give up?

"This girl's more than capable." What did it matter? Even when I was awake, my decision-making process was utterly flawed at worst, misguided at best. "I'll see you in the office."

Chapter 8 - Sloane

THE BROTHERHOOD OF Thieves? What sort of destination was that for a first date? Of course I'd heard of the place—everyone had. A decade ago, its name had been spoken in whispers, but in recent years, the bikers and criminals who'd once hung out there had moved on, and the Brotherhood had become achingly cool. The spit-and-sawdust ambience remained, but now the place was overrun with hipsters who wanted to take a walk on the wild side on Saturday nights. You could even buy "Brotherhood" merchandise on their website.

Or so I'd heard. I'd never been there, of course, but Leah had one of their patches sewn onto her leather jacket.

"Desmond wants to meet you there," she told me at ten o'clock. "It's just down the street from your house, right?"

"I'm not going."

"They don't take bookings, but you can hang out by the bar while you wait for a table."

"Or I could stay at home and watch *Game of Thrones*."

"Is that any good? I haven't seen it."

Neither had I, but I wasn't about to admit that to Leah. "I'm only on the first season."

"Do you want me to come over and help you with

your hair?"

"I'm still not going."

"Seven thirty. Don't be late."

Gardening had never been my favourite activity, but faced with the choice of tackling the jungle out back or going to the office where Leah might be lurking, I picked up a spade. Somewhere under all those weeds, there was a path to the overgrown patio that lay on the far side of the lawn. The lawn that was now knee-high.

When Lyndon was around, he used to mow the grass. He'd even planted a veggie patch, and for the two years we'd been together, I'd got used to eating fresh carrots and broccoli and potatoes. It had even helped me to lose a few pounds. But now the Jerusalem artichokes had turned into triffids, and the mere thought of digging them all out sent me reaching for the chocolate.

Was it too late to go to Venezuela?

Life with Lyndon had been easy. Straightforward. Too easy at times—apart from his views on food and animal welfare, he didn't really have opinions of his own. I suggested something; he agreed with it. Movies, music, sex, what to do at the weekend, politics, clothes. After a while, that got kind of boring, but it sure beat the aftermath of Kenneth and the awkwardness of every conversation I had with Logan.

I'd just started scraping the creeping grass off the concrete when my phone rang. This had better not be Leah trying to convince me to go on tonight's flipping date.

No, it was worse.

"Sloane?"

Why did my mother always say my name as a question? Since she'd phoned me, the fact that I'd picked up really shouldn't have been a surprise.

"Hi, Mom."

"I'm having a little get-together this evening, and I realised I forgot to tell you."

Nice to know where I lay on her list of priorities, wasn't it?

"It doesn't matter; I can't make it this evening."

"Why not?"

Because I didn't want to spend four hours eating Mom's burned offerings while she rehashed my failed love life and tried to set me up with her friends' sons.

"I have other plans."

"But I haven't seen you for a month."

There was a good reason for that. I didn't need another lecture on tolerance or forgiveness.

"How about I drop by one evening next week?"

"I'm making your favourite tonight. Fried chicken and gravy with strawberry cheesecake for dessert."

The mere mention of cheesecake made me cringe. "Sorry. Not tonight, Mom. There won't even be anyone my age there."

"Sure there will. I invited...people."

People? What people? "Mum, you didn't invite Kenneth, did you?"

"He's Linda's son."

A yes, then. "We broke up for a reason."

"He made a silly mistake, Sloaney."

"He cheated on me."

"Every man has his little indiscretions. Look at your

father and me—thirty-five years and still going strong."

If by "going strong," she meant they still lived in the same house and occasionally ate dinner together, then yes they were.

Three times in my childhood, he'd left us. Just walked out. The shortest disappearance had been for three weeks, and the longest for five months. I've had to watch my mom fret and mope, listen to her cry at night when she thought I was asleep. Every time a car drove past on the road outside, she'd run to the front door. Then she'd walked. Then shuffled. Eventually, she'd just looked up from her nest on the sofa with a forlorn expression.

At school, I'd turned to cookies as the rumours started flying. Why had my father left? Where had he gone? Was it him Shelby Carter's brother saw at the movie theatre with the checkout girl from the Spend 'n' Save?

The last time he'd come crawling back, I'd been fifteen years old, and I yelled at him for a full five minutes. How dare he keep doing this? Why did he keep hurting us? He'd said nothing. But Mom had welcomed him with open arms, and her smiles and laughter left me walking on eggshells in case he vanished again and left her miserable.

I wanted to see my mom happy, but Ruben Mullins had never been much of a husband, nor much of a father to me. Quite frankly, if he'd stayed gone the first time he went, I thought Mom and I might have actually been better off in the long run.

"I'm not getting back together with Kenneth. Not now, not ever."

"He's got a good heart."

No, he was just good at telling Mom what she wanted to hear. Like the time he claimed he'd donated his entire monthly sales bonus to the ACLU when I knew he'd done no such thing. And she giggled like a teenager every time he told her she didn't look a day over thirty despite the fact that she was fifty-three.

"There are plenty more single men in Virginia."

"Well, you haven't met one yet."

It'd only been a month, for goodness' sake. "As a matter of fact, I've got a date tonight."

"Really?"

Why did she sound so surprised?

"Yes, he's a cowboy, and he's taking me out for dinner at the Brotherhood of Thieves."

Why had I said that? To shock her? Probably.

"Sloane! That awful biker bar? A man got shot in the parking lot and bled to death. Don't you remember?"

"That was years ago."

"Kenneth would never take you to a place like that. I'm sure he wouldn't mind picking you up this evening if you don't want to drive. I'll ask him to stop off on the way."

"No! I won't even be here."

Which meant I'd have to go out with Desmond now. Because not only would Mom ask Kenneth to drop by my house no matter what I said, I also wouldn't put it past her to show up at the Brotherhood and interrogate Desmond. Lyndon had hated visiting my parents' place for dinner, and Mom hadn't been so keen on him either. His lack of shoes, lack of ambition, lack of a job... "How will he provide for you, Sloaney?" she'd asked on more than one occasion.

Never mind that I had my own career and earned decent money for a girl who'd messed up her last year of high school. An incident before my final exams had left me a nervous wreck, and I'd failed everything except geography, which was crazy because the only time I'd travelled outside of Virginia by myself, I'd gotten lost in the wilds of Kentucky and had to sleep in my car overnight.

Mom huffed out a sigh at the other end of the line. "Just make sure you're careful, Sloaney. And don't leave Kenneth hanging for too long—he won't wait forever."

Gah! I hung up and shoved my phone into my pocket. Was I somehow sending out "I want Kenneth" vibes without realising it? Why couldn't they get the message?

"Is everything okay, dearie?"

Edna's voice drifted over the fence, and I swallowed a groan. How much of that had she heard?

"Yes, everything's fine."

"Are you still having problems with that young man?"

"He's having a little trouble accepting it's over between us, and my mom isn't helping."

"How about some cake to cheer you up?"

"I really shouldn't."

"I've just finished making a Mississippi mud pie, and you know that's your favourite."

"Perhaps I could manage a small piece."

After all, I didn't want Edna to get lonely. When she first lost her husband, she'd been distraught, and I'd visited every day to check she was okay. I must have put on ten pounds in three months through those

chats. Luckily, I'd discovered the Greater Richmond Senior Center had an online chapter as well as regular meetings, and I'd helped Edna to enrol on her husband's old laptop. Now she had plenty of friends, and the centre had a fun program of activities to keep her busy, everything from computer classes to flower-arranging contests. Emmy didn't mind if I popped out of work occasionally to drive Edna to get-togethers.

And I didn't really mind spending time with Edna. Now that she'd mellowed out, she was fascinating to talk to, and I enjoyed hearing about her lifetime of adventures. She'd lived in eight different states, and when she was twenty, she'd hopped on a plane and travelled around Europe for two years, simply because she fancied a change. One piece of cake turned into three. Leah emailed me a photo of Desmond, who I had to admit was quite handsome, and before I knew it, the time had come to get ready for my date.

Think positive, Sloane. It can't possibly be as bad as dinner with Laurence.

CHAPTER 9 - SLOANE

TO DRESS UP or not to dress up? Seeing as I was going on this date under protest, I didn't feel particularly inclined to make an effort, but then I felt guilty because Desmond didn't know about Leah's meddling. In the end, I settled on indigo jeans with a fancy top and curled the ends of my hair. In his profile picture, Desmond had been wearing jeans and a checked shirt while holding onto a horse, so hopefully he wouldn't show up in a suit.

Besides, nobody wore smart clothes to the Brotherhood, right? I'd checked on the internet, and most of the photos showed overly cool twenty-somethings in designer denim and branded footwear. The casual-yet-costly look. My top was some fancy Italian label, a gift from Bradley, who spent half of his life shopping and the rest decorating, so at least I wouldn't feel totally out of place.

My phone buzzed with a message from Leah. *Have you left yet?*

Me: Just walking out the door.

Yes, walking. After all that cake with Edna, I needed the exercise, and if I cut across the park, the Brotherhood was less than a mile away. And going on foot would save me from hunting for a parking space, and worse, having to fit my car into it. Taking six goes

to reverse my Honda into a narrow bay under the scrutiny of Richmond's finest wasn't how I wanted to start the evening.

The Brotherhood was set back from the road, and I'd definitely been right to walk. Vehicles overflowed out of the small parking lot and down the side streets, and as the nicotine addicts clustered around the open front door turned their heads to look at me, I almost spun around and ran right back home. I didn't fit into a place like this.

But Leah hadn't sent me Desmond's contact details, and I could hardly stand him up, could I?

"What can I get you, beautiful?" the bartender asked once I'd been jostled and elbowed and somehow found myself at the front of the crowd.

"Uh..." Where did they get him from? A Hollywood movie set? The Mr. Universe locker room? "A diet cola, please."

"Surely you're not here on your own?"

"I'm supposed to be meeting someone."

He smiled and nodded. "Lucky man."

That bartender sure knew how to earn his tips.

Glass in hand, my next challenge was to find a table. Preferably one where I could see the door because Desmond was due to arrive at any moment. Seven thirty, Leah had said. I figured I could have one drink, maybe two, make a polite excuse, and still be home before it got dark. In June, that gave me plenty of time.

A couple got up to leave, and I almost tripped over my own feet in my hurry to reach their table. I dived for the closest seat, ignoring the glare of a leggy blonde whose stilettos had lost the race to my ballet pumps.

Victory was mine! But where was Desmond? I looked around the bar properly for the first time, and I could understand why it drew the crowds.

A group of men surrounded the pool table at the back, taunting each other, and beyond them, I glimpsed the famed "money wall." Visitors were invited to sign dollar bills and pin them to the smooth wooden boards, and when the wall was full, the cash got collected up and donated to charity. Last year, they'd raised over ten thousand bucks. But centre stage went to a sleek black Harley-Davidson, gleaming under spotlights on a revolving platform. I'd never ridden on a motorcycle before and most likely never would, but that bike would undoubtedly star in my dreams tonight, and probably those of every other woman in the place.

And at this rate, the Harley would be on its own, because there was no sign of Desmond. I checked the photo on my phone again. Nope, I definitely hadn't seen the handsome blond cowboy with cute dimples.

"Sloane?"

A brown-haired man perched on the seat opposite me. Tall and thin, he hadn't made the effort to shave, but then again, the fluff on his chin didn't really warrant it.

"Yes?"

How did he know my name?

"As soon as I saw your photo on that dating site, I knew it was you."

"I'm sorry, have we met before?"

"Not in person."

"You're not Desmond, are you?"

Because Laurence may have accused me of using a

flattering photo yesterday, but there was no way the man sitting opposite me and the man in Leah's picture were one and the same.

"Today, I'm Desmond. Just like today you're Sloane, Marilyn."

Marilyn? Marilyn was my middle name, after my grandma, but I never called myself that. I gave my drink the side-eye. Had somebody spiked it? Either that or I'd fallen off Planet Earth and landed in a parallel universe.

"I think there's been a mistake."

I tried to get up, but Desmond's evil non-twin grabbed my wrist. For a skinny guy, he was surprisingly strong.

"Let go of me."

"Look, I'm a reasonable guy. I just want my money back."

"Money? What money?"

"The money I sent for your breast enlargement surgery." He leaned back a little, taking a good look at my chest. "I have to admit they've done a good job, but cutting off all contact afterwards? Not cool, Marilyn."

I gasped as he reached his free hand over and gave one boob a good squeeze. "Hey!"

"Feel natural too."

"Get off!"

"Why? I paid for them. I think I'm entitled."

Both of Desmond's hands may have been busy, but mine weren't. I grabbed my drink and threw it in his face. Everyone turned to stare as he let out a howl, and I was so busy cringing, I forgot to duck as he slapped me. Hard. My ears rang as I tried to scramble away from him, but he still had hold of my wrist so I didn't

get very far.

Then a pair of hands prised Desmond's fingers away from me and gave him a hard shove.

"Leave her alone, you schmuck."

I might have still been blinking away stars, but I recognised that voice.

"Kenneth? What the hell are you doing here?"

"Don't worry, Sloane. I've got this."

Desmond swung at Kenneth, and the meaty *thud* as knuckles met flesh made me wince. Kenneth staggered backwards, clutching the top of his arm.

"Ow! You just broke my shoulder."

Kenneth had this, did he? Right.

"Butt out of my business, man."

"Not when you're hitting on my girlfriend."

"For the last time, Kenneth, we broke up."

As usual, he ignored me, and instead charged at Desmond, head down like an angry bull. Desmond doubled over, fighting for breath as Kenneth flailed away.

"Stop it! Both of you!"

Wait a minute—why was I defending either of them? Apart from the embarrassment factor, did I even care if they beat each other to a bloody pulp? Perhaps if I just slipped out the door...

"Fifty bucks says the preppy guy wins," one bystander said.

"Could you move over a bit?" a woman asked. "I'm filming this for YouTube."

Oh, heck. What if Mom found out about this? I'd never hear the end of it. Teeth gritted, I waded back into the fray and grabbed at Kenneth, but he wound his arm back to get another punch in and elbowed me in

the face.

Everything went black for a second, but someone caught me under my armpits and dragged me onto a chair. As my vision cleared, I became vaguely aware of the hot bartender striding past me and picking Desmond up in a bear hug.

"Get out of my fucking bar," he growled. "If I see you in here again, I'll kick your ass so hard you'll have to retrieve it from Idaho."

The crowd parted with groans of disappointment as the bartender carried Desmond towards the door, and I gingerly touched my face. Ouch. My eye was starting to swell up already.

"Are you okay?" Kenneth asked.

"Yes. No. I mean, I'm not sure. My face hurts."

A trickle of blood ran from his nose, and he dabbed at it with a napkin. "I should probably get an X-ray."

"I'm sorry. And thank you for stepping in." I gave my head a shake to try and clear the fuzz, and it felt as if I had a baseball careening around inside my skull. "Hang on—what are you even doing here?"

"Saving you from yourself. Your mother was worried."

"She told you where I was?" Stupid me, of course she did.

"With good reason, it seems. Honestly, what were you thinking going out with an animal like that? Sometimes, Sloane, you demonstrate appalling judgement."

"I know. I dated you for over a year, didn't I?"

"If your mother heard how ungrateful you sound, she'd turn in her grave."

"My mother's not even dead yet."

But she might be the next time I saw her.

"It's a figure of speech, Sloane. Luckily, I'm the forgiving type. Now that your 'date' has gone, we can sit down and have a civil conversation over dinner, although I'd be surprised if this dump served any decent food."

No, no, no, no, no. Kenneth did *not* get to charge back into my good graces like some bargain-basement white knight.

Think fast, Sloane.

"I've got no idea who that guy was. In fact, I've never seen him before in my life. My actual date is someone totally different."

"Then where is he?"

Uh, good question. I glanced up at the door, praying the bartender would come back and escort Kenneth to the parking lot as well, but no such luck. No, a different man appeared in the doorway, and my heart began to beat faster with hope, nervousness, and just a little bit of lust.

I raised one shaky finger and pointed in his direction. "That's him. That's my date."

My steps wavered as I staggered across the bar and clutched at the newcomer's arm like a lifeline. Kenneth had followed, and he looked understandably suspicious.

"*This* is your date?"

"Yes, absolutely." I peeped up into surprised brown eyes and attempted a smile. "Honey, you're late."

Please, Logan. Play along.

CHAPTER 10 - LOGAN

LOGAN TOOK ONE look at Sloane with her hair all mussed, her cheeks smudged with mascara, and her face swollen, and his hands balled into fists.

"Did this motherfucker hurt you, kitten?"

"Not on purpose."

So Kenneth *had* hurt her. That little shit was about to get intimately acquainted with the sidewalk. Logan took a step forward, but Sloane's grip tightened on his arm.

"Please don't. I'll explain, I promise, but can I sit down for a minute first? Kenneth was just leaving."

Too damn right he was. "Get out, and don't bother coming back. You're not welcome here."

"You can't tell me what to do, you Neanderthal. You don't own the place."

"Actually, I do."

Sloane gave a start and looked up at Logan, questioning. She needed ice on that cheek. Logan slid an arm around her waist and pulled her tight against him, as much to keep himself from pummelling Kenneth as anything else.

"Horse hockey," Kenneth said. "Sloane, this man's a liar and a thief. Did you know he stole my cufflinks?"

Sloane made a choking noise, but then Christian appeared at Logan's elbow.

"Need a hand, buddy?"

"I was just explaining to this gentleman that he's not welcome in our bar."

Christian took a step towards Kenneth, and the smaller man backed up in a hurry. Good move on his part. Back in high school, Christian had been on the wrestling team, and he still kept in shape. He could deal with Sloane's prick of an ex, because at the moment, Logan had more important things on his mind.

"Take care of this," he muttered, then dipped his head to kiss Sloane's hair, partly to annoy Kenneth but mostly because he wanted to. "Let's get you somewhere more comfortable."

People stared as he escorted Sloane through the bar, past his bike, past a giggling bachelorette party, and past the pool table, then through the door at the back marked *Private*. In Trey's office, Logan settled her into the leather swivel chair behind the desk and crouched down beside her.

"I'll be back in a minute. I'm just gonna get some ice for your face, okay?"

She nodded, staring vacantly at a spot on the wall behind him. What the hell had gone on before he got there? And more importantly, did he have to kill anyone?

In the kitchen, he ignored the staff and scooped ice into a bag, wrapping it in a tea towel to take some of the chill away before he jogged back to the office and held it gently against Sloane's cheek. She still hadn't spoken, and Logan recognised the signs of mild shock.

"What happened, kitten?"

He knelt at her side, holding the ice to her face as

she described the evening's events, and he didn't know where to start with processing things. What had Leah been thinking, setting Sloane up with a stranger like that?

"And you think it was a case of mistaken identity?" he asked.

"What else could it have been? I mean, it's not as though I've actually gotten a boob job."

No, she hadn't. Logan had spent the last seven years sneaking glances at her cleavage, and not only did her breasts look natural, they hadn't suddenly grown overnight.

"I know, kitten."

The term of endearment came naturally now, and he was surprised she hadn't called him on it again. Not that he'd stop. It suited her, Sloane the sweet little sex kitten, but if anyone used the name but him, he'd take their fucking head off.

"First Kenneth, now two disastrous dates in two days. I'm destined to be single for the rest of my life."

"Two? What was the other one?"

The story of Laurence came spilling out, and when Sloane finished speaking, Logan pressed her hand against the ice pack, drew his Glock 19 from his waistband, and dumped the ammunition out onto Trey's desk. Fifteen rounds from the magazine, and one from the chamber.

"So I don't get tempted," he explained.

"Please don't hurt anyone. It's over."

"Leah's still got internet access. Me and her are gonna have words."

"No! It's fine, honestly. I'll message her right now, see?"

Sloane pulled her phone out of her dinky little purse and tapped away at the screen.

"No more men," she read out. "I hereby quit dating in general and online dating in particular."

"Tell her to take down whatever profile she put up."

"Okay." Sloane added an extra sentence and hit the send button. "That's it. Done. Can I go home now?"

"No."

"No?"

Fuck it. He had Sloane here, alone, and he was going to keep her, at least for a few hours.

"What sort of douche would I be if I sent a lady home hungry? You came here for dinner, so I'm gonna get you dinner."

"I'm not hungry anymore."

"Well, I am, so you can stare at your food or watch me eat instead. Choice is yours. What do you want to order?"

"Anything. I'm easy."

If only. "Loaded burger? Fries?"

She tried to smile, but Logan didn't miss the way she winced. Fuck. "Back in five."

Talking to the chef took one minute, fetching a bottle of Advil from the first aid box took another, and then he made a brief detour out to the bar. Christian was back in position, no worse for wear from the evening's events.

"Did the little prick go quietly?" Logan asked.

"Stared after your girl when you walked her back inside, then he left in his fancy-ass car. Care to share what's going on?"

"Not sure myself, buddy. She said the first guy just showed up and grabbed her?"

"That's what it looked like from here."

"Motherfucker. Did you get his licence number?"

"Sorry. I tossed him onto the sidewalk, and he took off on foot. Must've been parked down the block."

Shit. If Logan asked Mack from the tech department to track the guy down online, she'd want to know why, and he wasn't sure how to answer that question right now. Yeah, he was interested in Sloane, but he didn't want to shoot his proverbial load too early and scare her off if she didn't feel the same way.

He'd just have to keep an eye on things. At least Sloane didn't seem particularly inclined to jump back into the dating game right away. That gave him time.

While Christian and the bar girls kept the masses at bay, he poured out two Cokes and headed back to Sloane. She hadn't moved from the chair, and when he appeared in the doorway, she gave him a wide-eyed look that made his cock twitch. Aw, hell. This had the potential to be more uncomfortable than his last date with Stacey the heiress, the one where he'd done the "let's stay friends" speech and she'd thrown a glass of wine over him.

"How are you feeling?" He fished the painkillers out of his pocket. "I brought these for you."

"Thanks."

Logan dragged up a wooden chair, close enough that their knees touched when he sat. Sloane didn't move away. Progress? Logan made a mental note not to joke about her sucking his dick tonight, because that sure hadn't gone down well last time.

"Food won't be long."

A tear dampened Sloane's cheek, and Logan felt the familiar rush of panic. On the plus side, at least his

cock softened.

"Uh, do you want more cheesecake?"

She shook her head, and a strangled sob of laughter escaped. "No, please. I felt so, so sick after that night."

"Then what can I do to make things better?"

She waved a hand and turned away, cheeks reddening. "Nothing. I'm fine."

"Fine? No, kitten, you're in denial." Oh, fuck it. Logan wrapped his arms around her waist and dragged her across onto his lap. "It's been a shitty day. I guess you just need to let it out?"

She nodded and buried her head in his shoulder, and he held her tighter. With any other woman, he'd have been ten miles away by now, but this was Sloane. He wanted her—warts, tears, drama, and all.

"I don't know what I'd have done if you hadn't walked in," she mumbled. "Kenneth wants us to get back together, but I'm not interested. Is there a secret man-code I don't know about? How can I get through to him?"

"Some men are idiots. Either they're stupid, or they're too blinded by their own self-importance to see the reality of the situation. With Kenneth, I suspect it's a mixture of both."

"What should I do if he tries again?"

"Call me. You've got my number, right?"

She nodded. Good. He'd programmed it into her phone years ago under some pretence at work, but not once had she dialled him. At least she hadn't pressed delete.

"But what if you're not there?"

"Phone someone else from work. Or Christian. We go way back, and he'll always help out if a friend's in

trouble."

"Christian's the bartender?"

"That's right."

"Do you really own this place?"

"One third of it. Mostly I'm a silent partner. I put a bunch of money in, but Christian and Trey run things."

"Trey?"

"Another friend. The three of us were in high school together. Trey went to college and got a marketing degree, I joined the army, and Christian knocked up a local girl and stayed here to take care of his daughter."

When Christian had to work late, Sienna would sleep over with Trey's daughter. They were close in age and practically inseparable. Thick as thieves. The three men kidded that if Logan ever had a daughter, they'd have to rename the bar the Sisterhood instead. A month ago, that hadn't looked too hopeful, but sometimes, things changed for the better.

"Won't the girl get upset if I call him?" Sloane asked.

"Sienna's mom ran out on the pair of them years ago."

"Oh. He seems like a nice guy."

"He is, but she wasn't a nice girl."

Yet another reason Logan had avoided emotional entanglements over the years. When Brandy upped and moved to California with a wannabe actor she'd known for less than a month, it had almost broken Christian. Looking after four-year-old Sienna was the only thing that had kept him going, and Logan never wanted to be in that position.

But with Sloane... Maybe the effort would be worth it.

A soft knock at the door announced the arrival of their food, and Logan didn't miss the look of disappointment on the waitress's face when she saw Sloane sitting on his lap. The young blonde had been flirting with him for months, and he'd played dumb every time. Never mix business with pleasure, Trey always told him, and so far he'd stuck to that rule, Sloane excepted. More than once, he'd jerked off in the bathroom at Blackwood after the team's monthly management meetings, the ones where she took the minutes and he got distracted.

He took a bite of his burger, but he barely tasted it as Sloane reached over and picked at her fries. Despite her earlier protestations, she ate, slightly awkwardly since she was still perched on his lap, but she didn't show any inclination to move and he wasn't about to suggest it.

"Food okay?" he asked.

"It's good."

"You sound surprised."

"I guess I am, a little. I mean, I know this place started off as a biker bar and then went hipster, but usually those places charge an arm and a leg for crappy food just because they can get away with it."

"People spend more if they're happy. You've never been here before?"

She shook her head, then licked a smear of ketchup from the corner of her lip. Fuck, now wasn't the time to be thinking of that tongue. Logan desperately replayed this morning's operations briefing in his head in an attempt to stop the blood flowing to his traitorous dick.

"Not my kind of place," she said.

"Why not?"

"Do I really have to spell it out?"

"Yeah."

Sloane took a deep breath. "Because I'm not like the people out there. They're all cool and pretty. Sexy," she whispered, blushing. "While I'm just kind of awkward."

"Kitten, half of them are grade A pricks, and you're prettier than all of those women."

She shrugged, dismissive, and Logan's blood boiled. She'd spouted the same bullshit about the girls in the office. Who had led her to think so little of herself? Given half the chance, he'd have shoved her up against the wall and shown her exactly how sexy he thought she was, but he feared that would earn him a knee in his junk. So he kept quiet and fed her another French fry.

Wyatt Earp once said, "Fast is fine, but accuracy is everything." Logan had been tiptoeing around Sloane for seven years, and now things were finally moving, he wouldn't go in for the kill until he was certain of success.

Which seemed unlikely to be tonight. The clock above Trey's cluster of framed certificates said two hours had passed, mostly in comfortable silence with a smattering of small talk, and the Brotherhood closed at ten on Sundays. In the old days, the more dubious clientele had propped up the bar until the early hours, but the new, trendy crowd woke early for yoga or organic juice cleanses or whatever. A year ago, they'd shortened the opening hours as an experiment, and profits hadn't suffered one bit.

"How's your face feeling?" he asked Sloane.

"Better. I think the painkillers helped."

She yawned, and Logan bit back a lewd comment. "Time to get you home to bed." Her own, unfortunately.

"Did you drive?"

"No, I walked. I'll call a cab."

"Don't worry; I can take you. My truck's outside."

"I must owe you a million favours by now."

"The only thing you owe me is a smile."

And he got one. When Sloane smiled, it didn't light up the room, it lit up the damn universe. Forget solar power and hydro dams—just keep Sloane happy and the world's energy problems would be solved.

Logan lifted Sloane to her feet and shuffled a bit to get the feeling back into his legs. Pins and needles had seemed a small price to pay for having her on his lap all evening, although he'd have preferred her slightly more naked.

But at least she didn't protest when he draped an arm over her shoulders and steered her out into the now-empty bar.

"Who came up with the idea for the money wall?" she asked.

"Trey. We wanted to help out some of the smaller charities that struggle to raise funds, and we were tossing around a bunch of ideas, and he said why not just get everyone to stick money up because it'll look great on Instagram."

"And the bike?"

"That was me. I was renovating my house, and I ran out of garage space."

"The Harley belongs to you? I thought it was only for decoration."

"No, it runs like a dream."

"Can I sit on it?" she asked, then looked horrified at herself for even suggesting it.

Logan laughed and lifted her onto the platform.

"Sure, kitten. Want me to take a picture?"

"Nuh-uh."

Dammit. That would have been a good one to file away in his spank bank.

Sloane swung one leg over the seat and grabbed the handlebars, grinning like a kid. That fucking smile would be the death of him. It made all rational thought disappear, which was probably why Logan came up with his next idea. Shrugging out of his leather jacket, he stepped up beside her.

"Put this on."

"What? Why?"

"Because it's cool outside at this time of night."

He unhooked a pair of crash helmets from the display behind the bar and settled one onto her head, tucking her hair back out of the way.

"Logan, what are you doing?"

"Taking you home."

Realisation dawned on her as he grabbed the keys out of the register and extended the ramp from the front of the platform. But by the time she thought to protest, it was too late. Logan got the other helmet fastened on his own head just in time to stop her from scrambling off the bike.

"On this thing?" she squealed. "Are you crazy?"

"Yeah, most people would say I am. Slide back a bit, kitten."

The engine started with a deep roar, and Logan hopped on board and kicked the bike into gear before Sloane could change her mind.

"Hold on," he shouted above the noise.

Sweet, compliant, that was his Sloane. She reached around his waist, clasping her hands in front, and fuck,

her breasts felt good squashed against him. And one hundred percent natural. Desmond or whatever his name was had been a total asswipe.

He waved to Christian as he gunned the bike out the front door, holding up two fingers to show he might be a while. His buddy just shook his head in amusement.

Sloane's thighs moulded around Logan's ass as he rode across the parking lot, and he wished it was his damn face. She lived a mile and a half away by road, and he'd savour every moment of the ride. Unless...

"Logan, why are we going left? My house is the other way."

"We're just taking a brief detour."

CHAPTER 11 - SLOANE

THE ALARM ON my phone blared out in the darkness, and I batted at it until it stopped squawking at me. It was too early to get up, and I wanted to relive last night's dream while I was still in that fuzzy state between sleep and wakefulness.

The dream where Logan had practically kidnapped me on the back of a Harley-Davidson and driven me halfway to Charlottesville so we could sit up on a hill and look at the stars. The dream where the vibrations of the motorcycle had done funny things to my insides and made me orgasm halfway along I-64 on the way home. The dream where I'd bitten my tongue to keep from crying out and loosened my hands around Logan's waist, only to realise a few seconds later that what I was touching wasn't his belt buckle.

He hadn't said anything about my errant hands when he helped me off the back of the bike outside my house, and I'd practically sprinted up the path. Perhaps it was a good thing I'd woken up after all.

I rolled over and stretched, then howled in pain when the left side of my face touched the pillow. In stunning clarity, the full chain of events from last night came rushing back to me. Un-Desmond, Kenneth, the fight, Christian's intervention, Logan's arrival, messing around on the bike, and omigosh, I really *had* felt up

Logan. Then I'd come home and felt up myself.

As Emmy would say, shitting hell.

Okay, okay, don't panic. Blackwood was a flexible employer. I could call in and take a personal day, then use the time to pack my bags and flee to Outer Mongolia. Well, perhaps not Outer Mongolia, because I didn't speak Mongolian. Maybe Alaska? Except Alaska was pretty cold, wasn't it? Even Kentucky would do.

I'd got the phone halfway to my ear when I remembered why I'd set the alarm early in the first place. Emmy was back this morning. And that meant I had a full day of catch-ups and meetings and phone calls and organising as well as the belated monthly management meeting, so I couldn't call in and I couldn't die of embarrassment because nobody else knew her schedule like I did.

Where was Logan? I called up his calendar and scrolled through to today's date. Oh, he was in the office too. Terrific.

Half an hour later, I'd taken a shower and made myself vaguely presentable, but I couldn't find any toothpicks to hold open my eyelids and I couldn't find my cat either. Of all the mornings for him to disappear.

"Nickel," I called out the back door. "Breakfast's ready."

Nothing. I battled through the yard, scanning left and right, but there was no sign of him.

Edna was out hanging up laundry, and she gave me a wave.

"Have you lost that cat of yours again?"

"Seems that way. He's probably off chasing birds." Or worse, mice. "I'll have to leave the back window open for him. Could you keep an eye?"

"Of course, dearie. I'll be in all day. Now, you get off to work and stop worrying."

Stop worrying? Right. How on earth was I supposed to face the man I'd inadvertently groped last night? He no doubt thought I was some desperate floozy. All I could do was hold my head high, keep my stilettos on, and pray I didn't end up with a damp patch on my panties. Again.

"You look like death warmed up," Emmy said when I walked into her office.

She, of course, looked like a supermodel despite having spent the last two weeks undercover in Libya. A little pale because she'd been wearing a burka the whole time, but stunning nonetheless.

"I didn't sleep so well last night."

"What happened to your eye? Do I have to kill anyone?"

Emmy smiled, but the scary thing was, I knew she wasn't entirely joking.

"No, no, it's fine. It was more of a misunderstanding."

"Hmm, some misunderstanding. You want a coffee?"

"Yes, please. Do you mind if I work at Black's desk today? It's kind of busy out there."

"Go for it."

With Emmy's husband still away, I got a brief reprieve from having to face Logan. Even so, I kept glancing through the glass wall towards his desk every time I saw movement, almost like a Pavlovian reflex. At

least I wasn't drooling, I suppose.

He didn't show up until a quarter to ten, wearing scuffed jeans and the leather jacket I'd borrowed last night. I leaned forward, squinting. Had he trimmed his beard? It tended towards scruffy, but it looked tidier this morning.

Stop it, Sloane. Do not give your libido any encouragement.

"Whatcha looking at?"

Busted. "Uh, for a moment, I thought I saw Ana, but isn't she in Lithuania?"

"Slovenia. She's not coming back until tomorrow. Are you ready for the meeting?"

No, not in a million years, but I held up my pad and the sparkly pen Bradley had given me last Christmas and forced a smile. "As I'll ever be."

In the big conference room, I grabbed the chair next to Emmy, and when Dan—Black's number two in the investigations department—meandered in, I waved her over.

"How are you? I haven't seen you in ages."

Thankfully, she took the bait and dropped into the seat on the other side of me.

"Crazy busy, but I haven't crashed a car for almost two months now, so it's all good. I hear Kenneth was being a dick again?"

"He was, but that's in the past now. Onwards and upwards."

"Indeed."

Logan was the last to arrive, sauntering in with a cup of coffee and a peach. He eyed me up as he slid into the last seat at the far end of the table, then took a bite and licked away a dribble of juice that ran down the

soft flesh. Straight away, my pulse began racing. Was he doing this on purpose? Because if he was, it wasn't funny.

"Everyone ready?" Emmy asked. "Nick, do you want to start?"

I picked up my pen and wrote *Management Meeting* and the date, but then Logan waggled his eyebrows and licked the damn peach. That...that... He *was* doing this on purpose, and if he kept it up, I might well take Emmy up on her offer to kill someone.

Beside me, Dan tapped my pad.

"Minutes?" she mouthed.

Darn it. Now Logan was messing with my work, and I couldn't afford for that to happen. While Emmy talked about budgets and operations and global mobility and statistical modelling, I scribbled notes I wasn't sure I'd even be able to read later and restricted myself to glancing up at Logan only once every five minutes. And half of the times I did, he was looking right back at me.

"Right, skills and drills," Emmy said. "Logan?"

Part of his job was managing the training for members of Emmy's Special Projects team, ensuring they practised together as often as necessary and kept up whatever qualifications they needed.

"I've got an exercise in Belize tentatively scheduled for the first week in November, and Nate's set up three new simulations in the kill-house that everyone needs to run through at some point over the next month."

"Individually?"

"In pairs. And I've got a plane arranged for anyone who wants to parachute next weekend. It'll be Evan's first jump since his accident, and Quinn's offered to

buddy up with him."

Emmy nodded towards Evan, who as international coordinator, also sat in on the meetings.

"How's your ankle holding up?"

"Good as new. I'm hoping to be back on active duty this time next month."

"As long as Dr. Stanton agrees."

"She will."

Emmy groaned. "Evan, tell me you and Kira aren't..."

"No, we're not. Not yet, anyway."

"Leave her alone. We like her working here, and you're incapable of anything more than a one-night stand. We can deal with the pissed-off women who turn up in reception, and the ones who cry, but if you upset Kira, I'll personally attach your parachute to your testicles and shove you out of a plane. Got it?"

Evan chuckled and gave her a salute. "Yes, ma'am."

"For fuck's sake," she muttered. "Anything else?"

Logan shook his head, and when the others turned back to Emmy, I kept staring long enough to get a smile. Darn it. I'd need to wring my freaking panties out after this. For a second, I imagined myself nibbling on his full bottom lip, that beard scratching against my chin, and then against other places. I clenched my thighs together as a rush of heat flooded through me. This was bad. Very bad.

Finally, Emmy closed the meeting, and I snatched up my scattered papers and hurried in the direction of the bathroom. Even so, Logan beat me there—I saw his sculpted ass disappearing through the door of the men's room farther along the hallway.

Inside the ladies' room, I locked myself in a stall

and hiked up my skirt, one hand already reaching inside my panties as I searched for the release I craved. Freaking heck. What on earth was I doing? Had I lost my darn mind? Definitely. And with Logan on the other side of the wall, probably with his jeans undone, I closed my eyes and brought myself to a quivering climax.

Yes, it was official; I'd gone insane.

It took a full five minutes for my legs to recover, and I forced myself to breathe slowly as I tugged my skirt down and made myself presentable. Was my face red? It sure felt like it. I checked in the mirror, and I could best be described as "glowing." At least my black eye took a little attention away from my cheeks.

My phone vibrated with a message on the way out of the bathroom, and my first thought of "I hope it's something dirty from Logan" made me wobble a bit.

But no, it was just Edna on her fancy new smartphone.

Edna: I haven't seen Nickel yet, but I've left a batch of cupcakes in a box on your counter, and another novel too.

Aw, she was always thoughtful like that. She joked that as I did most of her shopping, the least she could do was share the spoils. We often swapped books as well. It seemed that all generations enjoyed reading happily ever afters, even if I was yet to find mine.

Then another message popped up. An update?

No.

Kenneth: Look who stopped by to visit! I don't want him to get run over like the last one, so I think it's best that you come and pick him up. Shall we say tonight at seven?

He'd attached a photo of Nickel sitting on his couch, looking as if he wanted to swat something, and my vision turned red. That scumbag had taken my freaking cat!

How dare he?

I ducked into an empty meeting room and carefully placed my phone onto the table. Better that than throwing it against the wall. *Breathe, Sloane. Just breathe.*

"What's up, kitten?" Logan asked from behind me. "You're snorting like a pissed-off bull."

"I am not."

"Uh, you are."

"Well, can you blame me?" I thrust the phone into his hands. "Kenneth's catnapped Nickel!"

"Easy, easy."

One of Logan's hands came to the nape of my neck, rubbing away a little of the tension with one finger and a thumb while he studied Kenneth's ransom demand. My presence in exchange for the cat.

"Don't tell me 'easy.'" I leaned into Logan's touch; I couldn't help it. "Kenneth's like herpes. Once he gets into you, he never goes away. Although he didn't have herpes, thank goodness, because when we split up, I got tested for everything just in case and...that's too much information and I'm babbling again."

"We'll fix this tonight. No problem. You and me, okay?"

"How?"

"Let me worry about the logistics. I've got another meeting this afternoon, but I'll pick you up from your place at eight. Let the little shit stew for an hour first."

Logan made it all sound so easy. "But—"

"Trust me."

He may have been crude at times, and pushy, and so sexy he made me melt, but he'd never fibbed, not to me.

"I trust you."

CHAPTER 12 - SLOANE

I WISHED LOGAN had given me a tiny clue about his plans because I had no idea what to wear. What was appropriate attire for potentially burglarising your ex-boyfriend's apartment?

Skirts were out, that was a no-brainer, but should I go for jeans or sportswear? Not that I really wanted to wear yoga pants in front of Logan again. They showed every lump and bump and... Jeans it was. Black jeans and a black turtleneck with black tennis shoes. Should I wear gloves?

A knock at the door meant I had no time to hunt for them. I ran downstairs, yanked it open, and found Logan dressed in normal clothes—blue jeans, grey T-shirt, battered white tennis shoes.

"Okay, I feel like an idiot now."

"You should. Did you even check who it was before you opened the door?"

"Well, no, but..."

"Always check, kitten." He looked me up and down, slowly, and he didn't bother to hide it when his gaze lingered on my chest. "Where did you get your outfit? Ninjas 'R' Us?"

"Black's slimming, okay?"

"Sure. We can stop off and get you a few piercings and a tattoo on the way."

"Shut up."

He waved me ahead of him to the truck, and I felt his eyes on my bottom as we walked. Tell me I didn't have VPL? I'd worn boy shorts so I should have been in the clear, but that penetrating gaze made me oversensitive. Logan finally scooted past me to open the door, and I breathed a sigh of relief.

"Are you going to tell me the plan yet?" I asked once he'd hopped in beside me and started the engine.

"Simple. You set off the fire alarm, and when everyone evacuates the building, I'll go in through the balcony door and pick up Nickel."

"But Kenneth lives on the fourth floor."

"Which is why I brought a grappling hook gun."

"Seriously? I thought only Batman had one of those."

"Nate built it. He lives for this shit."

"How will you get through the balcony door, though? Kenneth keeps it locked."

"And the lock's a piece of garbage."

"How do you know?"

"I visited his apartment once before, remember? It's literally my job to notice that stuff."

I was way, way out of my league here. My job involved typing up the aftermath of Logan's adventures, not living through them.

"How am I supposed to set the fire alarm off? It's inside the building, and I threw my door fob and key back at Kenneth when I left."

"Easy. There's a button in the entrance hallway. Just hang around outside, smile sweetly at the first person to come by, and thank them when they hold the door open for you."

"That works?"

"Every damn time, kitten."

My heart pounded as I trailed a pretty brunette up the walkway to Kenneth's building. Logan was already in position around the back, hiding in the trees, and he'd looked totally relaxed as he strolled off. Me? My mouth was so dry I couldn't even swallow without coughing.

But as predicted, the girl held the door open, and my smile was genuine.

"Thank you," I croaked.

She gave me an odd look. "Are you feeling okay?"

"I'm just getting over a cold."

"Try lemon tea mixed with honey. I swear by it."

"Thanks, I will."

She jogged off up the stairs, and I hung around by the elevator for a moment to check nobody else was coming, then dialled Logan with trembling fingers.

"Ready?" I asked.

"All good here."

I screwed my eyes shut as I punched the fire alarm button, then speed-walked out the door. *Don't run*, Logan had said. *It looks suspicious.* Sirens wailed as I headed for his truck, parked in the far corner of the lot by the exit. A minute passed, then two, then five, and a hundred people must have been milling around outside the building, checking for smoke. I slumped down in the front seat, watching the drama over the dashboard. Where was Kenneth? Tell me he hadn't gotten wise to our little plan and stayed inside?

I let out a long, relieved breath when I spotted him

by the garbage dumpsters, talking on his cell phone. And then a fire truck arrived, which I felt kind of guilty about as well as the whole evacuation thing, but Logan assured me he was friends with one of the firefighters and it wouldn't be a problem. I understood free beer was involved somewhere along the line.

A month ago, I'd have relished the opportunity to ogle the fire crew up close, but a lot had changed in that time, and now I only had eyes for one man. Logan. And thirty seconds later, he sauntered towards the truck wearing a slim backpack I hoped contained Nickel.

"Did you get him?" I asked before Logan got halfway into the driver's seat.

"Pretty sure he's pissed at me. There was hissing."

"He'll forgive you. He was probably upset because he had to put up with Kenneth all day."

"Understandable."

Logan started the engine and pulled out of the lot at a sensible speed, and I undid the zipper on the bag, careful to keep hold of Nickel's collar so he didn't jump around the cab. Luckily, he didn't seem any the worse for wear, and by the time we got back to my place, he was curled up on my lap, purring.

"Once again, I don't know how to thank you."

"I already told you how." Logan cupped my chin with one hand and ran his thumb along my bottom lip. "Smile."

I didn't know whether to smile or spontaneously orgasm and instead, I ended up letting loose a high-pitched giggle that made Nickel tilt his head to one side in confusion.

"Better," Logan said.

He still hadn't moved his thumb, and I had a crazy

urge to suck it. What would he do if I did? I was strongly considering giving it a go when Nickel made a choking sound and horked up a slimy pile of kitty treats into my lap.

Oh, yuckety yuck. I had two choices: laugh hysterically or die.

Logan chose to laugh. "That cat sure does have an unfortunate sense of timing. Give me your keys, and I'll run in and get a roll of paper towels."

He jogged inside, leaving me to wonder whether I'd ever manage to have a normal day with Logan. Any other man would have run a hundred miles by now, but then again, Logan was just a friend. And friends helped each other out, right? I'd certainly do anything for him.

"Here we go." Logan scooped the worst of the mess into a garbage bag. "You go change, and I'll take care of the cat. And smile, kitten."

I did, but only because he told me to.

Upstairs, I gave up on the idea of being stylish. Logan had seen me with cat puke all over my legs, for crying out loud. Yoga pants and a tunic top would surely be an improvement, and at least the tunic covered me up.

Keeping the weight off had been a constant struggle, ever since I was a little girl. Each time Dad left, I turned to the cookies, and my teenage years hadn't been kind. I'd lost a whole thirty pounds while I was dating Lyndon, mainly because he liked hiking at the weekends, and if I was walking, I wasn't eating. I also knew how to recognise most of the native birds of Virginia and fifty types of wild flower.

But after he departed for South America, I'd piled the pounds back on, and Kenneth's love of restaurants

had only made the problem worse. Deep down, I suspected my looks had contributed to him straying, which was the main reason I hadn't put his tie collection through the waste disposal before I left.

A long sigh escaped my lips. What was the point in dwelling on things I couldn't change? Logan was in my house, and I couldn't just leave him on his own.

My slippers were cartoon cats, a gift from my mother last year, so I padded downstairs barefoot instead and found him sitting on the sofa with Nickel on his lap. Thankfully, my pet already seemed to have forgiven his rescuer for stuffing him into a bag.

Was it dumb to be jealous of a cat? Probably, but that didn't change the fact that I was.

"Hey."

Logan smiled up at me. "Hey."

Now what? I couldn't just stand there gawking.

"Uh, can I make you dinner? It's the least I can do. I'm not a great cook or even an average one, but—"

"I'd love dinner. What can I do in the kitchen?"

Bend me over the counter and take me from behind?

Sloane!

I shook my head to get rid of my filthy thoughts. Logan was only offering to help, but in my experience, men didn't help in the kitchen. Lyndon had taken over completely while Kenneth occasionally complained about the lack of seasoning. I didn't even know what to make. Something basic, that was for sure.

"Can you chop up an onion? And some tomatoes?"

Spaghetti bolognese was a safe option. Comfort food, filling, and I was pretty sure I had Parmesan cheese somewhere to grate on the top. As long as I

didn't set anything on fire... Two emergency call-outs in one night would be difficult to explain.

Logan leaned down as we walked out of the living room, his lips brushing my ear.

"Sure, kitten. I'll be your bitch tonight."

Aw, heck. I was in so much trouble here.

Once I'd got my racing pulse under control, cooking with Logan turned out to be a weirdly enjoyable experience. He chopped vegetables scarily fast, the knife flashing so quickly I could barely see the blade, while I browned the meat and boiled pasta.

"Do you cook much at home?" I asked.

"Just the basics. I've never had to learn anything more. In the army, someone else cooked, and then we bought the Brotherhood. Plus there's always food at the office."

"Where did you learn to chop like that?"

"Trust me, you don't want to know."

Logan was right—I didn't. But ironically, I felt safer with a trained killer in my kitchen than I ever had with an advertising executive or a vegan poet, and Logan did the washing-up too.

As we both sipped red wine—just one glass because he was driving and I absolutely wasn't getting drunk this time—the tiny part of me that still believed in fairy tales piped up with a worrying observation.

I could get used to this.

CHAPTER 13 - LOGAN

THE LAST TWENTY-four hours had been almost normal, Logan thought as he pounded along on the treadmill. According to the clock in the gym, it was still only seven a.m., which meant he had time to fit in a decent weights session before his first meeting. Only the catnapping drama had been a little out of the ordinary, but compared to some of the stuff Logan did on a regular basis, climbing up balconies barely warranted a raised eyebrow.

Dinner afterwards had been unexpected but...nice. Sharing a kitchen with a woman, eating good food... And when Sloane's nerves had settled and she'd relaxed, he thought she'd enjoyed it too. He choked back a laugh as he thought of the evening before. The impulsive bike ride had been two hours of heaven and hell. Heaven because Sloane had been pressed against his back as well as wrapped around him, hell because they'd both been wearing clothes and he'd had to concentrate on the road. Although he'd nearly crashed when she fondled his dick. Judging by how flustered she'd been afterwards, he had to assume that had been an accident, albeit a rather pleasant one.

And being in the office around her was purgatory too. Outside of work, she may have been loosening up a bit, but after the last incident with Kenneth on the

phone, Logan had to tread very, very carefully. Which meant no "accidental" brushes against her in the hallways, no innuendos at her desk, and definitely no dragging her into the bathroom because his damn hands wanted to peel her clothes off.

He lasted four hours before his willpower gave out. Four hours of surreptitious glances and a total inability to concentrate.

"Hey." Leah looked up as he perched on the edge of her desk. Not Sloane's—that would have been far too obvious. "Can I get either of you two ladies a drink?"

Leah beamed up at him. "Cappuccino, one shot of caramel, extra froth, and can you sprinkle some of that cocoa powder on the top?"

"I'm not a fucking barista. Sloane?"

"Huh?"

Well, that was disappointing. She wasn't even looking at him. Deliberate avoidance? Or did she just have a better game face than he did?

"Do you want a drink?"

"Oh, uh, thanks."

"Coffee?"

"Mmm."

This was more than messing around. What was up with her? Logan hopped off the desk and moved across a few feet to stand behind the woman who napalmed every one of his nerve endings.

"You okay?"

She kept staring at her computer screen. Facebook?

"I got a message."

"What kind of message?"

"A strange one."

Since she didn't seem to object, Logan leaned

forward to read it.

Hey Sloane!
Saw your profile on DateMe.com, but my account got terminated before I got a chance to hit you up. But then I found you on here! Fate, huh? Anyhow, I was wondering if you wanna go for a drink later?

As Logan watched, another box popped up.

Or how about tomorrow? Or the weekend? Anytime? I live just along the road from you.

"How did he find me on Facebook?" Sloane asked. "Why would he do that when there are a million other girls out there?"

Logan forced his jaw to unclench before he cracked a tooth. "I'm more concerned with the fact that he knows where you live."

Sloane had never had the darkest of complexions, probably because she spent most of her time in the office, but now she turned a shade paler.

"He can't know exactly where I live. I don't put my address on Facebook."

Logan's fingers brushed hers as he took the mouse out of her hand and scrolled through her profile page.

"You've got a picture of the front of your house. A check-in for brunch with the dickhead at the pancake place on Rosemount which is less than a mile away. A request for recommendations for a good lawn service that comes to your street. Anyone driving around that neighbourhood could find you in fifteen minutes."

The last of her colour drained from her cheeks.

"What should I do?"

"Delete all this, for starters." Logan didn't wait for her to do it herself, just began removing posts.

"Don't you think you're being a teensy bit alarmist?" Leah asked.

Where Sloane was concerned? "No."

"It's only a message."

"And what the hell does a guy do to get his membership terminated from a dating site?"

"Uh..." Leah clicked around on her own computer for a few seconds. "Okay, termination... *'Here at DateMe.com, we like to keep our terms simple. Anyone discussing or posting pictures of bestiality, paedophilia, extreme violence, scat or golden showers, fisting, or bloodletting will have their membership revoked.'* On second thought, why don't you delete Sloane's whole Facebook account?"

"Fuck," Logan muttered. "Did you take her dating profile down?"

"Right after she asked me to." Sloane turned her screen to prove it. "See?"

Oh, this just got better and better. Leah had lifted Sloane's Facebook profile picture to use as her headshot on the dating site. Anyone with Google could do a reverse image search and match the two. He tightened his grip on the mouse to stop himself from throttling the perky blonde.

"Sloane, you need to get a security system installed."

"But I live in a rented house. I can't start messing around with drills and stuff."

"Well, you need something. I'll speak to Nate."

"Do you really think it's a problem? Leah's right—

it's just a message. The guy probably sends twenty a day."

"I'm not taking that chance."

Leah tilted her head to one side and looked at him funny. "Why do you even care?"

Shit. Busted. Reeling in Sloane would be hard enough without the whole office watching their every move. Logan shifted closer to Leah and put an arm around her shoulders. "Because here at Blackwood, we're a team, and we look after each other. I'd do the same for you, except Sloane wouldn't be dumb enough to plaster your details all over the internet."

"I didn't realise—"

"Zip it. Help Sloane to change her Facebook settings to private while I go visit Nate. Make sure you block that guy. And do me a favour and get me a double espresso."

"Asshole," Leah muttered as he walked off.

Normal service: resumed.

Down in Nate's basement lair, Logan steeled himself for an interrogation. His bullshit might fly with Leah, but Nate was a whole other story.

As Logan swiped through the sliding door— bulletproof, of course—the acrid smell of propellant drifted out, followed by the soft *pop* of a silenced pistol. He meandered inside and found Nate pointing a .22 at a target on his private firing range. One of Blackwood's four directors, Nate was a former member of SEAL Team Six as well as Logan's old unit at the CIA. But despite being a master of modern warfare, he was most at home in his Batcave surrounded by gadgets and gizmos.

"What are you testing?"

"A smart pistol. It only fires if it's in range of a paired RFID chip, and it can be disarmed completely by satellite if someone undesirable manages to steal both components."

"Need a guinea pig?"

"Maybe in a week or two. I'm still refining the range. Is this a social visit, or did you want something?"

Nate didn't tolerate social visits very well, so Logan got straight to the point.

"Sloane's having man trouble."

"What, again?"

"Yeah. Leah signed her up for online dating, and a whole bunch of kooks are coming out of the woodwork. She needs a security system that she can install in a rented house, and quickly."

"Why do you care?" Nate put the gun down and scowled at Logan, but he scowled at everyone so that didn't mean much.

"Someone has to."

"First the visit to pretty-boy's apartment and now this? Is something going on between you two?"

Fucking Nate. Why did he have to be so perceptive?

"Why do you care?" Logan echoed Nate's words back to him.

"Because Sloane's a damn good PA, and if you treat her like she's disposable and she quits working here, Emmy'll remove your balls and mount them on a dartboard to give Sloane as her leaving gift."

Blunt, but the man had a point. Logan glanced down as the boys shrivelled involuntarily.

"I don't plan on hurting her. In fact, I'm trying to do the opposite here. Can you help, or can't you?"

"Yeah, I'll help. Just make sure you tread carefully.

I say that as a friend and also as a man who hates sponging bloodstains out of carpet."

"I'm on fucking tiptoes."

At the end of the day, Logan waited until the office had cleared out before he approached Sloane. Leah rarely stayed late, but Sloane usually worked until at least seven. Some might think she was inefficient, but Logan knew from talking to Black that she often took on extra tasks to help others out. She had nothing to prove and no need to ingratiate herself with anybody, so Logan suspected her willingness to go above and beyond stemmed from an ingrained desire to make people happy combined with a reluctance to go home. When she was with Kenneth, that had been quite understandable because who would want to spend an evening with that prick? But now? Logan hated to think that Sloane was lonely.

When the only people left on the third floor were the janitors and a small group of investigators huddled in a conference room, Logan sidled up to Sloane and dropped into Leah's chair.

"Almost done?"

Sloane minimised the Kitty Delights website and blushed. "Just leaving. Uh, I've finished working, I was only—"

"Doesn't matter. Here, I've got something for you."

He wheeled the chair leftwards until he was positioned behind her and swept her silky hair to one side. She flinched and then shuddered, but she didn't pull away as he'd feared she might.

"What is it?"

Logan didn't answer, just fumbled with the tiny catch as he fastened the necklace around her neck, then resisted the urge to press his lips against her soft skin.

Sloan reached up to feel the pendant, an abstract design of enamel swirls on a silver disc. Purple, blue, and red, the latter the colour of the plump lips Logan desperately wanted to kiss.

"A necklace?" she asked. "You got me a necklace?"

"It's Nate's handiwork. The middle circle's a panic button. Press it, and the cavalry will come."

The Blackwood control room would send whoever was nearest, but Logan intended to lead the charge. Until he was satisfied that Sloane wasn't in danger, he wouldn't be travelling any farther away than absolutely necessary. The new guys could take some of the load at work. Logan wasn't about to tell Sloane, but he planned to sleep on the sofa in Christian's office at the Brotherhood, just in case. What was a backache compared to the possibility of Sloane getting hurt?

"I don't want to make work for anyone," she said.

"Nobody minds. And I'm escorting you home each day for the next few weeks."

Logan had expected Sloane to protest, but all he got was a soft, "Thank you."

Fuck, she was scared. Logan hated that she was scared, and even more, he hated the men who'd made her that way. Leah wasn't in his good books either.

Sloane packed up, and all too soon, Logan was sitting outside her house as she climbed out of her little Honda. He had to grip the steering wheel to stop himself from following her inside since he really didn't have a good excuse for doing so. Not tonight. Not

unless the cat decided to bring another mouse in. For a moment, Logan considered appropriating a rodent from somewhere and letting it go in Sloane's house. In her bedroom, preferably. But he quickly shook his head, trying to clear that stupid thought. Had he lost his damn mind?

Yes, to Sloane Mullins.

As she walked up the path, all curvy ass and swishy hair, Aristotle's words rang true in Logan's ears: patience is bitter, but its fruit is sweet.

And he bet Sloane would taste delicious.

CHAPTER 14 - LOGAN

ANOTHER DAY, ANOTHER hard run in the morning followed by three hours in the kill-house, a martial arts session, and more paperwork than Logan cared to think about. As soon as this final meeting wrapped up, he could get back to the important things in life, like talking to the woman who'd been occupying his every thought since he said goodbye to her last night.

"Any volunteers for the Iraq trip?" Evan asked, looking straight at him.

A month ago, Logan wouldn't have hesitated to jump on the plane, but things had changed. Priorities, needs, wants... They'd all changed. Logan had spent his whole adult life on the job, but in the last few weeks, his world had shifted. Probably the planets had aligned or something, or at least, that's what his youngest sister would say. Nicolette was into all that astrology mumbo jumbo.

Evan was waiting for an answer, but before Logan could decline, Otto jumped in. Over the past year or so, Emmy and Black had begun bringing new blood into the Special Projects team, and he was one of the recent recruits. Four people so far—Cade, Slater, Otto, and Ryder—with the promise of more to come, and although it took effort to integrate the newcomers, they were needed. Every month, the workload got heavier,

and none of the long-standing members of the team were getting any younger, Logan included.

Perhaps that was what had escalated this obsession with Sloane? A desire to share the rest of his life with someone rather than going home alone or rolling out of some vacuous actress-slash-model's bed at three in the morning in case she felt the need to discuss babies over breakfast. Yes, that had happened, and yes, his dick had stayed limp for three days afterwards.

"I'll take Iraq," Otto said. "When do I leave?"

"Tomorrow evening, flying out of Andrews Field." Evan tapped at the screen on his tablet. "That's it for the overseas requirements. Does anyone have any other business?"

Logan let out a long breath of relief and shook his head along with the others. He'd be staying in Virginia for at least another week, and now he could go and see Sloane.

He found her sitting at her desk—no surprises there—and as he walked towards her, she smiled that insecure, flickery little smile he both loved and hated. Loved because it was cute, and hated because he wished she had more confidence in herself. Who had stolen that from her?

"Ready to go?" he asked.

"You're going to see me home again?"

"I said I would, didn't I?"

"Well, yes, but…"

People had let her down in the past, hadn't they? There and then, Logan vowed he wouldn't be one of them.

"Say hello to your new stalker, kitten. Until things settle down, I'm following you every evening, and if I

can't, I'll ask one of the other guys to make sure you get home safely."

Damn, she looked adorable when she got flustered. Her cheeks pinked, and those full lips twitched. Logan pictured them kissing their way across his stomach, lower, lower, until they wrapped around his cock.

"Logan? Are you okay?"

Now it was his turn to go red. How long had he zoned out for? "Sorry, just thinking about tomorrow's training exercise."

"Is it a hard one?"

Not yet, but if he'd carried on daydreaming for one more minute... Shit. He needed to be more careful around Sloane.

"Nothing too taxing."

"That's good." Sloane smiled again, wider this time. "I'm all finished here now. Are you done? If you're not, it's no problem to wait."

"Let's go. I didn't get groceries this week, so I'm gonna stop at the Brotherhood and pick up dinner. You want anything?"

"I didn't know they did takeout."

"They don't."

She crinkled her nose, undecided. "Maybe. Uh..."

"What?"

"Will there be anywhere to park?"

"For us, yes. There's a staff lot around the back. Just follow me in."

When they got to the bar, Logan was tempted to push for a date of sorts, but then he remembered it was two-for-one cocktail day. The place was packed, there were no available tables, the waitresses were rushed off their feet, and conversation was impossible over the

din.

"Stick by me," he half shouted in Sloane's ear.

She looked shell-shocked by the crowd, and he slid an arm around her waist to keep her close.

Keep your hand off her ass, Barnes.

He thought she'd break free as he opened the door to the staff area at the back, but she did the opposite, leaning into him as they walked to the kitchen. Perhaps they could keep walking? Out through the fire exit, along the street, into the park... They could find a quiet bench somewhere and spend an hour together, maybe two, just listening to the night and getting to know each other better. Would he get a slap if he tried it?

"What can I get you?" the chef asked, breaking the moment.

Sloane stepped sideways, and Logan cursed the man under his breath.

"What do you want to eat, kitten?"

"I guess I should have something healthy. Maybe a salad?"

That's what her mouth said, but the look of distaste on her face suggested otherwise.

"Give us two fully loaded burgers to go, side orders of fries and onion rings. Put some lettuce on Sloane's." He tucked his arm around her again. "Come on, let's get a drink while we wait."

"What if I wanted a proper salad?" she asked as he steered her along the hallway. "Lettuce doesn't count."

"You didn't want a salad."

Out at the bar, Logan waved at Christian, and a minute later, he came over with drinks—a small glass of white for Sloane and a beer for Logan. He took a mouthful while Sloane sipped. She was still tense as

hell, and Logan wasn't sure whether that was due to the number of people or the dating issues. Still, she was back by his side, *right* by his side, and he'd take any excuse to keep her there. Up close, she smelled sweet, citrusy, and he leaned in closer.

Only for Christian to guffaw from three feet away. "Dude, did you just sniff her hair?"

That asshole. Logan was gonna kill him.

Sloane took a step back, brow knitted in confusion. "Is he talking to you, Logan?"

Christian stayed just out of punching range and nodded. "The boy's sprung."

"Sorry? I didn't hear that."

Sloane went to move closer, but Logan pulled her back.

"Ignore him. Christian's the king of bullshit. You want to play pool?"

"I've never played pool before." She looked around, and her eyes lit up. "Can I pin a dollar on the money wall?"

Christian held out a pen, laughing, and Logan snatched it off him.

"Sure, kitten. I've got a whole bunch of dollars. Pin away."

Lucky escape.

Logan and Sloane had finally left the Brotherhood, bags of lukewarm food in hand. He followed as she drove her Honda through the quiet streets, wondering how he could invite himself in. A search for possible intruders? No, he didn't want to alarm her. A check for mice? That

could work, although dinner would be stone cold by the time he'd looked through every kitchen cupboard.

In the absence of a better plan, he would run with it. Sloane had a microwave, after all. But as they rounded the corner, fate finally threw him a bone, and he broke into a grin. Sloane did the opposite. Logan saw her mouth set into a flat line in the Honda's rear-view mirror, and a second later, his phone buzzed.

"Kenneth's outside my house," she hissed.

"I noticed."

There was no missing the little prick's cherry-red BMW with its W1NN3R vanity plate.

"I'm going back to Blackwood. I'll sleep in one of the pods."

The company had a dozen rooms available in case employees needed to stay overnight, and although they were perfectly comfortable and came fully stocked with bathroom shit, there was no way Sloane was sleeping in one.

"No, you won't. Park your car, and we'll get rid of him."

"How?"

Logan's smile grew wider. "Trust me. Do you trust me?"

She hung up without answering, but five seconds later, she pulled into her driveway. Yeah, she trusted him, and fuck if that didn't make him feel good.

Logan parked his truck behind Sloane's vehicle and avoided the temptation to give Kenneth the finger as he hopped out of the driver's side with his food. Sloane hesitated by her car, knuckles white as she gripped her own bag.

"Now what?" she whispered.

Fuck, that ass felt good under his hand. Soft, curvy, perfectly formed. He gave it a squeeze and Sloane made a little choking sound.

"W-w-what are you doing?"

"Showing Kenneth that you're not his anymore. Play along."

That flickery little smile came back, and Sloane tentatively slid an arm around his waist.

"Are you sure you don't mind? Him thinking you're with me, I mean?"

Logan would quite happily stick a poster on every street light, then tattoo her name across his chest if it made her happy. Too much? Yeah, probably.

"Give me your key."

Logan took her food so she could fish the key out of her shoulder bag, then guided her towards the front door. How much could he get away with? She hadn't seemed upset over his hand positioning, so when they climbed up the front steps, he swung her around to face him, her back against the door.

"Is Kenneth watching?" he asked.

She stood on tiptoes, and her gaze flicked over Logan's shoulder.

"Yes, and he doesn't look happy."

"Good."

Logan slotted the key into the lock, but he didn't bother to warn Sloane before he lowered his lips to hers. She'd only have come up with some half-assed reason why it was a bad idea, whereas Logan thought it was the best idea he'd had all day. And besides, she kissed him back. Only for a second before her eyes widened and she gave the sweetest little gasp, but her first instinct was definitely to kiss him, and Logan was

taking that as a win. Before she could say a word in front of Kenneth, Logan opened the door and lifted her inside, then slammed it behind him while she stared in shock.

"What was that for?" she asked.

"Just making things very clear for Kenneth." Logan sauntered into the living room, trying not to smirk. The ex-dickhead was toast. "Shall we eat?"

Sloane appeared in the doorway, gripping both sides of the doorjamb as she tried to string words into a sentence. Damn, that was fucking adorable.

"What... But... The..." She lifted an arm, dropped it again. "You're staying for dinner?"

"If Kenneth's hanging around, it would look odd if I left right away, don't you think?"

"I suppose."

"Sit down and pick out a movie, and I'll get drinks and flatware."

"A movie?"

"Unless you want to spend the evening in bed?"

He was joking, mostly, but Sloane still had a coughing fit. Logan thumped her on the back, then helped her over to the sofa.

"Easy, kitten. Just relax."

But she looked far from relaxed as he went to reheat the food. Had he overdone things? Sloane wasn't like any other woman he'd been interested in, and he was still finding his footing around her. Flighty, nervous, and with such low self-esteem that he needed a backhoe to find it—what had made her that way?

On the way back to the living room with the plates and glasses on a tray he'd spotted during the mouse escapade last week, Logan stopped to peer out the

narrow window beside the front door, just in time to see Kenneth floor it away down the road. His flashy electric car didn't even give the dickless wonder the satisfaction of a noisy getaway. Shame.

"Did you find a movie?" he asked Sloane.

She dropped her hand from her mouth and reached for the remote. "What? Uh, no, not yet. Did Kenneth leave?"

Should he tell the truth and lose his excuse to stay? Or opt for a tiny fib and hope he could get to know Sloane better? Logan knew what a good guy would do, but even his own sisters thought he was an asshole most of the time. Might as well live up to his reputation.

"Still there, kitten. Figure he'll get bored after an hour or two."

Oh, Logan was gonna go to hell for this.

CHAPTER 15 - SLOANE

I SAT ON the sofa and ran my fingers across my lips. Had I been dreaming or did Logan just kiss me? My lips didn't feel any different, but judging by the *clink* of dishes I could hear in the kitchen, Logan was definitely in my house, which meant I hadn't imagined the whole thing. Half of me wanted to freak out, and the other half wanted to send Kenneth a golf towel and a six-pack of organic smoothies as a thank-you gift for being in exactly the right place at the right time. The only question was, how could I get him to come back tomorrow?

"Did you find a movie?" Logan asked from the doorway.

I snatched my hand away from my mouth. *Don't let him know how much he affects you, Sloane.* The last thing I wanted to do was scare him off.

"What? Uh, no, not yet. Did Kenneth leave?"

"Still there, kitten. Figure he'll get bored after an hour or two."

Thank goodness. Did that mean Logan would stick around for two whole hours? I fumbled for the remote and clicked the TV on, cursing my lack of channels.

"What do you like watching?" I asked.

"I don't watch much TV. Just football occasionally."

"I really hate football." The mere thought of sitting

through a game left me cold. "Sorry."

"Then pick anything. I'm not bothered."

Oh, that was helpful. What if I chose the wrong thing? A game show, some reality singing thing, a documentary. Nope, nope, nope. Aha! An action movie. Gunfights, fast cars, a few explosions... That would make Logan feel right at home, wouldn't it? I mean, nobody told us PAs everything about Blackwood's operations, but I gleaned enough details to get nervous every time Logan left the building.

But for now, I tried to put work out of my mind. Tonight, Logan was here with me, and I wanted to enjoy every minute of his company, even if I did feel guilty for him giving up his evening to help me out.

"This movie?" I read the details from the guide. "'The year is 2023. When a crazed serial killer escapes from his high-tech prison, only three deputies stand between his murderous tendencies and the sleepy town of Westbrough. Can they recapture the notorious criminal before it's too late?'"

"Sounds good. You want ketchup?"

I loved ketchup, but I'd probably get it on my face and end up looking like one of the serial killer's victims as well as being utterly mortified. Spending time around Logan left me giddy, a weird, visceral reaction I still didn't quite understand. It wasn't as if I'd never had a boyfriend. I'd had several. And I'd eaten dinner with overly hot guys on more than one occasion, albeit mostly as a seat-filler when Blackwood had booked a table at a fancy event and somebody dropped out at the last minute. I'd even coped with Emmy's ex-boyfriend Jed acting as my escort, and until he'd met The One three years ago, he'd been a smart-mouthed man-slut

with octopus arms and hands that got everywhere. But just being in the same room as Logan left me tongue-tied.

So I shook my head. No, I didn't want to risk ketchup.

And that decision paid off when Logan finished his last mouthful, stretched his legs out, and settled back against the cushions with one arm behind me. His fingers brushed against my shoulder, burning through two layers of fabric, and I dropped a handful of fries in my lap. Shoot.

I must have stared at Logan's hand for a beat too long because he answered my unasked question.

"Just in case Kenneth decides to take a closer look. We should go for realism, and if I was spending the evening with my girl, we wouldn't be sitting at opposite ends of the couch."

"Realism. Yes."

I threw the fries back onto the plate and pushed the whole lot to the other side of the coffee table. One grease splotch was quite enough.

"You're not gonna finish that?" Logan asked.

"I'm full."

He gave a little shrug then jerked his head at his arm, raising one eyebrow as he did so. Blood rushed south, taking the last of my sanity with it. This might be the only chance I ever got to curl up on the sofa and watch a terrible movie with Logan. I was almost certain Kenneth wouldn't look through the windows, and he probably wouldn't come back again either after tonight's stunt.

I leaned back gingerly, and Logan curled his arm around my shoulders and pulled me closer. My pulse

raced, blood whooshing in my ears, but Logan just grabbed the remote from my lap and turned the volume up a notch.

"This is a sequel. Did you see the first one?"

"I don't think so."

"Don't worry, you didn't miss much. It was so bad, it was funny."

On screen, a man got shot with a pistol, flew three feet in the air, and his severed leg landed on top of a car. I'd only fired a gun twice, but even I knew that didn't happen. And beside me, Logan burst out laughing.

"See?" he said. "Shoulda brought popcorn."

"Do you want popcorn? I've got some of the microwaveable stuff in the kitchen."

"Why not?"

I levered myself off the sofa, and Logan's arm fell away. Muttered curses escaped my lips as I hurried to the kitchen—why on earth had I suggested an idea that involved moving from my happy place?

Good going, Sloane.

Sweet or salted? Sweet or salted? Sweet or salted? Oh, what the heck—I shoved both kinds into the microwave and grabbed a pair of bowls. Logan had better be hungry, but judging by the speed with which he'd eaten his burger, he'd undoubtedly inhale this lot too.

Three minutes later, I speed-walked back towards the sound of gunfire and screeching wheels emanating from the living room, but on the way, I snuck a glance out of the hall window. Dammit! Kenneth was nowhere to be seen. I paused, juggling the popcorn and two cans of Coca-Cola. Should I come clean to Logan? He

probably had loads to do at home. Laundry, weightlifting, entertaining a supermodel... The sensible thing, the *right* thing, would be to fess up and thank him for his time, then put his popcorn in a doggy bag and wave as he drove off down the street.

But tonight, Sloane the shameless hussy made an appearance, and I did my best to look innocent as I sauntered back to the sofa.

"Here you go. I might have made too much, but I can just throw the extra away."

"Nah, I'm starving. I ran sixteen miles this morning, and Toby was on the warpath so lunch was a chicken breast with organic spirulina, sprouted millet, and sautéed kale."

Toby was Emmy's nutritionist, and every so often, he'd get it into his head that the Special Projects team wasn't being healthy enough and go on a bit of a rampage. Out would go the cookies, the donuts, and the leftover pizza, and in would come the activated almonds, the organic apricots, and the coconut chips.

"I keep a stash of chocolate bars in my desk. Bottom left-hand drawer in the box marked 'Monthly Management Accounts.' Feel free to help yourself if Emmy hasn't got there first."

Logan's arm tightened around me, and I vowed never to let supplies run low.

"Thanks, kitten. I might just take you up on that offer. If you ever want dinner from the Brotherhood, just get what you want and put it on my tab. I'll let them know to expect you."

Dinner for a chocolate bar? That hardly seemed fair. And besides...

"I'm not sure I'd want to go there by myself. Not

again."

"Christian runs a tight ship. That was the first problem we've had in months."

"That's not what I meant."

"Then what *did* you mean?"

"I've already told you—I'm not exactly your usual clientele."

"Thank fuck for that. If all the women looked like you, I'd spend half my life there and never get any work done."

Was he joking? He had to be, and yet he didn't sound like it. "You don't have to gush fake flattery. I doubt Kenneth's listening at the window."

Especially as he was most likely tucked up in his apartment several miles away with a bottle of low-alcohol beer and some boring documentary. Or the news. He watched it constantly on a loop. Over and over and over.

Logan just tilted me back and I tipped right into him as I overbalanced. My left hand almost went into the popcorn, but I managed to redirect it to his thigh at the last second. His huge, well-muscled thigh that twitched under my fingers.

And no, hussy Sloane didn't take her hand away.

"Good," Logan said.

Good? Good what? Good that he didn't have to flatter me? Or good that Kenneth wasn't listening? As Logan caressed the top of my arm, I decided I didn't care. Instead, I leaned into him and pretended to watch the awful movie, all the time thinking of the man beside me, my real-life hero, and mentally undressing him rather than watching the shirtless wonders on-screen. His body heat seeped into me, and I might even have

sighed.

Oh, Sloane, you're gonna go to hell for this.

CHAPTER **16** - SLOANE

THE NEXT MORNING, I floated into work. Freaking floated. Like a feather, or a swan, or a... Emmy glided past on four-inch heels, waving as she headed towards the coffee machine. Okay, so beside her I was more of an empty oil drum bobbing around in the ocean, but I still felt pretty darn good.

Logan had stayed until the end of the funny-not-funny disaster of a movie, and when the credits rolled, he'd surfed through the channels and stopped on *Dirty Dancing*.

"Wanna watch this?"

"You like Jennifer Grey?"

"Who?"

"Baby." I pointed at her on the screen as she carried her watermelon.

"She's kind of skinny. I thought all chicks loved this movie?"

"We do."

Logan leaned forward, and there must have been something funky in that popcorn as well as all the bits of husk that were now stuck in my teeth because I could have sworn he kissed my hair. I didn't dare to move. Or breathe. And I almost choked when Logan's other arm wrapped around me. He didn't say a word, and I desperately tried to act as if this were perfectly

normal.

Normal. Right.

Last night, I'd won the man-candy lottery. The male equivalent of chocolate truffles and jelly beans and Starbursts, especially compared to Kenneth, who was the slightly shrivelled apple some joker snuck into your bagful of Halloween goodies.

"Where are you going?" Emmy asked from over my right shoulder.

Too late, I realised I'd walked right past my desk, done a lap of the office, and now I was heading for the fire exit.

"Uh, I ran out of staples."

"Staples?" Emmy asked as I veered left towards the stationery cupboard. "You didn't think much of Nate's 'let's go paperless' idea, then?"

"No, I think it's great, but you know how Mr. Johnson always likes a printed report."

Emmy grimaced because Mr. Johnson also liked her to turn the pages for him while he stared at her cleavage.

"Don't remind me." She held out a box in my direction. "Could you do me a favour after and take this down to Luther? It's my new pistol grip, and he said he'd fit it."

"Sure." I grabbed the box, only too happy to escape. "I'll do it right away."

Luther, Blackwood's armourer, had been a fixture at headquarters for as long as I'd worked there. In fact, I remembered him making me a cup of coffee on my first day, and I'd spilled half of it because my hands had been shaking so much. He must have been nearly sixty by now, and despite the fact he'd lost a leg in Iraq, he

still moved around faster than I did.

I took the stairs down to the basement in an effort to fit a tiny bit of exercise into my day, springing along, happy, but I soon stopped short when I heard voices ahead. Luther's Southern drawl and Nate's low-pitched mutterings.

"...and Sloane?"

What? Why had Luther mentioned my name? The package slipped out of my hands, and I only just caught it before it hit the floor and gave me away. Yes, yes, I knew it wasn't polite to listen in on private conversations, but I couldn't help myself, okay? Not that I could hear everything they said, only the odd snippet here and there.

"Twenty bucks says he will," Nate said.

He? Who was he?

"Not doubtin' that. For some reason, ladies find that asshole irresistible."

Nate bit out a laugh. "Never understood it myself. The first night Black and I met Logan, he showed up with three women and lent us the spares."

Logan? They were talking about Logan? And me? Tell me they weren't... I knew the Special Projects team wagered on all sorts of stupid things, office romances included. But the idea of them betting on me and Logan to do the nasty, as Emmy would put it, left me shaken. B.E.T. Three tiny letters, but they cut me to the core. B, and my breath stuttered. E, and the voices of my high-school classmates echoed in my head. T, and the blade thrust into my heart.

I retreated back to the stairwell on rubber-soled ballet pumps as memories came flooding back. My final year at Allenvale High, and the last time I'd gotten

involved with a man way out of my league. Reach for the stars, my mom always told me. Well, I did, and I got burned. I'd been in love with Joey McManus, and he'd claimed to feel the same way, right up until the moment he'd taken my virginity. Stupid. I'd been so, so, stupid.

Never again, I'd vowed. Never again would I fall for one of those oh-so-perfect men because it only led to heartache. When I stuck to the Kenneths and Lyndons of this world, a break-up became more of an inconvenience than a tragedy.

But for the last few days, I'd let my heart rule my head over Logan. I'd got caught up in a fantasy world of taut buttocks and sweet words and charming heroes who rode motorcycles and brought me cheesecake.

No more. *No more.*

I needed to throw a bucket of water over my libido and get back to reality. Logan was a nice guy. Kind. But even if his actions last night had been anything more than a show for Kenneth, which I found hard to believe and still felt kind of guilty over since Kenneth hadn't even been there for half of the evening, nothing could ever happen between the pair of us.

At that moment, following Lyndon's lead and doing a runner to South America seemed like the most sensible option.

"Planning a vacation?" Leah asked as she slid her phone into her bag at the end of the afternoon.

"Huh?"

She pointed at my computer screen. "You're looking

at flights to Ecuador?"

"Oh, yes, right. That's for Emmy."

"Are you okay? You've been distracted all day."

"Fine. Absolutely fine."

"I thought you might still be mad at me for the online dating thing."

Only a little. "Not at all. I've just got other things on my mind."

"Like Logan Barnes?"

My head swivelled in her direction so fast a nerve in my neck twanged. Ouch. "Whatever gives you that idea?"

"The way he looks at you? The way you look at him? The fact that you're both single and his ass was sculpted by Michelangelo himself?"

"There's nothing going on between me and Logan."

"Yet."

"Nor will there be."

"So you say." She glanced over my shoulder, grinned, and waved. "Speak of the devil. Don't worry, I'll make myself scarce."

"There's no need..."

Too late, she'd gone, and Logan was there in all his hotness. My resolve almost cracked, but I dug my fingernails into my thighs under the desk and forced what I hoped was a convincing smile.

"Hi."

"Ready to go?" he asked.

"Five minutes?"

"Sure. Wanna stop for food again on the way back?"

"Sorry, I can't."

Surprise flashed across Logan's face. I doubted he got many knock-backs, and even I was having second

thoughts as my mind warred with my body.

"Want company cooking?"

"I promised Edna I'd eat dinner with her tonight."

"That's a first—being ditched for a septuagenarian. How about tomorrow?"

"Maybe."

Maybe? *Sloane, you've* got *to get a handle on this.* Or at the very least, think up a more plausible excuse.

"Maybe?" Logan asked.

"I've got a lot of work to do, and it might spill into the evening."

His raised eyebrow asked, *Seriously?* but he didn't push me any further, and for that I was grateful.

"Okay. Five minutes, and I'll see you home."

Second thoughts? Now I was having third thoughts. Logan was no Joey McManus, and last night, I'd managed to be jittery and comfortable all at the same time. But tonight, I'd be dining alone because Edna went to the seniors' movie evening on the second Thursday of every month and she never came back before eleven. She had more of a social life than I did.

Part of me wanted to tell Logan not to worry about following me and avoid any temptation, but although I hadn't had any more strange messages, worry still niggled at me. How did other women manage to find their perfect matches online? Because surely quite a few of them must, or all of those dating sites would have gone bust years ago. Or were the testimonials they splashed across their front pages fake? Was the whole online dating scene just one big sham, a self-perpetuating myth sold to desperate souls who longed to find happiness?

I wanted to believe in the concept, because without

hope, what did I have left? But I shuddered at the thought of clicking on DateMe.com again. No, I'd carry on looking the old-fashioned way—you know, common interests, a shared connection. Except all I really did was work, wasn't it? Which brought me right back to Logan again. Gah.

I slammed the lid of my laptop down and shoved it into a drawer. I'd think about this tomorrow. Tonight, I'd devote my time to a good movie and possibly a pint of ice cream.

Yes, that was a good plan.

Chapter 17 - Sloane

"WANT ME TO check the house before I go?" Logan offered.

"I'll be fine." Because if I invited Logan in, I'd never ask him to leave. "Honestly. Edna spends Thursdays gardening, and she's good at keeping an eye on the place."

"Any problems, call me. You're still wearing your necklace, right?"

I fingered the pendant nestled above my breastbone. "Sure am."

He squeezed my hand before taking a step back, and a rush of warmth and regret flooded through me. Everything was messed up inside. Jumbled. But then he backed up another step, and resolve battled through the rest of my feelings and came out on top.

I needed space to think.

The rumble of Logan's truck engine receded into the distance as I walked inside, leaving only silence. With Edna out, I didn't even have the faint sound of her TV coming through the wall for company, and the loudest noise in my home was the hum coming from the refrigerator. Where was Nickel? I'd left the window cracked open, so he could be anywhere. Occasionally, he even got stuck at Edna's if he snuck inside and she didn't notice.

"Nickel?" I called out. Nothing.

He liked to go outside, but he never ventured farther than a couple of backyards away. What was it they said about pets being like their owners? I tipped Kitty Krunchies into a bowl and rattled them out of the back door.

"Nickel? Dinner time."

Only silence.

Well, he'd come in when he was hungry. Unless he finally decided to eat one of those darn mice he kept catching. I relished the breeze drifting in as I turned on the tiny TV beside the microwave to give myself some company. News...infomercials...a reality show... Finally, I settled on a sitcom rerun and got out a package of pasta. Then I put it back. I was hopeless at judging quantities, which meant dinner for one always turned into dinner for two, and my jeans were quite tight enough already. A baked potato would be much healthier, and I could run the vacuum cleaner around while it cooked. Then I needed to put the laundry on.

Except before I could get the vacuum cleaner out of the hall closet, the doorbell rang. An involuntary buzz ran through me. Had Logan come back? I rushed to check through the peephole, only to find a stranger standing there. A man around my age, hair slicked back above a face whose tan looked to have come from a salon rather than the great outdoors. His red-and-black checked shirt was pristine. A city cowboy. Who was he? For a moment I thought of Desmond and his fake photo, but this guy's hair was brown rather than blond.

My heart thumped, but ignoring him would have been rude and he'd probably seen my shadow through the little frosted glass panel at the top of the door.

Besides, he didn't look like a murderer, more of a car salesman.

Once the chain was securely in place, I opened the door a crack. "Can I help you?"

"I'm here to see Jeff Peterson?"

"I think you've got the wrong address."

"You don't have a dining table for sale?"

"Sorry, but no." Mine came with the house, and the chipped wood had seen better days. Nobody in their right mind would pay money for it.

"This isn't 107 Walnut Road?"

Ah, a simple mix-up. "No, this is Walnut Avenue. People make that mistake all the time. Walnut Road is about two miles in that direction." I realised he couldn't see me and opened the door as wide as I could with the chain on, then pointed again. "That way. East."

"Apologies for disturbing you, ma'am. Have a good evening."

"You too."

Okay, panic over. I was so jumpy nowadays. All the little problems this week had added up, leaving me drained and liable to overreact at the smallest thing. *Relax, Sloane.* I poured myself a glass of red and took a sip to calm my nerves before I started the chores. Mom always used to sing whenever she got stressed, and with Edna out, the noise didn't matter, so I belted out Gloria Gaynor as I pushed the vacuum cleaner around the hallway. Yes, I'd survive. I'd been through worse and come out the other side.

Have you ever been swimming in the sea and trodden on something weird that's not supposed to be there? Where first your heart seizes, and when your limbs start working again, you do that crazy mad dash

out of the water in case it's a shark or a prehistoric monster?

If you have, you can imagine how I felt when I backed into the man standing at the foot of my stairs. First came that moment of "no, this can't be real," followed by paralysis, and then I leapt for the kitchen door, heart pounding.

I didn't make it.

He grabbed my wrist and yanked me back, and I caught a glimpse of red and black as he threw me face-first onto the floor. *The cowboy.* I opened my mouth to scream, but he smushed my face into the carpet.

"Don't make a sound."

Blood gushed in my ears as he put a knee on my back, holding me down. Why? What? *Who was he?* And more importantly, how the hell was I going to get out of this one?

I'd sent Logan away. The one man who could have helped me, and I'd sent him away. Then my fuzzy brain remembered the pendant. I tried to push the button, but when I bent my hand underneath myself, the cowboy pulled it back. The chain snapped, and the whole necklace flew across the hallway and landed by the side table where I kept the mail.

"Keep still, Marilyn. Or should I call you Sloane?"

Marilyn? This was the second man to call me Marilyn in a week. What was going on? I didn't understand, and as he snapped one handcuff around my wrist and clicked the other around the bannister, the only thing I knew for sure was that I was in big trouble.

My shoulder burned as he shoved me backwards against the stairs, and I got my first good look at him as

he rocked back on his heels.

Earlier, I'd thought he looked plain, nondescript, but now his eyes glittered with anger. Or madness. Perhaps both.

"W-w-what do you want?"

"First, I want my money back. Then I want all the things you promised me. You don't lead a man on like that, then walk into the fucking sunset. Nobody does that shit to Jerry Olson and gets away with it. I always get my woman. *Always.*"

I went to scream again, and he punched me hard in the jaw. My ears rang, but the noise was eclipsed by Jerry's howl of pain as Nickel flew down the stairs and launched himself at the man's face, claws out. But my brave little cat's efforts were short-lived. With a yell, Jerry tore him away and kicked him across the hallway, where he hit the wall with a sickening *thump.*

Please, Nickel, be okay.

He lay still for a few seconds, then staggered towards the kitchen, but on the way, he stepped on... Did he? Oh, say he stepped on the pendant. Would one little kitty paw be enough to activate it?

All I could do was hope as Jerry straightened up.

"Thought you were so clever, didn't you? Hiding behind your fancy computer and preying on innocent men."

I almost choked. "Innocent? You just broke into my house."

"You left the window open and the key in the door lock. Couldn't have been easier."

Oh, heck. I thunked my head against the wall, wondering how hard I'd have to hit it to knock myself out. How could I have been so stupid?

"B-b-but you've handcuffed me."

He shrugged. "You told me you enjoyed men being rough. Or did you lie about that too?"

"I don't know what you're talking about."

"Stop lying!" he roared.

Okay, okay, don't antagonise the psycho. I tried meek instead. "I'm sorry."

He stepped forward and bent a little to cup my cheek. When I jerked my head away, he dug his nails in and glared at me.

"I liked you, Marilyn. I thought you were different from the others, but you're not. Women only ever want one thing."

"What thing?"

"Money. I sent you cash to repair your car and bought you a plane ticket. Three hours I waited at the airport, but you never showed up."

I still didn't know what he was talking about. I mean, obviously he'd got me confused with somebody else, but I didn't want to ask for more details in case it made him angry again.

He knelt now, and warm breath washed over my face. Yuck—he was a smoker.

"Where I'm from, nothing comes for free. If a man gives a woman money, it's a down payment for services not yet rendered." He caressed my cheek again, only this time his hand meandered lower and brushed against my breast. "And I intend to collect."

Oh hell, oh hell, oh hell. I couldn't breathe. Couldn't. Freaking. Breathe.

His hand went lower, lower, and I writhed away, pulling at my cuffed wrist, but whoever built this house had done a solid job because the bannister didn't even

rattle. I tried kicking, then punching, but that only earned me another slap that made me see stars as he tore at my top. The flimsy fabric ripped, and his sick smile as he stared at me in my bra wasn't something I'd ever forget. His body weight held me against the stairs, and I couldn't move an inch.

"We're gonna have fun, Marilyn. You and me, we're gonna have fun."

"Please no," I whispered as he fondled me again, this time touching my bare flesh.

He didn't stop, and I couldn't watch. I screwed my eyes shut, bile rising in my throat, but suddenly Jerry's hand disappeared, then his weight, and my eyelids flew open when I heard a splintering crash.

What the...?

Jerry lay crumpled on the remains of my side table, and as Logan rained blows down on him, he curled up in a foetal position, whimpering. Then Emmy was there, and Ana, the pair of them pulling Logan away from his prey. I thought he was going to take a swing for Emmy too, such was his fury, but then Ana kicked his legs out from underneath him and he landed on the floor with a *thump*. Before I could blink, Emmy had him in some sort of armlock.

Seconds. The whole thing had taken seconds, and now there was total silence. None of the Blackwood team was even breathing hard.

I'd worked with Emmy for years, but I rarely saw her or any of the other Special Projects people in action. Her eyes were cold and clinical as she assessed the scene, but Ana's were worse. Her dead expression made my guts clench, even though she was on my side. I leaned to my left and vomited.

"Let me up," Logan growled.

"Only if you keep your hands off our new friend here," Emmy told him. "I don't have the time or the inclination to deal with a murder charge tonight."

Ana poked Jerry with her foot. "He's unconscious."

Emmy kept herself between the two men when she released Logan, and before I could properly process what had happened, my hand was free and I was curled into his lap. My arms wound around his neck of their own accord, hanging onto my lifeline.

"Are you okay?" he murmured.

I shook my head, and then the tears came. A whole river of them, gushing out and soaking Logan's black T-shirt.

"I-I-I'm sorry."

He hugged me tighter, kissing my hair. "Nothing to be sorry for, kitten."

But there was. Even now, bruises were beginning to form on his knuckles, streaks of red and purple and a trickle of blood.

"You got hurt."

He followed my gaze. "This? This is nothing. I've had worse in training."

Someone settled a blanket around my shoulders, and I looked up to see Emmy.

"What do you want us to do with him?" she asked. "Do you want the police involved, or shall we deal with it?"

Good question. My first instinct was *send that man to jail*, but years of working at Blackwood had taught me to look at situations like this from another perspective. I swiped at my tears with my fingers and forced myself to think. I didn't have any lasting

damage, just a swollen jaw and bruises on my wrist from the handcuff. Jerry hadn't broken in. Logan's only damage was to his knuckles, and Jerry looked like tenderised meat. If the cops came, who were they most likely to arrest? That's right: Logan. Even if we could persuade them of Jerry's guilt, any court case would drag on for months, and he'd probably get off with a slap on the wrist.

"Can you deal with it?" I asked Emmy.

Beside her, Ana smiled, and that scared me more than anything.

"Sure, we'll deal with it."

Logan shifted underneath me. "Let's get you out of here." Another kiss, this time to my forehead. "Good thing you pressed the button when you did."

Oh, hell. Nickel!

"I didn't. The necklace came off and Nickel stepped on it. Jerry kicked him across the hallway, and I think he might be injured."

"Did you see where he went?"

"To the kitchen."

"The cuntnugget's called Jerry?" Emmy asked.

"Jerry Olson, he told me. He could have been lying, though. He kept saying I'd stolen money from him, and something about a plane ticket, and—"

"We'll sort it out. Go with Logan and look for the cat, yeah?"

Logan lifted me up and set me on my feet, one arm wrapped around my waist to steady me. I tugged the blanket tighter together, all too aware that I was half-naked.

"Here." He peeled off his T-shirt and held it out towards me. "Put this on."

My legs buckled a bit because not only had the evening's events left me shaken, now I had the glorious sight of Logan's torso to contend with. Emmy helped out by poking my hands through the armholes, and I inhaled Logan's scent. A hint of aftershave, sandalwood maybe, but mostly the shirt just smelled of him. Funny how the small things could make a bad situation better, wasn't it?

"Let's go search for Nickel," Logan said. "I'm sure he'll be okay."

I hung onto him as we headed for the kitchen. My legs wouldn't have held me up otherwise.

CHAPTER 18 - LOGAN

FURY COURSED THROUGH Logan's veins as he helped Sloane into the kitchen. Part of him wanted to go back into the hallway and finish what he'd started—bodies weren't that hard to hide if you knew how—but the realist in him knew that wasn't a good idea. Firstly, because murdering a man in Sloane's hallway wouldn't exactly endear Logan to her, and secondly, because no punishment he could inflict would be worse than what Emmy and Ana could dish out. Yes, he'd leave this one to the masters.

"Does Nickel have somewhere he goes to hide?" he asked.

Sloane took a few seconds to answer. Was she going into shock? Logan paused in the kitchen to check her colour under the lights. Pale as fuck. Shit. Sloane wasn't used to dealing with this kind of stuff, and as long as Logan lived, he vowed she never would be. He'd take care of her, starting with ice for her face.

"He rarely goes farther than the yard."

"Do you have a flashlight?"

"In the cupboard next to the back door."

It was still light outside, but Sloane's yard looked like a fucking jungle with all the overgrown trees and weeds. She clung to Logan with one arm and pressed a packet of frozen peas to her jaw with the other as he

shone the light under bushes and behind the carcasses of plants whose chlorophyll had long since departed this earth. From the way her fingers trembled, he knew what she was thinking.

"He'll be okay, kitten."

"He was limping, and he couldn't run very fast."

"It might have been the shock of what happened."

"I left the window open," she whispered. "For Nickel, and that man just reached in and unlocked the door."

Logan stroked her hair as anger flared inside him again. "Shh. Don't blame yourself. Nobody but that fucker is responsible for what he did."

"But—"

"Did you see movement?"

"Where?"

Logan crouched next to the shed. "Behind that tree stump."

The whole thing was covered in cobwebs, but one side of the tangle was ragged, as if something cat-sized had recently crashed through.

"I can't see him," Sloane said.

"I'll take a closer look. Talk to him, would you? He knows your voice." And Logan would rather avoid getting clawed by an upset cat if at all possible. No matter what he'd said to Sloane, his hands really fucking hurt.

As he reached into the darkness, a spider the size of a dinner plate skittered across his arm and Sloane leapt back three feet. Her voice hitched as she chattered away to the cat, telling him she loved him and tomorrow they could do all his favourite things. Was it bad that Logan wanted to be a cat right now?

His fingers touched fur, and the cat wriggled farther away. Logan closed his hand around the scruff of Nickel's neck, trying to avoid the legs Sloane thought might be injured.

"Easy, little guy. I won't hurt you."

Logan withdrew his arm, pulling the trembling cat and a couple more spiders with it. He batted them away as Sloane dropped to her knees beside him.

"Is he okay?"

Logan didn't need to be a veterinarian to see that one of Nickel's hind legs was sticking out at an unnatural angle, but he didn't want to alarm Sloane any more than necessary.

"I think we should take him to the animal hospital."

The poor little bastard squeaked in pain as Logan stood up and headed for the house, Sloane following at his heels. He couldn't vault over the fence to the street the way he'd come in, not with a cat in his arms, which meant they'd have to go out through the house since Sloane's side gate was overgrown with brambles. And they'd have to walk through the hallway. Logan really didn't want to see what Emmy and Ana were doing to Jerry Olson, and he wanted Sloane to witness it even less. On the bright side, he hadn't heard any screams.

He soon found out why.

"What the hell are you doing?" Logan asked from the kitchen doorway with Sloane tucked safely behind him.

They'd used a technique known as the Savaki Meat Hook, a form of torture invented by the old Iranian secret police, the SAVAK, and used in Tehran's Evin Prison in the 1970s. It involved stretching a man's arms straight out behind him, tying them at the wrists, and

using a rope to raise them higher, higher, until the victim was standing on tiptoes, with a meat hook through the knot and a pulley attached to the ceiling. Men tended to talk real fast in that position.

Emmy and Ana had improvised with the cable from the vacuum cleaner and Sloane's upstairs bannister, but Jerry still looked pretty uncomfortable. Silent, though, because they'd duct-taped his mouth closed.

And now Emmy was sitting on the floor folding a paper aeroplane while Ana leaned against the wall and poured out a shot of vodka.

"Mr. Olson here isn't so keen on talking, so we need to persuade him." Emmy turned back to the little fucker, whose black eye had swollen up nicely now. "Shall we have another try?"

She ran the wing of the plane down Olson's exposed left arm, once, twice, three times, then Ana stepped forward and poured the vodka over the paper cuts.

Okay, now Logan understood the need for the duct tape. Olson's howl came out as a strangled moan, he turned bright red, and his eyes bugged out. Sloane tried to peer around Logan, but he covered her eyes.

"Don't look, kitten. Let's get Nickel to the veterinarian."

"What are they doing?"

"Come on, let's go."

Luckily, the cat raised his head and let out a quiet whimper that drew Sloane's attention as they hurried through the hallway. At least Emmy and Ana weren't making too much mess.

And whatever Olson had to say, Logan knew he'd talk.

Logan's only pet had been a hamster purchased by his mom to teach the Barnes kids about the concept of death, which had duly obliged by kicking the bucket. He liked animals, but being in the military and then working at Blackwood made owning one impractical. Still, he wouldn't mind spending more time with Nickel. And his owner.

Sloane was curled into his side at the moment, quiet, still a little tearful as they waited in the empty reception area of the animal hospital. Logan couldn't blame her. The emergency veterinarian on duty had taken Nickel straight into surgery to pin his broken leg, and although the prognosis was good, it was obvious Sloane was still beating herself up over it. Logan too, if he was honest. He should have insisted on staying this evening, even if he'd sat in his truck outside, but instead, he'd driven to the Brotherhood to drown his sorrows after Sloane knocked him back. Thank fuck he'd only been halfway through his first beer when the alarm went off.

And thank fuck Emmy and Ana had barged through the front door when they did, otherwise he'd have been burying a body and grovelling to Sloane to forgive him for all the bloodstains.

Logan's phone vibrated with a message, and he shielded the screen from Sloane as he read what Emmy had to say. They'd had one brief conversation earlier, on the phone just after Nickel went into surgery. Logan had filled her in on recent events, from Kenneth's selfishness to Leah's idiocy with the online dating site

to the fight at the Brotherhood.

EB: Done here. Someone's coming to clear up the mess.

Logan: Olson?

EB: On his way back to West Virginia in the back of Ryder's truck. But there's a bigger problem, and that means Sloane mustn't be left on her own tonight.

Logan: I'll stay with her. What problem?

EB: Will explain tomorrow. Mack's looking into things right now, and we should know more in the morning. My office at 9.

Logan: With Sloane?

EB: Best not.

Shit. That meant the news wasn't good. Was it too late to book plane tickets to Europe? The South of France was nice at this time of year. Or Lake Como in Italy. One of the guys at work had a house there they could borrow, and—

"Is that Emmy?" Sloane asked.

"Yeah."

"What's happening?"

"Everything's fine."

"Fine?" Sloane rounded on him, bristling. "How can you possibly say that? A man tried to rape me, my cat's on the operating table, and there might well be a body in my house."

Logan only heard one word in all of that, and it made him see red. "Shoulda killed that fucker when I had the chance."

Perhaps he could call Ryder and ask for a favour? There were plenty of remote spots between Richmond and West Virginia.

But Sloane uncurled his fists and slid one hand into

his. "Thank you for coming. I'm sorry—I shouldn't have snapped. Uh, *is* there a body in my house?"

"No. Emmy and Ana got whatever answers they were looking for, and Olson's on his way back to the swamp he came from."

Was Logan worried about the man returning? Not really. No one who'd faced off against that pair would willingly set foot in the same state again.

The veterinarian came out, still wearing a pair of blood-covered scrubs, but he was smiling, which Logan took as a good sign. Sloane gripped his hand tighter, and Logan gave hers a reassuring squeeze.

"Miss Mullins? The operation went well. Nickel's awake now if you'd like to see him."

"Yes, please."

The little cat was groggy, but he managed a weak purr when Sloane petted him. She'd told Logan what he'd done while they waited, how he'd attacked Olson then raised the alarm, albeit by accident, and Logan owed Nickel a whole truckload of catnip. He'd never grumble about the mouse episode ever again.

The veterinarian yawned, and when Logan checked his watch, he saw it was almost two in the morning.

"Time to go home?" he asked Sloane.

She managed a shake of the head. "More like time for me to get in my car and drive to Florida. I'm so, so sick of this month."

Logan was only half-sure she was joking. "We can go to Florida if you want."

"We?"

He steered her out of hearing range of the hospital staff. "Wherever you are, I'm gonna be sitting outside your bedroom door with a gun, kitten."

"Really?"

"Nobody's getting near you. Trust me. Do you want to stay in a hotel? Or at Emmy's place?"

"Yes."

Logan sensed a "but" coming.

"But..." See? He hadn't spent years watching Sloane for nothing. "But then he'll have won, won't he? If that psycho scares me out of my home, he'll have won."

"I don't think anyone would judge you if you spent one night elsewhere."

"Emmy wouldn't run."

"You're not Emmy."

Fuck, wrong thing to say. Sloane's face crumpled as Logan grabbed a virtual spade and attempted to dig himself out of the hole he'd made.

"And that's a good thing, kitten. Emmy has to lock herself in her fuckin' bedroom so she doesn't kill people in her sleep. But if you want to go home, then I'll take you." He tried to make her decision seem rational. "It's probably not a bad idea to stay close to the veterinarian." Shit, that made it sound as if the cat was gonna die. "So we can pick Nickel up as soon as they call."

She seemed to consider that for a few seconds. "Logan?"

"Yeah?"

"Could you sit inside my bedroom? There's a window, and..."

"I'll stay anywhere you want, kitten. Anywhere."

Back at Sloane's place, Logan started off in an old armchair, watching her outline as she lay in bed. His Colt .45 sat in his lap, and if anyone decided to pay a nocturnal visit, they'd feel its wrath. He'd kept many

silent vigils over the years, but never over a woman he was in love with. Because if he cared to admit it, he'd more than liked Sloane for a long time, and this last week had only cemented his feelings. He might not deserve her, but he wanted her.

And when he heard her sobbing quietly at four a.m., he slid off the chair and lay down beside her, one hand tentatively placed on her hip over the quilt to see if she'd react. And she *did* react. She dragged his arm tight around her chest, close to her pounding heart, and nestled back against his stomach.

After the events of the previous evening, Logan shouldn't have smiled in the darkness, but smile he did. With Sloane in his arms, he just couldn't help it.

CHAPTER 19 - LOGAN

LOGAN SKIPPED HIS morning workout in favour of taking Sloane for breakfast on the way to the office. She only picked at her New York cheesecake pancakes, and he couldn't help noticing the way she glanced at his knuckles every ten seconds. He should have worn gloves.

"Nothing's broken, kitten."

"Me. I'm broken. Everything I touch turns to shit." She pushed the plate away. "And I'm not even meant to be eating cheesecake."

Sloane rarely swore, so that was a strong statement from her.

"It's been a bad few weeks, I'll give you that, but things'll get better. We'll make sure they do. Blackwood's a team, and we always have each other's backs."

"But I'm only a secretary, not one of you guys."

Logan dropped his fork, and it bounced off the plate and fell onto the floor. The waitress rushed over with another, but he ignored her hand as it brushed his and focused on Sloane.

"Don't ever belittle yourself like that. Everyone in the company's important, from Emmy and Black to the guy who refills the damn toilet paper. Because I may be pretty good in combat, but..." Okay, perhaps this was a

bad analogy. "But I also need to wipe my ass."

Sloane burst out laughing, and for the first time since yesterday afternoon, her sweet smile came back. Not such a bad analogy, after all. Logan reached across the table and took her hands in his.

"And you're not just important to Blackwood, you're important to me."

"Can I get you anything else, sir?"

Damn that perky waitress with her flirtatious glances and fuck-awful sense of timing.

"Just the check."

Her face fell at Logan's sharp tone, and she backed away, apologising with her eyes. But the moment was lost. Sloane had pulled her hands away and was already halfway out of her seat, blushing.

"We should get to the office."

"Kitten..."

"I can't be late for work."

"You got attacked in your own home last night. I think they'll understand if you take a personal day."

"Would Emmy take a personal day?"

"No, but Emmy's half-cyborg."

And the other half was pure bitch.

"I don't want to be at home, okay?"

"I've got one meeting at nine, and then I'll take you out somewhere. Didn't you say you wanted to go to Florida?"

He tried for light-hearted, but Sloane wasn't buying it.

"Meeting? What meeting? You don't have a meeting on your calendar."

"You've been checking my calendar again?"

Sloane turned from pink to red. "Maybe just the

occasional glance." She folded her arms across her chest, which did everything for her cleavage. "That's my job."

"I check your calendar all the time, but mainly because I'm nosy." And if Logan knew where she was every hour of every day, he could accidentally run into her more often.

She still wasn't buying it. "What meeting?"

"Just a last-minute thing with Emmy."

"About Jerry Olson?"

"Yeah."

"Why wasn't I invited?"

"The discussions may not be pleasant."

"I'm living in the middle of this, Logan. I want to know what's going on."

He didn't want her getting nightmares, but last night's bad dreams had come with favourable side effects. Logan could still feel Sloane wrapped around him as he desperately willed his cock not to harden this morning. *Forget it, Barnes.* No, he wouldn't use dirty tricks to get her into bed. But he *would* do everything in his power to shelter her from the nastiness in the world.

"I promise I'll tell you what we discuss. How about over lunch? We can go to Claude's." Women raved about that ridiculously expensive French place. "I bet they serve fancy cheesecake."

"Okay."

Okay? Logan was a little surprised when she gave in so easily, but he'd take the win. And the filet mignon that came with it.

"I'll make a reservation."

At Blackwood's headquarters, Logan walked into the office Emmy shared with her husband just as Black slammed the phone down.

"Everything okay?"

"You remember Miriam?"

Nobody who'd met Black's aunt could forget her. She got raging drunk at every party she showed up to, and someone usually had to carry her out to a cab.

"I thought you told her not to contact you?"

"I did, but either she got too drunk to remember or she just ignored me." He glared at the phone. "There are ninety-five billion nerves in the human body, and that woman manages to get on every single fucking one of them."

"Do you want me to get rid of her?" Ana's voice came from the doorway. "I could make it look like an accident."

"Honestly? I can't be bothered to deal with the paperwork right now. It's easier to keep hanging up on her."

Ana shrugged. "Whatever you prefer."

Emmy walked in behind her, followed by Mack with her laptop and Sloane with a tray of coffee. One, two, three, four, five cups. Who else were they expecting?

Logan realised when Sloane sat herself down on the leather couch in the corner and picked up a cappuccino.

"What are you doing?" he asked, even though he already knew the answer. He should have realised she'd pull a stunt like this when she'd gone quiet earlier. Lust

played havoc with his intelligence. But at the same time, he had to be impressed by her devious side.

"I want to know what's happening. I've got a right."

Emmy crouched beside her. "We just don't want to see you upset."

"Upset? I'm already upset," she shrieked. "I couldn't get any more freaking upset."

People in the office beyond turned to stare at them, and Ana took a seat beside Sloane.

"Tell her. She might as well find out sooner rather than later."

"Thanks, I think." Sloane looked more sick than anything else.

Black glanced at his watch. "Fine, but we need to hurry this up. I've got another meeting in half an hour."

Mack hooked her laptop up to the larger monitor on Black's desk, and a minute later, photos of Sloane filled the screen. Logan recognised most of them from her Facebook albums. Not that he'd been studying them or anything. More of an occasional glance. Okay, so he might have saved a couple of them to his phone, but it wasn't as if he'd used them as his screen saver. Mostly because he thought she might notice.

He sat on the arm of the couch beside her, and she chewed her lip as she watched. Logan wanted to carry her out of the room caveman-style so she wouldn't have to go through this, but firstly, the others would ask questions, and secondly, Sloane would probably kick him in the nuts.

"Mr. Olson had some interesting things to say last night," Emmy started. "It seems he first met Sloane, who he knew as Marilyn, on a dating site aimed at blue-collar workers from the southern states. This was seven

months ago. They got talking online, and he wanted to meet up in person, but Marilyn kept coming up with excuses. Her car needed repairs, so he sent her money, but then she claimed she was too nervous to drive such a long way alone. He offered to come to her, even took time off work, but she cancelled at the last minute. Sick cat, apparently. Finally, she said she'd fly in to meet him, so he paid for a ticket and she never showed up. When he checked with the airline, he found she'd spun a convincing tale and got the ticket refunded to her."

"I didn't do any of that, I swear."

Emmy managed a smile that was sympathetic rather than cunning. A minor miracle. "We know you didn't, honey, but somebody using your picture did."

Mack took over, clicking through various other screenshots. "Somebody's been using your photos to catfish men. They strike up an online relationship, then convince their marks to send money with various sob stories."

Sloane's jaw dropped. "They *what?* But why me?"

"Because you're pretty, honey," Emmy said. "And in a girl-next-door sort of way, not a 'this chick's gonna be high-maintenance' way. Men go for that. Right, Logan?"

"Right."

Logan answered automatically, and Black's lip flickered up at one corner. Those assholes had to be running a pool on him and Sloane by now, surely? Which week did Black have?

Sloane just looked dazed as Mack continued.

"We've found 'Marilyn' on six sites so far, smaller ones, all targeted at a particular geographical area or demographic. Clever, really. It helps whoever's doing

this to stay under the radar. But when Leah signed Sloane up on DateMe, it seems some of the previous victims spotted her, which explains the problems of the last few weeks."

"Jerry Olson?" Logan asked.

Emmy nodded. "He saw the photo, recognised her, and then used her real name and photo to find her on Facebook."

"And paid her a visit," Logan growled.

"Indeed. He'd been planning it for over a week. Of the six sites, one's where she met Jerry, and we think another might relate to Laurence. Christian gave us the security camera footage from the bar, and Desmond, or whatever the dude's real name is, doesn't appear to be on any of the other four, so we're missing at least one. Assuming someone took the bait on each, we're potentially looking at seven pissed-off dudes as a minimum."

Mack's phone pinged, and she glanced at the screen. "Make that eight. Agatha just found another site."

"What about the source?" Black asked. "Whoever's doing this is close enough to Sloane to know her middle name."

"Perhaps not. It's on her Facebook page. Remember Bradley's silver-screen-themed fancy-dress party? The one where Sloane went as Marilyn Monroe? Someone made a joke out of it. And the post was set to public, so..."

Black's eyes rolled halfway around before he caught Logan glaring at him and stopped.

"Tell me that fucking account's been sanitised now."

"I did it myself," Mack told him. "But unfortunately, the damage is done. Whoever's running this scam is posting from behind a proxy server. We'll find them, but it may take time."

"Which means Sloane needs security for the time being. Either a team, or—"

"I'll do it," Logan said.

Black grinned for a brief second. "Thought you might."

Yeah, they were definitely running a pool.

CHAPTER 20 - SLOANE

ALL THOSE PICTURES of me on the internet. All those men, and I hadn't even realised. Why hadn't alarm bells rung louder on that strange date with Desmond? I'd thought it was a simple case of mistaken identity because, let's be honest, I did tend to attract weirdos, but the reality was far, far worse.

And now people I cared about had been dragged into the mess too. Logan's knuckles were practically black, and Mack had been up all night judging by the dark circles under her eyes.

"Are you okay?" Leah asked as I slumped into my chair.

"No."

"I heard what happened, and I'm so, so sorry about putting you on that dating site."

"In a way, it was a good thing," Logan said from behind me. "If it hadn't blown up now, whoever stole Sloane's identity could have carried on for months, and the pressure would have kept building."

"What are you gonna do?" Leah asked.

My brain was barely functioning at the moment. It was as much as I could do to get dressed this morning.

"I guess I'd better sort out my emails. Then check Emmy's and Black's travel schedules, and I promised I'd help Bradley sort out a hotel in Milan, and there's a

report to type up for Hoffman Leisure, and—"

Logan held up a hand. "Stop. Just stop. You're gonna do the bare essentials, and then I'm taking you out for lunch, remember?"

"Lunch?"

"We discussed this earlier. Claude's? You agreed to it."

I screwed my eyes shut, trying to remember what I'd said. "I wasn't thinking straight."

"Too late. Claude's expecting us at twelve thirty. Leah, you can do the rest of Sloane's work today, can't you?"

"No problem."

"We leave at twelve. Don't be late."

The butterflies started at eleven thirty, battering my belly with their wings. Logan had disappeared to do his own "bare essentials," as he put it, and the dirty part of me imagined him naked in the locker room downstairs as I stared at my computer screen.

I'd tried backing away from him yesterday, and look where that had got us. We'd both ended up hurt, he'd taken care of me, and now I wanted him more than ever. He'd spent the night wrapped around me in bed, for goodness' sake! Or rather on the bed, but even with both of us fully clothed, my heart had been beating so hard I'd feared I'd have a coronary.

And now he was walking in my direction, hair still damp from the shower, wearing not his usual jeans and T-shirt but a button-down shirt, flannel slacks, and a smile that would melt a chastity belt.

"Ready to go?"

I'd flung on the first thing that came to hand this morning, a navy-blue wrap dress that left me feeling woefully underdressed, at least on the outside. The comfortable underwear I wore day-to-day had all been in the laundry basket, so I'd worn one of the fancy lace sets Kenneth had bought me at the beginning of our relationship, and now it was starting to itch.

"Can we stop at my house? I should change into something nicer. And I need to sort out my hair, and do my make-up, and..."

"No time. You're beautiful as you are."

Beautiful? Did Logan Barnes just call me beautiful? Leah fanned herself with her notepad, and when I didn't get up, she shoved me out of my chair.

"Go! I'll look after things here."

I'd taken two steps when she hauled me back by my purse strap.

"Wait! You might need this."

"Did you just shove a condom into my bag?" I hissed.

She shrugged, unrepentant. "Don't do anything I wouldn't do. And I want all the details!"

Logan's smirk said he'd caught that whole exchange, and I wanted to die. Not in the way Jerry Olson might have intended last night, more of a graceful collapse into a pile of ash that would scatter into the wind along with my embarrassment.

But that didn't happen, so I trailed Logan to the parking lot instead, withering under the weight of everybody's stares. Did they all know what had happened yesterday? I hated my private life becoming public gossip.

"Smile," Logan said as he opened his truck door for me. "We'll sort the problems out. Today, your only job is to enjoy lunch."

I thought that would be impossible, but when we got to the restaurant, Claude showed us to a quiet table for two at the back, hidden from prying eyes by a screen of plants. I'd eaten there half a dozen times with Kenneth and once or twice with Emmy, who visited so many times she ran a tab, and I suspected she'd pulled some strings to get us seated in that particular spot. I really did have the best boss. Unorthodox, maybe, but I never wanted to work for anyone else.

"I'll make you a special lunch," Claude said. "Not something from the menu. Are there any foods you don't like to eat?"

Logan shook his head, and Claude looked at me.

"I'll eat anything."

"Good to know," Logan murmured as Claude walked away.

"I heard that."

I pretended to be grumpy, but secretly, I liked Logan's dirty side. For a few blissful seconds, I wondered what it would be like to have him whispering filthy words in my ear, arms around me as we—

"Sloane?"

Darn it, I had to stop daydreaming. "I'm fine. Just wondering what Claude's going to cook."

"That's a relief. For a moment, I thought you were imagining what you'd like to do to me naked."

"I wasn't... I didn't..." My cheeks burned up, and I was tempted to press my glass of chilled water against them.

"You're cute when you try to deny things, kitten."

"Can we just talk about something else?"

"Sure. What do you want to talk about?"

"You. Let's talk about you." We'd worked together for years, but I knew so little about him. Just snippets I'd overheard and the basics from his company profile. Logan had always been a very private man.

"I'm not all that interesting."

"Well, I think you are. Tell me about Logan Barnes. Did you grow up in Richmond?"

"Partly. I was born in Anaheim, but we moved to Richmond when I was thirteen because my dad got a new job."

"Your sister went back to California?" I recalled the birthday gift I'd sent to his niece.

"All three sisters, and my folks too, but I joined the army instead of going with them."

"Why?"

"Originally, it was gonna be me and Christian, but then he ended up with Sienna instead. I offered to stick around, but he told me I was an asshole and I needed a bigger asshole to kick some discipline into me." Logan snorted a laugh. "He's not right about much, but I have to give him that one."

"So you enlisted on your own?"

"Yeah. Did the training, got deployed to Iraq, then Afghanistan, drank beer, went on patrols, shot stuff, avoided dying, then my captain suggested I apply to join the Rangers. Fuck. I always thought I was tough, but the training nearly killed me."

"I'd have collapsed on the first day. Probably before breakfast."

"Nah, you wouldn't have. Breakfast was at five a.m."

"Getting into the Rangers must have been worth the pain, huh?"

"Yes and no. I enjoyed the operations, but I hated the politics. Certain people wanted to fast-track me to Delta Force, and one of the commanding officers didn't like that idea so he made my life hell."

"Why?"

"A power trip. Jealousy. Racism. Take your pick."

"Racism?"

"My mother's Syrian. That was why they wanted to fast-track me in the first place. Because I grew up speaking Arabic and I know a lot about the region."

"I'm so sorry that happened to you."

"I'm not. If it hadn't been for him, I'd probably still be in the army instead of working for Blackwood."

"You quit because of him?"

"Not exactly. One day, I snapped and punched him, and I was drowning my sorrows in beer and women the week before my court martial when I met Black and Nate. The rest, as they say, is history."

"Black fixed things?"

"The officer got court-martialled for shooting at a civilian in Afghanistan, and I got a job in Black and Nate's old unit. Joined Blackwood when I got out."

"I'm glad you're here," I said softly.

"Me too."

Claude brought our appetisers, delicious mini cheese balls that had a fancy name I totally missed because I was too busy staring at Logan. I bet he tasted better than the food. This was the first time I'd been taken out to an upmarket restaurant where I cared more about the man I was with than the ambience or what I was eating.

At least, until the couple at the next table began speaking after the main course, and when I say "speaking," I mean arguing. Logan put a finger to his lips as their voices grew louder through the screen of greenery.

"I need another drink," the woman slurred. "You never let me have any fun."

"You're drunk, Janice."

"I'm not drunk. I'm celebrating."

"Celebrating what?"

"Martina Harden's country-club membership got revoked. That bitch always hated me."

"What did she do?"

"Tried to set fire to her husband's girlfriend's tennis dress."

"I'd have thought she'd have got off with a warning."

"The girl was wearing it at the time. The tennis coach she was screwing threw her into the swimming pool to put the flames out. Now gimme another drink."

The man sighed. "One more glass of champagne, and then we're done."

Logan grinned at me and dropped his voice to a whisper. "This place has more drama than a Netflix original." He reached out to trace my lips with a finger. "That's better—you're smiling."

Because I was with Logan. And possibly, just possibly because the waiter had just slid a perfectly caramelised crème brûlée in front of me.

"Thanks for bringing me. I didn't think I'd enjoy it, but I am."

"I'm not sure whether to take that as a compliment or not."

Thankfully, my phone rang before I could stuff my foot any farther into my mouth, and I snatched it out of my purse.

"Hi, it's Julia from the Sutherland Animal Hospital."

"Is Nickel okay?"

"Better than okay. He's eating well, and it was a straightforward repair, so he can go home just as soon as you're ready to pick him up."

"I'll be there soon." How long would it take me to finish lunch, get home, pick up my car, and drive to the veterinarian? "In around an hour?"

"Perfect! He's such a lovely little kitty."

I hung up and spooned a mouthful of dessert into my mouth, chewing slowly. After the escape to Claude's, it was time to return to reality.

"What's up?" Logan asked. "Bad news?"

"Not really. Nickel's doing good."

"Then why do you look as though your husband's mistress just interrupted your tennis match?"

Trust Logan to make me smile again. "Because Nickel can go home now, which means I have to as well, and I was kind of hoping to stay somewhere else tonight."

A hotel, maybe, or one of the sleep pods in the office. Last night, the adrenaline had still been flowing and I'd been determined not to let Jerry Olson break me, but today... A girl was allowed to change her mind, wasn't she?

"Well, that's good, because you're both staying at my place," Logan said.

I choked on my last mouthful of crème brûlée. "What?"

"Your security's not up to scratch, and I need to get some sleep too. Nate built my monitoring system, and it'll alert me if a mouse coughs."

"But... But..."

"You can pick up clothes and cat food on the way. Don't worry—I'm not expecting you to sleep naked. Unless you want to, of course. I'm not gonna say no."

I was still gaping like a goldfish when Claude came over to say our meal was going on Emmy's tab. Logan wanted me to stay in his...his man cave? I'd heard rumours that he lived in a cabin buried in the freaking woods, far from anywhere and totally alone. I'd be trapped. A man like Logan could eat a girl like me for breakfast.

"I can't believe—"

The sound of a slap stopped me mid-sentence.

"For the record, I faked it every time!" the woman at the next table shrieked.

I squinted through the foliage, and her husband simply shrugged. "What makes you think I was screwing you for your benefit?"

He ducked as she threw her wine glass at him, and as it smashed on the floor, she was already storming off.

Logan slid his arm around my waist. "Just for the record, kitten," he murmured, lips close enough to brush my ear, "I'm all about a woman's pleasure."

Be still my throbbing lady parts. Perhaps being eaten for breakfast wouldn't be so bad after all.

Chapter 21 - Sloane

NICKEL MIAOWED INSIDE his cat carrier as we trundled along Logan's driveway. The ruts made my teeth rattle, and the tree branches meeting overhead gave the whole approach an atmosphere of gloom. A lopsided pair of rusty gates blocked the way, and I was amazed they were still standing, but as we approached, they swung open on silent hinges. Not a single creak. Odd.

Then we rounded a bend, and the pitted blacktop gave way to a perfectly smooth surface. The trees thinned out, and I glimpsed a clearing with a stone sculpture in the centre. Pretty. A moment later, the house came into view, and I let out a gasp. The L-shaped ranch dominated the space, pale green in colour with cream and brown accents. Manicured lawns stretched to the trees, and sunshine glimmered off the rippling surface of the pool at one side.

Logan pressed a button on his keys, and a door in the separate three-car garage rolled up.

"So, what do you think of the place?" he asked.

"It's not what I was expecting."

"I don't like to make it look too nice out front. Attracts the wrong sort of attention."

He parked the truck and opened my door for me, revealing his inner gentleman once more, and the last

of my resolve melted away. The things he'd said and done for the past few weeks—they couldn't all have been in jest, could they? The sweet words, the kind gestures, the little touches that might have been innocent on their own but put together added up to something more. He really did like me.

I still didn't understand why, but I'd take it.

And I'd give myself.

I clutched Nickel's carrier while Logan grabbed my bag and Nickel's litter tray, and the bolts on the front door shot back when he peered into the retina scanner beside it. Blackwood used the same system for after-hours access at headquarters.

"Can you add me to the system so I can get in and out?"

"Already done."

"You knew I'd be coming here?"

"Yes."

I didn't really know what to say to that, so I didn't say anything, just gripped the handle on Nickel's carrier tighter and followed Logan into the hallway. The place was about as far from the bachelor pad I'd imagined as it could get. Pale wood floors with the occasional rug, pastel walls, and plenty of windows to let the light in. A trio of cream leather sofas clustered around a log burner in the living room. And his glass dining table was a whole lot nicer than my chipped wooden one.

"I've got three guest rooms, but one of them's set up for Fantasia. If you like Disney, feel free to use it." He dropped my bag next to a door I assumed led to the sleeping wing. "I thought we'd put Nickel in the mudroom. The veterinarian said he needed to be

confined in a small space, right?"

Logan had a mudroom? That was so...so...civilised. Had I fallen down Alice's rabbit hole a month ago and somehow not noticed? I'd gone from semi-living with a cheating jerk to temporarily shacking up with a man who probably wore a cape and went joyriding in the Batmobile in his spare time.

"Yes, the mudroom. Makes perfect sense."

Nickel had his leg tightly wrapped in a blue bandage, and when I opened the door of the carrier, he gingerly stepped out and sniffed around. The room was spotless, not a speck of dirt anywhere despite its purpose.

"Do you have a cleaner?"

"How did you guess? She comes Tuesdays and Fridays."

"And a gardener?"

"Every Thursday."

I couldn't even find my back gate. Suddenly, I felt utterly inadequate, but Logan didn't notice because he was on his knees petting Nickel.

"I think he likes me."

"I know how he feels," I blurted, then clapped a hand over my mouth. "Oops."

Logan froze for a second then climbed to his feet, walking towards me until I was forced to back up. My ass hit the wall, but still he kept coming until there was only an inch of space between us. His kind expression had disappeared, replaced with a heated gaze and a dangerous mouth.

And when he kissed me, I had to hang onto his arms to stop my knees from buckling.

His lips were gentle at first. Soft. But when he

licked the seam of my mouth and I yielded, he became more forceful, taking everything and demanding more. My embarrassing gasps and whimpers—he swallowed them all.

I wrapped my legs around him as he carried me into the hallway, and I thought he'd keep going, through to the bedroom, but he stopped to re-arm the security system. At least one of us was still thinking straight.

"Secure." He pressed me up against the wall again, and this time he arched his hips into me. Holy moly, Christmas had come early. "Your mouth tastes so sweet, kitten. I bet you taste good everywhere."

I unbuttoned his shirt as he kissed my neck, and as his lips trailed along my collarbone, they left a fiery path in their wake. How had I ever tried to resist this? The man was more addictive than crack. I only hoped I measured up. The likes of Kenneth and Lyndon had in no way prepared me for a man like Logan, but right now, all I wanted to do was touch him, so I closed my eyes and blindly carried on.

"I'm glad we took the afternoon off," I whispered.

Logan chuckled against my shoulder and it tickled. "Wonder who's gonna win the pool?"

I froze. Of all the words Logan could have said to me, he'd picked the six that turned my veins to ice. I knew he didn't mean anything horrible by them, but even as he tugged at the tie of my dress, a rogue tear slipped out.

And of course, Logan noticed. "What's wrong?"

"Nothing."

"Kitten, you're crying. Do you want me to stop?"

I shook my head, but I couldn't speak because then

the dam would break. Why did my past have to rear its ugly head at the most inopportune moments?

Logan kissed me again, and I tried to kiss him back, but the heat and passion of a few moments ago had disappeared.

"Talk to me, Sloane." He tugged the edges of my dress together. "What did I do? If you don't tell me, I can't fix it."

"You didn't do anything wrong. It's something somebody else did a long, long time ago, but I can't get the memories out of my head. This is all me, not you."

He carried me through to the living room and sat on the sofa, holding me sideways on his lap with his arms loose around my waist. Even when I screwed up, he was kind.

"I mentioned the pool in the office. Is that what upset you? It's nothing personal—they bet on everything, and the guys all knew I was gonna make a play for you sooner or later."

"They did?"

"I couldn't keep my eyes off your ass."

Even though he could be crude, his honesty still made me smile. And if we were going to get through this, I knew I had to be honest with him, no matter how much it hurt. I slumped against his chest, eyes fixed on the far end of the sofa because if I had to look at him while I bared my soul, I'd never speak.

"I was eighteen, and his name was Joey McManus. The star quarterback at Allenvale High, and my biology lab partner. He made me nervous at first, but he was nice to me, and when we had to dissect a frog, he did the cutting and didn't even laugh when I ran to the bathroom to puke. After that, we started eating lunch

together. He quit sitting at the cool table with the other jocks for me. *Me.* Sloane Mullins, the chubby nerd who couldn't name a single reality TV show but who knew all the answers in physics." Logan's arms tightened around me, and I sniffled against his shoulder. "I bet you sat at the cool table."

"Mostly, I was smoking behind the janitor's storage shed with Christian and Trey."

"You smoke?"

"Not anymore. Not for years." Logan tucked a few strands of hair behind my ear. "Kitten, you don't have to talk about this if you don't want to."

"No, I need to get it out." I sucked in another breath. "Anyhow, Joey and I started dating. He asked me to prom. I went to football games, and I tried so hard to love the game even though it secretly bored me. And then..." I took a deep breath, forcing the air in because it felt as if my throat was closing up. "Then I slept with him. It was my first time, and I was all over the place because I didn't know what I was doing, but it happened, and it was... Let's just say, I couldn't understand what all the fuss was about. Still can't, if I'm honest."

"Give me a week, and you won't be saying that."

There was no arrogance in Logan's statement, only sincerity, and I believed him. Even now, when I was a sobbing, shaking mess, he still made my blood run hot. I pressed a kiss against his shoulder before I carried on.

"The next day, Joey didn't answer my messages or my calls, and when I got to school, he blanked me. It turned out he'd made a bet. Every player on the varsity football team roster would pay him a hundred bucks if he took my virginity. He got two thousand dollars, and

I got a crushed heart. So now you understand why I freaked out when you mentioned the pool at work, and that's also why I was cold yesterday. Because I overheard Nate and Luther talking about it."

"Sloane, I'm so sorry."

"There's nothing you need to be sorry for. Like I said, it's all me."

"I'm sorry on behalf of mankind that you got treated that way. I won't pretend I'm a saint because I'm not, but when you give me your heart—and I do mean when, not if—I'm gonna treat it with the care and respect and love it deserves."

Now I began crying harder, good tears mixed with pain, and Logan just held me, occasionally kissing my hair while I sobbed. But I wasn't finished yet.

"It got worse."

"Fuck."

"Joey had to prove he'd delivered on the bet, so he filmed the whole thing with a hidden camera. Everybody in my high school saw the damn video, even the teachers judging by the way they looked at me. The football team had T-shirts made with 'Is that gonna fit?' written across them. Red with white block letters. I can still see them now."

"Is that why you always went for the safe option afterwards? Men like Kenneth with tiny dicks?" Logan looked a little sheepish. "Shit. Sorry."

A snort of laughter escaped, but there was truth in his words. "I guess I picked men who couldn't hurt me because I didn't like them enough to love them. That's why you scare me so much."

I ended on a whisper, and Logan captured my lips in a searing kiss.

"Don't be scared, kitten. Full disclosure: there're cameras all over the house as part of the security system, but they're turned off. I'll show you how to check that."

"I trust you." I closed my eyes so I could finish without getting distracted. "The Joey mess happened right before my final exams, and I failed almost everything. On the day of my physics paper, I went to use the bathroom right before it started, and every stall had a picture of my naked butt taped to the back of it. I walked out and never returned. My parents were furious."

"They didn't support you?"

"Dad spent most of his life chasing women who weren't my mom, which didn't leave him much time to care about his daughter. And Mom said I should suck it up, that I should be proud of my body and hold my head high. But I couldn't. I just couldn't."

"And the teachers? What did the principal say?"

"Oh, boys will be boys. He wasn't about to do anything that might jeopardise the football team's chances, and like I said, Joey was the star quarterback."

"Wait a second. You don't mean *the* Joey McManus? Joey McManus who won the Heisman Trophy?"

"That's him. Now you know why I won't watch football. And also why I became a personal assistant. Originally, I wanted to be a physicist, but I lost my place at college."

Funny how it got easier to talk about as I went on. My tears were drying up, probably because Logan hadn't judged me or run screaming. No, he simply hugged me. We must have stayed like that for ten

minutes, until my breathing calmed down and I could think straight again.

"Now what do we do?" I asked.

The moment we'd shared earlier had been lost, and I wouldn't have blamed Logan if he just wanted to have a quiet meal and go to bed. This wasn't what he'd signed up for.

"You want my honest answer or the one you want to hear?"

"What's the one I want to hear?"

"I'll cook you dinner, kiss you goodnight, and show you to your room, all gentlemanly."

"And the truth?"

"I want to back you up against the nearest wall, remove your underwear with my teeth, and lick your pussy until you scream my name."

Oh. My. Goodness. What was I supposed to say to that? A thousand words whirled around in my mind, but only two fell out of my mouth.

"Do it."

"What?"

"Do it. Me. Just do me." Darn it, all logic had gone again. "Please?"

Fortunately, Logan knew how to interpret my ramblings, because two and a half seconds later, he slammed me back against the wall by the door, kissing, sucking, even biting as he freaking devoured me. He was right—there was nothing gentlemanly about it, but I couldn't get enough. Something ripped as I grabbed at his shirt, and I broke a nail trying to get his jeans undone. But before I got at the goods, he tore my dress in two and dropped to his knees. I hung onto the doorjamb for dear life as he made good on his promise

and peeled off my panties with his teeth. My bra had disappeared somewhere along the way too.

Naked before him, I didn't feel any of the shame I used to feel with Kenneth. It was impossible with the way Logan looked up at me, setting me aflame with his gaze as he slowly took all of me in. His eyes finally locked on mine, and he didn't break the connection as he went in for the kill with his tongue.

Okay, he definitely didn't need a week to prove his earlier point. More like two minutes. The orgasm that tore through me left me on the floor in his arms, mostly speaking gibberish as he held me close. But I managed to get one word out.

"Bedroom?"

"Too damn fucking right, kitten."

Chapter 22 - Sloane

SUNRISE FOUND ME clinging onto one edge of Logan's bed because he sprawled all over the place and took up most of it. And he was big. Big everywhere. More of a giant starfish than a man, really.

"Logan?"

"Mmm."

"I'm about to fall on the floor."

He wrapped one arm around my waist and dragged me across his chest, opening first one eye and then the other as he kissed me.

"Morning, kitten. Sleep well?"

Yes, for a whole three hours. "I'm so tired."

"You can stay in bed today. I'll just wake you up for sex occasionally."

"Are you always this charming?"

"Pretty much, yeah. I'll bring you food."

He was joking. I saw the glint in his eyes. Although right now, his offer sounded quite good to me, even if I did feel slightly...worn. Logan didn't seem to be suffering any ill effects from our exertions, though, judging by the tented sheet beside my right hip.

Of course, he didn't miss my glance.

"Feel like another ride? Or do you want me to do the work?"

Morning sex? Another new thing for me. Lyndon

had always risen with the larks to meditate while Kenneth preferred to wake up with the newspaper and a latte. I pinched myself in case I was dreaming.

"What's that for?" Logan asked.

"I'm just having a hard time believing that I'm here with you. That you're with me."

"What can I say? I'm a tits-and-ass guy."

He was so much more than that, but I was getting used to his crudeness now, and I figured I should play him at his own game.

"I guess that makes me a six-pack-and-cock girl."

One quick move, and I was underneath him. "Sure does." He squashed my breasts together, staring at them. "I love these tits. One day, I'm gonna fuck them. Then I'm gonna come all over them, push them up to your mouth, and watch you lick it off."

I didn't know whether to slap him or beg him to do exactly that right then. In the end, I just gave a little sigh and lay back, exhausted but still so, so needy.

"Do with me what you will, Mr. Barnes."

On Saturdays, I usually went to Blackwood and so did Logan, but ten o'clock found us sitting at his kitchen counter, wearing one outfit between us. I had the shirt; he had the pants.

"Do you think we should go to the office?" I asked.

He slid a much-needed cup of coffee towards me. "Why?"

"Because... I guess because we always do? And shouldn't we help with my, uh, case? Situation?"

"Agatha's looking into things. I already talked to

her while you were in the shower. She's found your picture on two more websites, and she's hacking into the accounts as we speak."

"Oh."

"Which means we can do whatever we want today."

"What do you usually do at the weekends? When you're not working, I mean."

"Use the gym. Go for a swim. Hang out at the Brotherhood. Go on dates sometimes. You?"

"Not swimming." I shuddered. "Or the gym. Occasionally I go out for dinner or watch TV. Groceries, cleaning, all the boring stuff."

"What's wrong with swimming?"

"Nothing per se, it's more the thought of wearing a bathing suit in public."

"We can swim today. I've got a pool."

"I didn't bring a suit. In fact, I'm not even sure the ones I have fit anymore."

"Who said anything about a suit?"

"You can't be serious?"

"I live in the middle of a fucking forest, Sloane."

"I'm not sure—"

I didn't get a chance to finish before he picked me up and carried me outside.

"Stop. Stop! I just had a shower."

"Then you can just have another one."

He didn't even pause before he jumped into the pool, and I came up spluttering as he trod water and laughed. That asshole!

"I'm going to kill you."

"Gotta catch me first."

Of course, Logan swam like a fish, and after a fruitless chase, I clung to the side of the pool, out of

breath with my hair plastered in rat-tails around my face. He soon joined me, minus the breathless part, and his hair looked artfully mussed instead of horrendous, but rather than an apology, I got, "Your shirt's gone see-through."

This man was going to frustrate the heck out of me, but as he peeled away the offending garment and gripped my butt under the water, I decided I didn't care. I'd take Logan with all his faults and his filthy mouth and his assholic tendencies, over and over again, in any way I could get him.

On Sunday evening, I sipped a glass of wine as the sun went down. Logan had one of those old-fashioned swings on his back porch, and we'd curled up there under a blanket after dinner. Two days with him, and I felt different. Lighter inside. Possibly outside too since we'd spent the morning walking around his property while he checked the sensors for the security system.

This weekend had been an escape. An escape from the internet nightmare, an escape from my past, an escape from life in general. Would things change when we went back to work tomorrow? Would Logan come to his senses and realise I truly was just that awkward girl who didn't quite fit?

He took a long sip of his beer as he twirled the ends of my hair with the fingers of his other hand.

"What are you thinking?" he asked.

"Nothing."

"Which means everything."

Why did he have to be so perceptive? "Only that I

don't want this weekend to be over."

"It's not over."

"But soon it will be. What if everything changes tomorrow?"

"Between us, you mean? Nothing's gonna change, kitten. Tomorrow, I'll want you more than I do today, and today, I wanted you more than I did yesterday. Now that I've had a taste, I'll never get enough."

"But I'm no Emmy. You should be dating Superwoman."

Logan burst out laughing. "Is that what you think? That I want a girl like Emmy? Couldn't be further from the truth, gorgeous. Women like her and Ana and Sofia and Dan leave a trail of destruction wherever they go. At the end of the day, I just want to come home and relax with a hot woman and a cold beer. Come here." He lifted me over to straddle him. "Believe me when I say I want you."

Right then, I did. I could feel the evidence between my legs.

Logan had my wrap dress open in less than a second, and when he pulled my bra down and drew one nipple into his mouth, I breathed a long, drawn-out moan.

"I need to get you more of these tie-up dresses," he said, pausing to look up at me. "And those tight skirts you wear to the office. I like them too."

"You should stick with sweatpants. No underwear and no shirt."

"Noted. I always knew there was a dirty girl hiding inside you. I just needed to set her free."

He wriggled down his pants—yes, the sweatpants that didn't leave much to the imagination—produced a

condom from somewhere, and before I could contradict him, he'd pushed my panties to one side and lowered me on top of his cock.

In two days, I'd gone from hell to heaven. Logan hit precisely the right spot as I rocked my hips, and I kept my eyes open as he kissed me. I wanted to remember every moment of this evening. The smoky aroma of food cooking on the grill, the chirping of the crickets as dusk fell, and the soothing warmth of the man I'd basically fallen in love with.

Please, Logan, don't break my heart.

CHAPTER 23 - LOGAN

LOGAN SAT ON the floor in the mudroom, drinking his morning coffee with Nickel on his lap.

"How're you feeling, little fella?" The cat raised his head, and Logan scritched behind his ears. "You want more salmon?"

He hadn't really known what to feed Nickel, but with Sloane still in bed, he figured fish was a safe bet. They needed to leave for work in an hour, and he wanted Sloane to sleep for as long as possible. She'd been exhausted last night, and he had to accept some responsibility for that. Okay, all the responsibility.

But he finally had his woman in his house, and like a kid with a shiny new toy, he couldn't stop playing with her. Twenty minutes, and he'd take her a cup of coffee. That should give them enough time for a quickie in the shower, and they could pick up breakfast on the way to the office.

It was a good plan, but the quickie turned into a not-so-quickie that left them both running out to his truck with Sloane still trying to fasten her necklace. Officially, they didn't have set working hours, but Sloane had a conference call scheduled with some of their colleagues in Japan, and Logan had a nine o'clock meeting he couldn't be late for. Actually, it was more of a test-slash-demonstration of a simulation system for

their training facility. One that used virtual reality
headsets rather than their current holograms and
added extra layers to the experience with smells and
vibrations. It would be a massive upgrade and a
considerable investment, but one that could potentially
pay dividends in the future.

"We can get breakfast at the office," Sloane said.
"That'll save a few minutes."

"Is there proper food there this week?"

Or was the kitchen still filled with kelp smoothies
and avocados? Logan hated avocados. People raved
about them, but to him, they tasted like compressed
grass only slimier.

"I've got Frosted Flakes in my desk drawer. In the
box marked 'Operations Reports.'"

"I love you."

Sloane giggled. What if she realised he wasn't
joking? He didn't think she was ready to hear those
words yet, and when they hit the road, he found out he
was right.

"Logan?"

Her tone said this was something *he* didn't want to
hear.

"Yeah?"

"When we get to the office, can we not let everyone
know we're together? It's not that I don't want them to
find out, but they're going to stare, and just for a few
days..."

"I get it."

Logan didn't like it, but he got it. While the feelings
between them might have been building for a long
time, the start of their actual relationship had been
sudden, and it had happened in a week when Sloane

had been forced to deal with a ton of drama. Then there was Joey McManus. No wonder she hated being the centre of attention.

Just thinking of that little fucker made Logan grip the steering wheel so hard he glanced down to see whether it had bent. McManus would pay for what he'd done. Not this week, not next week, but soon.

He forced himself to let go with one hand so he could squeeze Sloane's. "I'll keep out of your way in the office as long as you're back in my bed tonight."

"Thank you."

But Logan hadn't made any promises about digital contact, and he sent the first message before he went to his meeting.

Logan: I can still taste you.

He watched Sloane as she read it, then felt kind of guilty when she spat coffee over her desk. *Sorry, sweetheart.*

But he wasn't sorry enough not to type out another message as he walked to the conference room.

Logan: And I can still feel your lips around my cock.

Sloane: We're in the office!!!!!

Logan: So don't squirm too much in your seat. Could get messy.

Would she or wouldn't she play along? How far could he push her? Nothing came through from her for almost three hours, but then his phone buzzed as he took off his VR headset and tried to calm his heartbeat. The test simulation had been a blast, quite literally, but it was still early days.

Sloane: I'm in a different seat now.

Logan: Is it waterproof?

Sloane: No, but Leah isn't staring at me anymore. I miss the taste of you.

So his little kitten *did* want to play along. Logan itched to type out a response, except Nate glanced across at him and he couldn't afford to get distracted in this meeting. But Sloane's words had already had an effect on him, and it only took him a second to snap a selfie of the shadow in his sweatpants and send it with a single word.

Logan: Soon...

By the time he got back to his desk, he had a message waiting, and it turned out Sloane had gotten into this game more than he ever dreamed she would. And she must have paid a visit to the bathroom because she'd sent a picture of those fantastic tits, albeit still ensconced in a fancy bra.

Sloane: Hurry up...

Now Logan was the one with the problem. He slid his chair farther forward so his desk hid the evidence. Where was Sloane? She hadn't been kidding when she said she wasn't at her desk. Her chair was empty, her computer screen dark.

Logan scanned the room, searching for the familiar brown hair or a splash of the pale pink top she'd put on that morning. Nothing. Then he spotted her favourite coffee mug, a dainty thing decorated with multicoloured cats that Bradley had given her one Christmas. Black and Emmy were out, and she was sitting at Black's desk, hidden behind his oversized computer screen.

Well done, Sloane.

She didn't know it yet, but she'd picked the perfect spot.

Logan spent an hour in the gym, then hunted down Agatha. She'd found another dating profile, but she hadn't had any luck with tracking the perpetrator, and today, she'd gotten distracted by a fraud case. Secretly, Logan didn't mind the delay. Sloane was safe at his place, and as long as the culprit was on the loose, she'd stay there.

For the rest of the afternoon, he dialled back on the smut, sending mildly filthy messages and grinning like an idiot into his fuck-awful smoothie. But at five o'clock when people started leaving the office, he could take it no more.

Holding a sheaf of papers in front of himself to hide his painfully hard cock, he sauntered over to Black's office and pushed the door open.

"Hi."

Sloane's eyes snapped up. "What are you doing here?"

Her, if he got his way. "Just came to say hello. How much work do you have left?"

"About another half hour."

Perfect. He pushed her chair back a foot, slid her laptop to one side, and sat on the desk in front of her. Those beautiful brown eyes widened as they took in the outline that was all too obvious through his sweatpants. He normally wore jeans to the office, but for Sloane, he'd made an exception.

"Logan, what are you doing?"

The hint of panic in her voice only made him harder. "You said you missed the taste."

"Are you serious? Tell me you're not serious?"

Logan shrugged. "Why not?"

"Because we're in the office and this is my boss's

desk," she hissed.

"He's not here."

"There're still loads of people out there. Somebody else might see."

"No, they won't."

"You don't know that."

"Yeah, I do. Why do you think Black rearranged the furniture a few months back?"

The filthy old bastard had got Logan to help him one weekend, and they'd checked all the angles. Logan wouldn't be the first man to get blown at this desk.

He held his breath, waiting to see what Sloane would do, and his patience paid off. Slowly, slowly, she slid his waistband down until he sprang free.

At the first touch of her velvety lips, he almost busted a nut, but he forced himself to think of all sorts of unsexy things. Statistics on the new-model Ford pickup. The trees he needed to plant before winter. Elvira in accounts.

"Hey, reckon we should call up Kenneth and let him listen?"

Sloane gagged, and his cock popped out of her mouth as she started giggling. "He could use it as an instructional for his secretary."

Oh, now her sense of humour was shining through. Logan was going to like the new Sloane.

"But that would mean sharing you, and I'm not going to." He tucked himself away temporarily, pulled her up, and gave her a gentle shove towards Emmy and Black's private bathroom. "Let's finish this."

"You can't be—"

"Where you're concerned, I'm always serious. Go, quick, while nobody's looking in this direction."

She stumbled into the bathroom, legs adorably wobbly like a baby fawn's, and Logan quickly followed.

"Fuck, kitten. You're not wearing any panties."

"It was supposed to be a surprise."

"Trust me, it's a surprise."

Holy shit, she was dripping. He tore open a condom with his teeth and did the necessary, lifted her up against the wall, and lowered her onto his cock. Office sex was a first for him, but with Sloane in the building, it wouldn't be the last time he got dirty at work.

"You're a difficult woman to stay away from."

"I hardly got anything done all day."

"You get bonus points for doing me."

"You're such an asshole, Logan."

He grinned, unrepentant. "But I'm *your* asshole."

Logan bet the bathroom had good soundproofing— Black would have made sure of that—but even so, he swallowed Sloane's cries as he thrust into her. Their first time, she'd been nervous, a little hesitant, but now she was starting to let her guard down and he loved raw, unfiltered Sloane.

She went rigid as she came, her muscles tightening around his cock and sending him over the edge as well. Heaven in a prim little dress with no panties on.

"I can't believe we did that," she whispered.

"I'll give you frequent reminders to refresh your memory."

"You're crazy."

"Better than boring. Half an hour, right? Want to pick up a pizza on the way home?"

She gave her head a delicate shake as he set her on her feet and rearranged her dress, but it was more "I can't believe this guy" than an outright no.

"Pizza?" he asked again.

"No anchovies on mine."

Just extra sauce.

They nearly got away with it. Sloane finger-combed her hair while Logan disposed of the condom and drank a few mouthfuls of water from his cupped hands at the sink. Sex with Sloane counted as an extra workout and left him thirsty. He watched her in the mirror, smiling at her flushed cheeks and sleepy eyes. Were her lips sore? They looked a little red. If he kept kissing her like that, he might need to shave off his beard because he didn't want to leave her skin chapped. He'd always thought he looked too young clean-shaven, but now that he was thirty-seven, knocking off a year or two mightn't be a bad thing. Then again, the beard came in useful for undercover work in the Middle East. When was he next going overseas?

He was still debating the merits of facial hair when Sloane opened the door to leave, and he bumped into her as she froze in front of him.

Oops.

"Hey, how was Atlanta?" Logan asked.

Black looked across at them from his desk, one eyebrow raised. "How long has this been going on?"

"This particular instance, or...?"

"You two, together."

"About two days and eighteen hours."

Black turned to his computer and clicked the mouse a few times. "Fuck. Luther won the pool again."

"Nice bathroom, by the way."

"Emmy's rather fond of it."

Logan gave Sloane a nudge. Was she okay after Black's mention of the pool?

"Kitten, can you finish your stuff tomorrow? Or at home?"

A single nod.

Logan grabbed her laptop and purse and steered her out of the office. "Then let's go get pizza."

Chapter 24 - Sloane

I COULD ONLY imagine what my colleagues were thinking as I scurried through the office behind Logan. My cheeks burned, my hair looked as if Logan had been pulling it—because he had—and we both reeked of sex.

And worse, my freaking boss had seen us slinking out of his darn bathroom.

"What do you think will happen?" I whispered to Logan as I clambered into his truck.

"About what?"

"We got caught!" My voice rose to a shriek, and I quickly checked around to see if anyone else had heard.

"Only by Black."

"*Only* by Black? What does the company handbook say? Is sex in the office a disciplinary offence?"

"If it was, all the directors would have to fire each other."

"Black looked pissed."

"That's his normal expression."

"Really pissed."

"Only because he lost the pool." Logan pressed a button on the steering wheel, and a dial tone filled the cabin. "No anchovies, right?"

How could he even think of eating? "I'm not hungry."

He ordered two pizzas anyway, plus a side of

chicken wings and a pint of cookie dough ice cream.

"Don't you listen to anything I say?"

He reached over and squeezed my thigh. "Not when you're talking bullshit, kitten."

The only reason I didn't strangle him was that my phone rang. And it was Emmy.

"H-h-hello?" Had Black told her what happened?

"I understand congratulations are in order?"

"Sorry?"

"You and Logan? I'd have preferred if you could have held off for another week, but such is life."

"You mean—"

"But there's some bad news."

Oh heck, here it comes. "Please, just tell me."

"Bradley overheard Black telling me about you two —that bathroom's soundproofed, by the way—and now he wants to throw a bloody party. I'd suggest leaving the country."

The volume was loud enough for Logan to hear, and he started laughing.

"Told you," he muttered.

"I can't leave the country. Nickel broke his leg, and he's still recovering."

"I'll hold Bradley off for a week or two, but you've got loads of vacation stored up. Use some of it."

"Emmy, I—"

"Gotta go. Don't worry if you're late tomorrow— Alex is making me run a fucking marathon first thing, so I'll probably crawl in around midday."

Aaaaaaaand...she was gone.

A week passed, and I gradually began to get used to spending my evenings with Logan. Half the time, he drove me insane, but the other half, I wanted him so fiercely I thought I'd lose my mind. He gave off these weird pheromones that made all my synapses misfire. It was like living on a roller coaster, but the rush of being with him was addictive.

Everyone in the office knew now, *everyone*, and some joker kept leaving sex toys on my desk each morning. I couldn't even be mad because Logan knew exactly what to do with them. And I'd only been back to my house once, to pick up more clothes and do Edna's grocery shopping since she'd been laid up with a cold all week.

"So you found yourself a new man?" she asked when I apologised for not being around much.

"I did."

"That's good, dear. I wasn't so keen on the last one. My husband, God rest his soul, always said the only men who wear shiny suits are charlatans and bigamists."

"Logan doesn't wear shiny suits, thank goodness."

Or any kind of a suit. Mostly, he didn't even wear clothes.

"Sounds like a keeper. Did you buy those tiny sausages I'm fond of?"

"Two packages."

"You're a gem, dear."

Nickel was recovering too. He had the run of Logan's house now, and he got around remarkably quickly with his bandage when he wasn't high on the family-sized bag of catnip Logan had bought for him.

Life was good. A little too good. Because all good

things come to an end, and with Dan now helping Agatha to investigate the catfishing, it was only a matter of time before it was safe for me to go home again.

"Are you okay?" Logan asked on Monday morning. Sun streamed in through the bedroom window behind him, highlighting every peak and trough of his muscles.

"Absolutely fine. Why?"

"Your sweater's on inside out."

Darn it. "I just got distracted."

"By what? And don't say my naked ass because you've seen that plenty of times."

What should I tell him? Every woman's magazine I'd ever read said men hated women with insecurities, and I had more than a few of them. But Logan was staring at me, waiting, so I couldn't say nothing.

Then something slimy landed on my foot.

"Yeuch! What was that?"

Nickel looked extraordinarily pleased with himself as the frog hopped across the bedroom floor, and I felt like kissing him. Nickel, not the frog. Saved by my cat again.

"Looks like a green tree frog," Logan said. "There's a pond in the woods out back, so they often come to visit."

Logan picked it up to show me, and I beat a hasty retreat into the bathroom and slammed the door. Discussion: avoided.

Or so I thought.

I'd forgotten I was dealing with Logan, master of strategy and an expert at reading his prey. He waited until I'd got into his truck to go to the office, then he locked the doors.

"You didn't answer my question."

"What question?"

He sighed and turned to me. "Kitten, what's distracting you? You've been quiet all weekend."

"I don't know. I guess... I guess I'm just thinking about our future. Where it's going."

For the first time ever, I saw a flash of nervousness in Logan's eyes.

"Where do you think our future's going?" he asked.

"This past week's been crazy. I mean, I ended up living in your house with no warning whatsoever, and it's been amazing, but I don't know if that's what you signed up for, and if it isn't, then things could get awkward at work, and I hope we can act like adults, and..."

He just stared at me, which was hardly surprising given the word vomit coming from my mouth.

"Why are you writing us off when we're only just beginning?"

"Because..." I hated talking about the serious stuff. *Hated* it. "Because I'm scared. Scared of this ending, and every day we spend together, I like you more." I swallowed, feeling sick, and voiced the question that terrified me. "Where do *you* see our future going?"

He took a deep breath and gripped the steering wheel, staring straight ahead even though the engine wasn't turned on yet.

"I see you coming home with me again tonight, although I can't guarantee you'll get much rest. I'll make you come once, twice, three times, and then you'll fall asleep with your head on my chest. And in the morning, I'll put whatever frog or mouse or bird Nickel's brought us out into the backyard and make us

breakfast. Then we'll go to work. And the next day, and the day after. Sometimes we'll stay at my place, sometimes we'll stay at yours. At the weekend, I'll let you out of bed long enough to take you on a proper date —dinner, a movie, whatever—and afterwards I'll kiss you breathless at the side of the road because I won't be able to last the whole drive home without tasting you. Rinse and repeat.

"And in six months, if you haven't gotten sick of me going away for work and also being an asshole, then I'll wake up at your place one morning and get pissed off because my favourite shirt is at my house and I'm not, and I'll ask you to move in with me when your lease is up because I don't want to live alone anymore. And in a year, eighteen months maybe, some punk will look at you sideways in a bar, you'll get mad at me when I punch him, then I'll put my ring on your finger because I want every other asshole to know you're mine. There. That's how I see things going."

I couldn't speak. I couldn't even breathe. Did Logan Barnes just talk about getting married? My mind stuttered like a car on its last drop of gas.

"Five months," I managed to get out.

"What?"

"My lease is up in five months."

He squeezed my hand, then started the engine. "So you'll move into my place permanently in five months."

"Okay."

Logan flashed me a grin. "You're agreeing?"

"You didn't sound as if you were giving me a choice."

"I'm not. I'll kidnap you otherwise."

"What, and tie me to your bed?"

"Sure, if you like that kind of thing."

"Stop being an asshole, Logan." But being tied up? Hmm... That might be kinda hot. "Do you have rope?"

Five months couldn't pass fast enough.

Chapter 25 - Sloane

I'D JUST GOTTEN my first cup of coffee when Agatha waved me over to her desk. Logan and Dan were already there, staring at the screen.

"We're tracking access to each account, but whoever it is hasn't been online all week. This newest one hasn't been accessed for nine days. Our catfisher's working the sympathy angle here. This time, her house got flooded due to a faulty washing machine, and she's having to work overtime, which means she can't fly out to meet our victim. But get this; she knows how to talk dirty."

I skimmed over the passages, and they would have made a porn star blush. But one of them seemed oddly familiar.

"Uh, I think she copied that one from a romance novel."

"Really? Which one?" Agatha asked.

"*My Secret Commando*. Or maybe *The SEAL and the Secretary*."

"How do you know?"

My cheeks burned. "I might have read them."

Logan's hand brushed over my ass, and he leaned down to murmur in my ear. "Want me to wear my fatigues this evening?"

Thanks to our talk in the truck, I was feeling a little

more secure now.

"Would you mind?" I whispered back, then focused on the screen again as I tried not to grin like an idiot. Imagining Logan in his uniform would have to wait. "Hold on, go back a bit." Agatha scrolled up, and I peered closer. "Where the hell did that picture come from?"

There I was, lying out in a frilly pink bikini, wearing the Gucci sunglasses Bradley had given me for my twenty-seventh birthday.

"Thought you said you hated swimsuits, kitten?"

"I do. I've never worn that one anywhere but in the privacy of my own backyard, and always alone. That's my freaking lounge chair!"

"Who took the photo?"

"I don't know!"

"Kenneth?"

"I wasn't with Kenneth then."

"Someone else?"

"Lyndon. I was dating Lyndon. But he doesn't even have a cell phone, let alone a camera."

Agatha looked incredulous. "What kind of person doesn't have a cell phone?"

"He's a vegan who wears pleather shoes and eschews all modern technology. We broke up when he moved to Venezuela to live in the jungle."

"How tall is your fence?" Dan asked.

"Why does that matter?"

"Because from the way the shadows are falling, your house is on the right-hand side of that photo. And you live in a duplex, right?"

"Right."

"So your garden's narrow. Whoever took that shot

was either up against your fence or in the garden next door."

"In Edna's garden?"

"The fence is about four feet high," Logan said.

"But Edna hardly ever has visitors. Just the occasional tradesman and one or two people from the senior centre."

"Well, either one of them must have taken that picture," Dan said, "or Edna herself did."

"Edna? You think Edna's behind this? She barely knew how to turn on a computer until..." A groan escaped my lips. "Until I taught her. Then she started taking programming classes at the senior centre. And I might have passed some of my romance novels on to her as well."

"I think we need to take a look at her computer. Does she go out much?"

I sagged back against Logan, scarcely believing what I was hearing. There had to be another explanation. Edna was a friend. She baked me cakes and watched my house when I was out. She wouldn't betray me like that. Would she?

"Sloane?" Logan said. "Does Edna leave the house much?"

"She often goes to the senior centre."

"What about tonight? Where will she be?"

"Uh, what day is it? Monday? She goes to the potluck supper at the senior centre on Mondays. Six thirty until nine."

"Then we'll take a look tonight." Dan gave my arm a squeeze. "Don't be upset—we could be wrong."

But her tone said she didn't think so.

"This is gonna be the easiest sneak 'n' peek I've ever done," Dan said.

We were sitting in my kitchen—me, Dan, and Agatha—and Logan was trailing Edna to the senior centre to make sure she didn't come back unexpectedly. Her friend William had picked her up at a quarter past six, which gave us plenty of time to check things out. We didn't even need to break in because I had a key.

"This still feels wrong," I told them as we went through the narrow gate between our two backyards. "Why would she need to scam people? She gets rent from me every month, and I know her husband left her some insurance money."

"Who knows? I once tracked down a multimillionaire who used to steal from his hosts at parties for kicks. He had this room in his house filled with everything from salt shakers to diamond necklaces. Said buying things wasn't fun anymore because he could afford anything he wanted."

"Edna's not exactly loaded."

Dan turned the key in the lock, and the back door swung open. "Let's just take a look, shall we?"

Inside, Agatha headed straight for Edna's laptop, which she'd left open on the little desk in one corner of the dining room, next to the bookcase. I followed Dan as she meandered around the house, opening and closing cupboards and rifling through papers with her gloved hands. She even checked in the toilet tank and flipped over each mattress before carefully smoothing out the bedclothes again. It obviously wasn't her first

rodeo.

"*I* feel like the criminal here," I whispered.

She patted me on the hand, also gloved. "Oh, sweetie. Compared to most of my jobs, we were practically invited. Hey, look at this." Dan thumbed through a folder full of bank statements she'd found in the guest room's closet. "She's blown through all the insurance money, and now she's overdrawn."

"Guys," Agatha called from downstairs. "I've got in."

By the time we skidded to a halt beside her, Agatha was scrolling through Edna's browsing history. DateMe, Buster's Bingo, Plenty of Fish, Lucky Ladies Bingo, Hearts 'n' Minds, Fantasy Bingo.

"Reckon we've got our motive," she said. "Dating sites and online bingo. Fifty bucks says she's addicted to gambling."

"Edna?" I scoffed. "She only goes to seniors' bingo for the free crab cakes."

"She told you that?"

"Just a couple of months ago."

Dan nodded. "Makes sense. Covering her tracks."

I didn't want to believe it, but Edna's passwords were stored for one-click access, and when Agatha began checking her accounts, the horrible truth revealed. All the conversations Edna had participated in pretending to be me. The thousands she'd lost to online gambling sites. The emails from her bank demanding she clear her overdraft. I might not have wanted to believe it, but the evidence was laid out in front of me. I'd been betrayed by one of the few people I considered a friend.

Dan checked her watch. "We'd better leave."

"Two minutes," Agatha said. "The hard drive's almost copied. I can finish analysing it back in the office."

What was the point? I'd seen enough of Edna's secrets already, and I felt quite sick.

"What happens now?" I asked.

Dan steered me in the direction of the back door. "Now, we go home."

They stayed with me until Logan got back, and he took one look at my face and hugged me tight. "I'm so sorry, kitten. It sucks when people we care about hurt us."

"What should we do about it?" I asked.

Dan shrugged. "Depends on your goal. Restitution? Revenge?"

"Revenge? Edna's seventy-four years old!"

"So she should know right from wrong by now."

"Logan, help me out here."

"Why is everyone looking at me? I'm no good at shaking down old ladies." Logan clenched his fists. Unclenched them again. "Even if I am so fucking pissed about what she did to you."

"I think she needs help rather than prison," Agatha said, the voice of reason. "If she's got an addictive personality, she probably can't help herself any more than a drug abuser can."

My emotions battled it out in my head—anger, disbelief, pity. But I also remembered Edna's kind side. The way she fed Nickel when I worked late. The cookies she baked for me. All the board games we'd played to take my mind off Lyndon when he left.

"I feel sorry for her more than anything. Does anyone offer rehab for bingo addicts? Is that a thing?"

Dan shrugged. "Probably. Did you know one of Nick's celebrity clients is undergoing treatment for a Facebook addiction? If there's a therapist for that, I bet there's one for bingo."

"Want me to look it up?" Agatha asked.

"Yes, please. I should talk to her. Explain why what she's doing can't carry on and offer to help. What do you think? Logan?"

"I think you're too fucking sweet, kitten, but I'll back you up with whatever you want to do."

"Will you come with me to see her?"

"Just don't expect me to talk about knitting patterns and crochet."

CHAPTER 26 - SLOANE

WE WENT BACK to Logan's place that night, partly because Nickel needed dinner but mainly because I wanted to get away from my house and think. Edna's betrayal stung ten times worse than Kenneth's. Wasn't there supposed to be some kind of girl code, no matter the age difference?

"Still fretting?" Logan asked after I'd lain awake in his arms for an hour.

"It just hurts. Why does everyone I get close to outside of work stab me in the back?"

"I'm not gonna stab you in the back, kitten," he mumbled, seemingly half-asleep. "I love you."

I went rigid. Did those three words just leave Logan's mouth? Or was I dreaming?

"Sorry?"

He kissed me on the forehead. "Don't make me say it again. I've never said that to anyone else, and I'm trying not to panic right now."

Panic? I was trying not to pass out.

"Why would you panic?"

"In case you don't feel the same way."

"I love you."

Logan grinned, teeth white in the moonlight, and I burrowed against his chest, feeling his heartbeat against my cheek. When I was sad, he made me happy.

When I felt weak, he gave me strength. When I felt fear, he gave me love.

Now I could finally fall asleep.

"Would you rather visit Edna this evening?" Logan asked the next morning. "A few hours won't make much difference."

"I just want to get it over with."

My zipper stuck as I tried to do up my dress, and he swept my hair to one side and fixed it for me, finishing with a soft kiss on the nape of my neck.

"Have you thought about what you're going to say?"

"Yes. No. Sort of. I want to tell her that what she's been doing isn't okay. That to her, it might just be a little game on the computer, but there are real people being affected by her deception. Did Agatha send over that info on Gamblers Anonymous?"

"Yes, and I've printed it all out."

"And you're sure you don't mind coming with me?"

"I'll always have your back."

After "I love you," those were the best words I'd ever heard come out of somebody's mouth. For so long, I'd sought out company because I didn't like being alone, but I'd never truly understood what it was like to be one half of a whole. Now I did.

"Then let's do this. I feel so sick, I can't even eat breakfast at the moment."

Several times on the drive to Edna's, I almost asked Logan to turn around. I didn't so much have butterflies, more caterpillars eating at me from the inside out. People said Emmy thrived on confrontation, but if I

had to do this every day, I'd wither and die.

Logan turned the corner, and Edna's house came into view. An ordinary day on our quiet street, except for...

"Why is there a police car parked outside Edna's place? Did somebody call the cops? I thought Blackwood was handling this?"

He looked as confused as I felt. "None of us called them, I swear."

"Then why are they here?"

"We'll have to ask them that."

A bead of sweat trickled down the back of my neck as Logan parked in my driveway, and when he helped me out of the truck, I looped my arm through his so my knees wouldn't buckle. Had somebody else found out about Edna's little secret? I didn't want her to go to jail. I just wanted her to get the help she needed.

A cop climbed out of the car, unfolding his lanky frame from behind the wheel before he walked over. There was no swagger in his step, and he didn't look particularly happy to be there. That made two of us.

"Sloane Mullins?"

"Yes?"

"You live next door to Edna Burrows?"

"Yes?"

"I'm afraid I've got some bad news. Mrs. Burrows passed away last night."

"She what?"

At first, I thought I'd misheard, but the cop's sombre face hammered his words home. Edna dead? But...but...she'd seemed so sprightly for her age. So healthy.

"According to the folks at the senior centre, she put

you down as her next of kin."

Logan held me up as I tried to process the news. Edna was dead? No, she couldn't be. I'd just talked to her the day before yesterday, and she'd looked healthy as anything.

"What happened?" Logan asked.

"She went to bingo yesterday and won the jackpot. Twenty thousand dollars. From what I understand, she was celebrating when her heart gave out." He shook his head, incredulous. "Talk about bad luck."

"More like karma," Logan muttered, and I elbowed him in the ribs.

The news left me numb. Of all the ways I'd imagined this going, burying Edna wasn't one of them.

"What do I do now? We weren't related, but she doesn't have anyone else."

"There were no suspicious circumstances, so you'll just need to claim the body and arrange a funeral if you choose to hold one."

"Of course she needs a funeral." I felt my eyes start to prickle. "How do I even claim a body?"

Logan wrapped an arm around my waist, holding me up. "I'll deal with all that."

The cop backed away, no doubt relieved to escape as the first tear rolled down my cheek. "Have a good day, ma'am."

A good day. Right.

He drove off, leaving me shell-shocked on the sidewalk. Edna was gone. This whole sorry episode had ended in the most horrible way imaginable, and now I couldn't talk things out with her or help her through her problems. I'd had enough of the rabbit hole now. I wanted to get back to the real world.

"Want me to drive you home, kitten?"

I nearly pointed out that I lived right next door, but then I realised he was right. Home was with Logan now. My heart lived in a sprawling ranch house in the middle of a forest. But today, I didn't want to be there alone.

"Can we just go to the office?" I asked.

"The office? You don't want to take the day off? Emmy would understand."

"Work helps me to feel normal, and I really, really need that this morning."

Logan bent to kiss me on the forehead, and I knew he understood.

"Then let's go to Blackwood."

At Edna's wake, I stood in one corner with Logan, watching the clusters of people dotted around the room. This gathering gave a whole new meaning to the phrase "fifty shades of grey." Apart from one lady who'd dyed her hair an adventurous shade of pink, the only colour in the room came from the bright red bingo machine in the far corner.

Emmy had volunteered Bradley's services to plan the send-off—payback, she said, for the time he'd organised her funeral and given her a shiny black casket decorated with diamantés. I'd suggested a low-key affair, but he'd consulted with her friends at the senior centre and apparently they'd disagreed.

And now he clambered onto the makeshift stage by the buffet.

"Ladies, gents, do you all have your bingo cards?

It's time to put the fun in funeral!"

"This has got to be the most tasteless get-together I've ever been to," Logan whispered. "And I once went to a cremation where the dead dude's wife and mistress got into a catfight over who got to keep the floral arrangements."

"Maybe we could sneak out?"

"Good plan."

Logan shuffled sideways, but we only got halfway to the fire exit before Bradley spotted us. "Sloane, do you have a card? Somebody give her a card."

An octogenarian with perfect pin curls passed me a bingo card and pen, and a man with a comb-over waved us into two empty seats. After much clomping of walking frames and creaking of false hips, Bradley tapped on a glass with a knife.

"Now, I never had the pleasure of meeting the lovely Edna, but bingo was her favourite game, and I'm sure she's here with us in spirit. Let's start with a toast. Everybody raise your glasses to Edna."

Murmurs of "To Edna" came from around the room, and one old gent had a coughing fit when his champagne went down the wrong way. Once he'd popped his false teeth back in, Bradley declared us ready to start.

"Okay, so each of your cards has a whole selection of items you might find at a funeral. The first person to get a line wins dinner for six at Betty's Diner, and the grand prize is a weekend for two at Caesars in Atlantic City. Are we ready?"

A chorus of agreement came back at him, and he pressed a button on the bingo machine.

"Aaaaaand...the first item is a priest!" Bradley held

up a ball with a tiny cartoon figure drawn on it. "While we're here, let's have a round of applause for Father Robert, who did an excellent job with the service today."

And so it continued in all its cringeworthy glory. Edna's friend William won the meal at Betty's, and I thought for a minute that the woman who won the trip to Caesars was going to follow in Edna's footsteps. Everyone heaved a sigh of relief when she stopped clutching at her chest.

"If I die before you, promise you'll just stick me into a hole in the ground," Logan whispered. "No party."

"Don't talk like that."

"Just sayin', kitten."

It really hit me at that moment. Logan trusted me with the big decisions, and this thing, this relationship, it wasn't just a flash in the pan. It was serious. Real. We'd gone beyond sex and dirty talk and being the subject of office gossip, and I no longer had insecurities about what everyone might think. There wasn't just Logan and Sloane anymore. There was *us*. I shifted my seat closer to Logan's, and he tucked an arm around my shoulders while marking off a casket on his second bingo card with his other hand. We were playing for a customised walking stick now.

"I love you," I whispered into his ear.

"Love you too, kitten." He reached over to my card. "Hey, you missed the wreath."

I thought the shindig was over when the band began to pack up, but as we slunk towards the exit, an elderly man tapped me on the arm.

"Miss Mullins?"

"That's me."

"My name's Sheldon Bernstein. I was a friend of Edna's, but I was also her attorney. She asked me to give you this if anything happened to her."

He drew a long white envelope out of his pocket and passed it over, together with his business card.

"Thank you."

Sheldon patted me on the hand. "We'll speak soon."

Back at Logan's place, I spent an hour that evening staring at the envelope with my name written on the front in Edna's old-fashioned cursive. It was the second unexpected letter I'd gotten that week—after Logan had had a word with my regular Wednesday-night phone pervert, the guy sent a box of candy and a note saying he was very sorry but he'd just liked the sound of my voice.

I had a feeling Edna's letter wouldn't be so easy to digest. Should I open it? I wanted to, but at the same time, I didn't. Would it reopen old wounds?

In the end, Logan got bored with waiting.

"Want me to read it for you?"

"No, I should do this."

Maybe it would give me closure? There were still so many things I'd wanted to say to her at the end, some good, some bad.

"Any time today's good, kitten. Dinner's almost ready."

See? Pushy. But sometimes I needed that. I slit open the envelope with Logan's pocketknife and slid out a single sheet of white paper, spread it on my lap, and began to read.

Sloane,
After Theodore died, I didn't know what to do with

myself before you came into my life. For so many months, I was lost and alone, but you gave your time and your effort to help an old lady live again. I made so many new friends, learned new things, and saw the world in colour once more.

Although I didn't always make the best decisions, I'm so glad I chose you out of all the people who applied to move in next door. I just wanted to take this last chance to say thank you for everything you did for me. That's why I'm leaving both houses to you.

We only have one life, Sloane, and I hope you enjoy the rest of yours.

Edna

When I got to the end, I read both paragraphs again, then a third time, trying to take everything in.

"She's leaving me two houses?"

"Sure seems that way."

Among all the news and weirdness, I could only think of one thing. "But we said I'd move in with you when my lease ran out. What happens if I don't have a lease?"

Logan put the letter on the coffee table before my tears made the ink run and scooped me onto his lap.

"I don't give a fuck about lease or no-lease. You can move in with me whenever you feel ready."

"I never want to leave."

"Then don't leave." He hugged me tighter. "Are you okay with the rest of what she said?"

"I think so. She didn't mention the gambling or the catfishing specifically—do you think that's what she meant by bad decisions?"

"Maybe. Or perhaps she didn't see what she did as a

crime? It's easy to think that way on the internet. Catfishing, digital piracy, assholes who spew hate on Facebook—people don't realise there are real people behind the screen who are hurting."

"I guess. I don't think she was a bad person at heart."

"Good people don't always make the best choices, like she said."

But for once in my life, I'd made a great choice. Despite all the pain and heartache of the last month, I wouldn't want to change anything other than Edna's passing because now I had Logan.

She was absolutely right. We only had one life, and I intended to live the remainder of mine to the fullest.

EPILOGUE - LOGAN

"NICE KNOWING YOU, boys."

Logan gave his testicles one last glance before he zipped up his suit pants because depending on what happened over the next few hours, he might not have them for much longer. He and Sloane had survived a lot over the past three months—Kenneth, Edna and the dating debacle, meeting each other's families, moving in together—but this would be their biggest test yet.

"Kitten, are you ready?"

"Almost."

Which meant he still had at least twenty minutes to change his mind. He paced the living room, stepping over Nickel and their new cat, Quarter, as he went. They hadn't intended to get another pet, but it had shown up in the front yard at Sloane's old place one morning last month, scrawny as fuck and crying out for food, and when nobody responded to the flyers she pinned up all over the neighbourhood, she'd decided they were keeping it. Logan didn't argue. He'd give Sloane anything she wanted.

Thanks to Bradley, Sloane's two houses were renovated now—repaired, freshly painted, and tidy since some dude with a dumpster had removed all the shit from Sloane's backyard, including the damned spiders. She was renting out Edna's former home for

extra income, but because Logan's girl had a heart the size of Texas, she'd decided to offer the other half of the duplex to Emmy's charity. Three teenagers who hadn't had the best start in life would now have a roof over their heads until they could afford their own apartments.

And thanks to Mack and Agatha, Blackwood had tracked down all the men Edna had catfished, and Logan made reparations. Well, mostly. He'd paid a visit to Desmond, the guy who'd shown up at the Brotherhood, and threatened to break the guy's face if he ever breathed air in Virginia again. But for the rest, he'd repaid the money they'd lost and advised that perhaps they be a little more careful in the future.

Sloane certainly would be. She'd even taught a class at the senior centre to warn of the dangers of online scams. Logan was so damn proud of her—she'd bounced back after the drama, and every day he loved her more.

He only hoped she felt the same way about him tomorrow.

Footsteps sounded, heels clicking on the wooden floor, and Sloane came into view wearing a bright red dress that showcased those perfect tits. Bradley had chosen her outfit, and Logan owed the man a cigar. Or a sea salt protein massage, which was what he'd been raving about incessantly this week.

"Do I look okay?"

"If you looked any more okay, I'd be tearing you out of that dress and we wouldn't be going out at all."

She'd lost weight since they started dating. Over ten pounds so far, and although Logan didn't care what size she was, he did like the extra confidence she'd

gained as a result. When she first started coming to the gym with him in the mornings, she'd only walked on the treadmill, but now she jogged and occasionally went swimming too. Little did she know she'd be spending next week in a bikini. Or out of it—Logan wasn't fussy.

"Will you tell me where we're going yet?" she asked.

"It's a surprise."

"Do I have to stand up for long? I don't know what shoes to wear."

"Pick something comfortable." But not too comfortable, because if she decided to run away, he wanted to be able to catch her. "Maybe small heels?"

The limo was waiting outside, complete with champagne and a privacy screen. The latter was very necessary because things would only go one of two ways tonight—either they'd be getting up to some serious filth on the way back, or Sloane would be yelling at him.

For the millionth time, Logan asked himself whether this was a good idea, but too much work by too many people had gone into this to quit. Wheels were in motion now, and there were no brakes.

"Is it a restaurant?" Sloane guessed as she snuggled against his side in the car. "Are we going to that new Greek place?"

"I'm not telling you."

"The theatre? A concert? Some sort of fundraiser?"

"You'll just have to wait and find out."

He kissed those delectable lips to distract her and also because it might be the last chance he got, then she grumbled at him while she retouched her make-up. Nearly there. This was worse than a nuclear fucking

countdown.

Logan saw the moment when Sloane realised their destination, and his heart sputtered as her face fell. Her pretty smile disappeared, and the cold dread that replaced it turned his guts to ice.

"Allenvale High? You brought me to my old school?"

"You've got one last demon to face. Your high school reunion."

Her jaw dropped. "Are you crazy? You know how I feel about what happened here. The last thing I want to do is go back."

Fuck. Sloane did that twitchy thing with her eyes that meant tears were imminent, and Logan felt like a massive shit. He grasped both of her hands in his, pleading.

"Which is exactly why you need to go inside. You look like a goddess, you've carved out a successful career, and nobody has a bigger heart than you do. It's time to hold your head high and show those assholes what you've made of yourself."

Her voice dropped to a whisper. "What if he's here?"

It didn't take a genius to work out who she was talking about. "McManus?"

She nodded, biting her lip.

"Then we'll face him together. Do you trust me?"

Another nod.

"I love you. Always remember that."

Sloane was shaking visibly as Logan unpeeled her fingers from the armrest, but they couldn't give up now. Because McManus was the guest of honour tonight, the returning star set to cast his tarnished glow

over all those he looked down on. The invite had come through Sloane's Facebook profile a month ago, a short message from an old classmate, a cohort from math society according to the note. *I doubt you'll want to go, but I didn't want you to think you weren't invited.* Sloane didn't use Facebook anymore, but Agatha kept an eye on her account in case any more men wormed their way out of the woodwork, and she'd told Logan about the reunion. He'd been about to delete the offending words when he had an idea. A stupid, devious idea. Clearly he'd been hanging out with Emmy for too long.

Logan may have trimmed his beard, but he hadn't visited the barber for a while—other things kept distracting him, and by things, he meant Sloane—so tonight, his hair covered his earpiece nicely. A Stars and Stripes lapel pin hid the matching camera, and Agatha would keep him updated on developments so he could make his move at the right moment. Who knew, maybe they could even enjoy the party while they waited?

The instant they walked through the door, a woman wearing a dress she'd probably stolen from her sixteen-year-old sister rushed up and pressed a glass of something fizzy into each of their hands, her face screwed up as she squinted at Sloane.

"Sloane Mullins?"

Sloane nodded, her mouth a tight little line.

"You look great. I mean, really *great*." Bitch seemed surprised. "And who's this adorable man?"

Logan had been called many things in his time, but adorable wasn't one of them, even by his grandmother.

"Logan Barnes." He held out a hand, and the

woman clung onto it the whole time Agatha was speaking into his ear.

"Candace Scott. She was dating one of the defensive ends at the time of the incident. Rumour has it, she was the girl who stuck the pictures up in the bathroom stalls."

Nothing on the internet ever disappeared completely, and Agatha had found social media messages going back years. Now Candace giggled and flicked her hair, still holding onto Logan's hand. He gave it a tug to free himself, then leaned in close.

"Those are great veneers. I mean, really *great*. Good cosmetic dentists are so hard to find."

He steered Sloane away, leaving Candace open-mouthed, unsure whether she'd just been insulted or not. Probably it would take her a while to figure it out.

Sloane still hadn't spoken when they stopped in front of the next guy. From Blackwood's research, Logan recognised him as another football player.

Agatha came back again, sounding perky even though she'd been up since five a.m. "Colby Lendowski, wide receiver. Got sidelined by a knee injury in college, and now he works as a host on TKMZ. It's an internet radio station, broadcasts in Virginia, West Virginia, and Kentucky."

Logan thumped the man on the back, resisting the urge to laugh when the jackass spluttered beer onto his shirt.

"Colby Lendowski, right?"

"Uh, yeah. Do we know each other?"

"Sloane's told me all about you. Love your show, man. Keeping my fingers crossed that you survive the cutbacks. Hear they're gonna be pretty tough."

"Cutbacks? What cutbacks?"

Logan made an "oops" face. "Perhaps I shouldn't have said anything. Hey, there's Drew Harvey."

"Ex-tight end," Agatha reminded him. "Works as a catalogue model, his wife's eight years younger, and she's screwing the pool boy."

"His name?" Logan whispered.

"The pool boy? Uh, Brett Baker."

Drew was one of those men who looked down on everyone around him despite his small stature, and Logan took pleasure in standing a little straighter so Harvey was forced to crane his neck back. The sleaze stared at Sloane's tits first, then her face. Was he actually wearing make-up?

"Sloane Mullins?"

Another nod, and her knuckles had gone white where she clutched the stem of her glass.

"Well, well, well. Haven't you changed? If you'd looked like that back when we were students, we might have gotten to know each other better."

Logan forced his fists to unclench. One. Finger. At. A. Time. That took some balls, hitting on Sloane in front of him. Balls Logan would be forced to remove if the fucker tried it again.

Finally, Sloane found her tongue. "I prefer men with brains, Drew, and it seems you still don't have any."

"Easy, kitten." Logan grinned, relieved that she'd broken her silence at last. "She's turned into a little tiger, hasn't she?" No answer required. "*Rowr*. You're Drew Harvey, right?"

"Have we met before?"

"We share the same pool cleaner, I believe. Brett

Baker? Anyhow, he asked me to pass on his regards to your wife."

"My wife? My wife barely knows Brett."

"Sorry, man. I guess it's true what they say—the husband's always the last to find out."

Three down, and a whole roomful of fun still to be had. They left Drew staring after them, wide-eyed, and as Logan led Sloane away, she clutched at his shirt.

"What are you doing? Why are you saying these things?"

"I'm reminding some of these people that they're not quite as great as they think they are. You're worth a hundred of any of them, and I don't want you to forget it."

"But how do you know who they are?"

"Research." He tapped his ear. "Plus Agatha's feeding me intel."

Her lips flickered at the corners, and the vice around Logan's chest eased off a notch. He knew then that his balls would survive to come another day.

"Is Drew's wife really cheating with the pool cleaner?"

"You got it, baby."

She clapped one hand over her mouth and giggled. "What else do you know? Tell me, tell me."

Logan spotted a mass of blonde curls in his peripheral vision. "Emma-Jane de Verio, head cheerleader. Got busted for prostitution in her second year at college. Apparently, one of the professors tried to hire her and the cops caught them both."

"Ohmigosh! And she's right over there." Sloane pointed with her pinky finger. "My math group thought she was sleeping with the hockey coach, but we never

knew for sure."

Agatha's voice came through Logan's earpiece again. "I've just uploaded the McManus video. Facebook, Twitter, YouTube, and his own website. Plus I've changed his passwords and sent the file to all the major news networks and his boss."

"Keep me posted."

"Of course. Mack's off to make popcorn."

While they waited for the main event, Logan guided Sloane around the room, telling her stories while they nibbled on canapés. There were a few people she seemed to genuinely like, but mostly, Logan could see why she'd hated school so much. As they meandered, Agatha kept up a running commentary: ten thousand views, twenty, thirty, forty.

And then it happened. They turned around from the buffet table, and Sloane walked right into Joey McManus. He stared down at her, his expression pure arrogance.

"Sloane Mullins. Didn't expect you to show your face here tonight."

Logan played innocent. "Why wouldn't she come? Doesn't everybody love their high school reunion?"

"I don't know if she told you, buddy..." McManus put his hand beside his mouth and stage whispered, "Me and her, we had a thing once."

"Yeah, she told me. We don't have any secrets, do we, kitten?" Logan gave Sloane a squeeze, but she'd gone rigid again. "It's always fascinating to see how your old classmates have turned out, isn't it? Some go on to be captains of industry, or great humanitarians, or groundbreaking scientists. Some even become movie stars. I love movies, don't you, Joey?" Agatha took her

cue, and the cheesy yearbook photos disappeared from the giant screen in the auditorium, replaced by a surprisingly clear picture of a hotel room. "Especially home movies."

McManus turned white as he walked into shot, his arms around two women, neither of whom was his pop-star girlfriend. In the alcohol-fuelled scenes that followed, McManus managed to snort cocaine and go on a drug-filled rant against his NFL team owner, as well as revealing that he clearly stuffed his underwear during those semi-naked photoshoots he got paid the big bucks for.

The two women remained enigmatic, faces out of shot, and stripped no further than their underwear as they spoke in soft southern accents, encouraging McManus into a hole he'd never dig his way out of. When Logan first saw the tape, he'd given the girls a round of applause, but he shouldn't have been surprised at the final result. Emmy and Sofia were professionals. Sofia had done this shit many, many times before, aided by Emmy on occasion, and even though it made Black grumpy as fuck to see his wife in that position, they'd do it again. Now Logan owed the pair of them a whole lifetime of favours, and he'd pay up gladly.

By the time the tape faded out, McManus was sitting on one of the indoor bleachers with his head in his hands. His arrogance had disappeared, leaving only a coward who hid behind his ego. Logan didn't feel the least bit sorry for him.

"Hope you've got a good lawyer, *buddy*."

Sloane was still trembling as Logan bundled her into the car, and he gathered her into his lap, hoping

she wouldn't be too pissed. Yes, he'd gone in hard with McManus, but the man had deserved it. As far as Logan and Agatha could ascertain, he'd never shown an ounce of remorse for ruining Sloane's life in high school, while she'd spent a decade suffering in silence.

"Kitten, are you okay?"

"Did you do all that?"

"I didn't dress up in the fancy underwear."

She jabbed him in the ribs. "You know exactly what I mean."

"Yeah, I arranged it."

"Was that Emmy on the tape?"

"And Sofia."

"I can't believe they did that for you."

"They didn't do it for me; they did it for you." When Logan had been musing over the best scheme for revenge, Emmy had offered to help in any way she could. She thought a lot of her assistant. "And now it's over."

"I don't know how to feel. I want to laugh, but then I feel guilty for feeling happy. Do you think Joey will lose his job?"

"Probably. The guy who owns his team is anti-drugs, so I can't see him tolerating the coke, let alone the personal insults. When we planned the video, all we were aiming for was a few compromising shots with the girls, but then the rest of that shit happened..." Logan shook his head in disbelief. "Fuck, it was gold."

"I can't believe he said such horrible things about his boss."

"Nobody asked him to." He cuddled her close. "Are you mad at me?"

Sloane sighed. "I should be. But honestly? It's the

most amazing thing anyone's ever done for my birthday."

"Your birthday's not until tomorrow, and I've got something better planned."

"Really? I don't think anything— Hey, we've gone past the turn for home."

"That's because we're going to the airport. Want to join the mile-high club, kitten?"

Logan had borrowed Emmy and Black's private island for a week. Just him and Sloane, plus a mile of sandy beach and a crystal-clear sea. Logan had packed for both of them—seven economy-sized boxes of condoms for him, and a very tiny bag with hardly anything in it for Sloane. His idea of paradise.

She twisted on his lap and pressed her lips to his, turning the smooch into a fierce kiss before they broke apart for air.

"The mile-high club?" Sloane smiled her new smile, the confident, sexy one. "With you? Don't mind if I do."

What's next?

My next book will be *Sphere*, a novella in the Blackwood Security series...

Sphere

When Bradley forces Emmy to take a day off work and go to an amusement park with her friends, he promises it'll be a fun day out. But it turns out the escaped monkeys are just the beginning, and before Emmy's even finished her first cocktail, she finds herself planning perhaps the most unusual rescue operation she's ever been involved in. Thank goodness she brought her gun...

For more details: www.elise-noble.com/sphere

If you haven't tried the Blackwood Security series yet, why not start the Blackwood story from the beginning with Pitch Black?

Even a Diamond can be shattered...

After the owner of a security company is murdered, his sharp-edged wife goes on the run. Forced to abandon everything she holds dear—her home, her friends, her job in special ops—she builds a new life for herself in England. As Ashlyn Hale, she meets Luke, a handsome local who makes her realise just how lonely she is.

Yet, even in the sleepy village of Lower Foxford, the dark side of life dogs Diamond's trail when the unthinkable strikes. Forced out of hiding, she races against time to save those she cares about. But is it too little, too late?

You can get Pitch Black for FREE here:
www.elise-noble.com/pitch-black

If you enjoyed Nickel, please consider leaving a review.

For an author, every review is incredibly important. Not only do they make us feel warm and fuzzy inside, readers consider them when making their decision whether or not to buy a book. Even a line saying you enjoyed the book or what your favourite part was helps a lot.

Want to stalk me?

For updates on my new releases, giveaways, and other random stuff, you can sign up for my newsletter on my website:
www.elise-noble.com

Facebook:
www.facebook.com/EliseNobleAuthor

Twitter: @EliseANoble

Instagram: @elise_noble

If you're on Facebook, you may also like to join Team Blackwood for exclusive giveaways, sneak previews, and book-related chat. Be the first to find out about new stories, and you might even see your name or one of your ideas make it into print!

And if you'd like to read my books for FREE, you can also find details of how to join my advance review team.

Would you like to join Team Blackwood?

www.elise-noble.com/team-blackwood

END OF BOOK STUFF

Freaking hell. I'm writing this at the end of March, and in the space of a month, the whole world's descended into chaos. Three months ago, a coronavirus was one of those things that I might have learned about in high school biology once, an irritation that caused a few sniffles and not much more. Now? The virus that causes COVID-19 is 0.1 microns in size and it's brought life to a standstill.

I've been stuck in my house for two weeks now (self-isolating because I've been ill), and from my desk, I've made one interesting observation. Many of the people who for so long have been put on pedestals really aren't that great. Most of the wealthy are all holed up in their mansions (or shunning social distancing in favour of West Hampstead farmers' market) while the people they look down on are busy keeping society going. Nurses, carers, grocery store assistants, refuse collectors, delivery drivers... Many of these essential workers earn minimum wage. I sincerely hope we give them the appreciation they deserve going forward.

And in this difficult time, who have many stuck at home turned to for entertainment? To artists. To singers, actors, podcast hosts, writers (I might be a bit biased on that one), and painters. Yet so often, art is

taken for granted.

Question: why do we spend more on war than on science?

There have been some bright points—more people adopting dogs because they've realised what awesome company they make, a sense of community as neighbours help each other out more, and less pollution as we stop driving our cars so much. Fingers crossed that these changes will last beyond the pandemic.

I'm hoping that by the time you read this (another month), things might have got a little more "normal" again, although I know for me at least, the new normal won't be the same as the old normal. Having this time to sit back and take stock of life and the world in general has definitely opened my eyes to so many things. It's always darkest before dawn, and, I'd love for the post-coronavirus world to be an improvement on the previous one.

Thank you to everyone who's helped with this book —Nikki for editing, Abi for designing the cover, John, Lizbeth, and Debi for proof reading, and Jeff, Renata, Terri, Lina, Musi, David, Stacia, Jessica, Nikita, Quenby, and Jody for beta reading.

My next book will be a Blackwood Security novella —Sphere—a little extra novella before Alaric's books come out later in the year. The editing on those is taking ages because they're all long and they need to be done together so I can ensure continuity because as those who see my early drafts will know, timelines and names are not my strong point!

Happy reading, and stay safe,
Elise

Oᴛʜᴇʀ ʙᴏᴏᴋs ʙʏ Eʟɪsᴇ Nᴏʙʟᴇ

The Blackwood Security Series
For the Love of Animals (Nate & Carmen - prequel)
Black is my Heart (prequel)
Pitch Black
Into the Black
Forever Black
Gold Rush
Gray is my Heart
Neon (novella)
Out of the Blue
Ultraviolet
Glitter (novella)
Red Alert
White Hot
Sphere (novella) (2020)
The Scarlet Affair
Quicksilver
The Girl with the Emerald Ring (2020)
Red After Dark (2020)
When the Shadows Fall (TBA)

The Blackwood Elements Series
Oxygen
Lithium
Carbon

Rhodium
Platinum
Lead
Copper
Bronze
Nickel
Hydrogen (TBA)

The Blackwood UK Series

Joker in the Pack
Cherry on Top (novella)
Roses are Dead
Shallow Graves
Indigo Rain
Pass the Parcel (TBA)

Blackwood Casefiles

Stolen Hearts

Blackstone House

Hard Lines (TBA)
Hard Tide (TBA)

The Electi Series

Cursed
Spooked
Possessed
Demented
Judged (2020)

The Trouble Series

Trouble in Paradise
Nothing but Trouble

24 Hours of Trouble

Standalone
Life
Coco du Ciel (TBA)
Twisted (short stories)
A Very Happy Christmas (novella)